*Add This to the List of Things
That You Are*

ADD THIS
TO THE LIST
OF THINGS
THAT YOU ARE

Chris Fink

The University of Wisconsin Press

The University of Wisconsin Press
728 State Street, Suite 443
Madison, Wisconsin 53706-1428
uwpress.wisc.edu

Gray's Inn House, 127 Clerkenwell Road
London EC1R 5DB, United Kingdom
eurospanbookstore.com

Printed in the United States of America

This book may be available in a digital edition.

Library of Congress Cataloging-in-Publication Data
Names: Fink, Chris, 1971- author.
Title: Add this to the list of things that you are / Chris Fink.
Description: Madison, Wisconsin: The University of Wisconsin Press, [2019]
Identifiers: LCCN 2019009204 | ISBN 9780299326203 (cloth: alk. paper)
Subjects: LCSH: Wisconsin—Fiction. | LCGFT: Fiction. | Short stories.
Classification: LCC PS3606.I5365 A6 2019 | DDC 813/.6—dc23
LC record available at https://lccn.loc.gov/2019009204

This is a work of fiction. Space and time have been rearranged to suit the convenience of the
book, and with the exception of public figures, any resemblance to persons living or dead is
coincidental. The opinions expressed are those of the characters and should not be confused
with the author's.

For my family

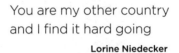

You are my other country
and I find it hard going

Lorine Niedecker

Contents

*Add This to the List of Things
That You Are*

Whistle or Lose it

Whoa Boy whinnies outside, and Timothy's lying face-to-carpet in the living room of his sister's rented farmhouse in Blue River, Wisconsin. His face has oozed enough puss that it's become stuck to the carpet. He peels it away and he's so drunk still he doesn't really feel it, just hears it, that sound you only hear when you're peeling something from carpet. It's an old calico number, once a shag, either good at disguising stains or just one big stain. Timothy sits up and gauges the damage with his fingertips. The air smells both succulent and burnt, as if a pig is being roasted. It comes to him now that a pig has already been roasted, and this is just the aftermath. Yesterday. Last night. The pig split and burnt to celebrate his sister's nuptials.

No one else is awake in the house. Dusty sun streams into the room through the blinds. Whoa Boy whinnies again, wanting grain. Behind that sound is the distant murmur of the milk pump. Gust must be out doing his chores.

Timothy's sick to his stomach and full of dread. His face feels like it must look. Like a cake left out in the rain, the Old Gent will say when he comes downstairs. A sure bet. Mornings like this, head a flaming cocktail of alcohol and ruptured flesh, Timothy imagines his

3

brain inside his skull, gray and wrinkled, afloat in the pickling fluid. It's a generic brain, looking like any brain afloat in a blue jar. But something's wrong with it you can't see from the outside. It must be dissected.

Before anyone else awakes, Timothy had better come up with a story to explain his face. It's as if he has a cue ball crammed inside his cheek, and lacerations from his teeth, especially that broken molar, lace the inside of his cheek. The colors too must be impressive.

Whoa Boy whinnies again. It's the gift horse, alone in the cow yard, girdled still by the gaudy red ribbon. Timothy's alibi is delivered by the next whinny. Whoa Boy did it. They had been talking about riding him anyway, before they got too drunk. The horse liked to charge up hills and chase deer in the tall grass of the back forty. But Whoa Boy was only green broke, a two-thousand-dollar horse that still refused the saddle and the bit. Cord and Timothy tried to teach him, but they were as green as the horse.

This will be Timothy's story: He took Whoa Boy for a trot, the horse bucked, scraped him off on a tree, his foot caught in the stirrup, and he was dragged until his face looked like this. Then Whoa Boy stopped to eat grass.

He had better cut the ribbon before he tells his story.

From upstairs come the sounds of someone else awake. These old farmhouses, you can hear everything. First there is the tossing and turning in bed, then the solid announcement of feet planted onto the floor. Then the pacing around the room as the body assembles its clothes.

Who will it be?

Timothy showed up late to the pig roast. Like most things he did, this late arrival was calculated. He skipped the whole business at the courthouse. To Timothy's view, the courthouse ceremony justified Cord's later drunken appraisal of second weddings. Skipped the whole rolling out of the pig roaster too, not to mention the earlier butchery. Cord hired one of the Nutt brothers to grill the pig. Hillbilly has a pig roaster he trailers behind his three-quarter ton, calls it Nutt's Famous Roast-a-Shoat and lets it out to weddings, funerals, graduations. Of course, when Timothy pulls up everyone is standing around admiring the black thing, already drinking beer out of plastic cups, getting an early start. It is as if the Roast-a-Shoat is the central event here, and the wedding is just an accoutrement one pulls out to garnish a cooked pig.

Timothy discreetly parks his small Toyota pickup in the shadow of one of the three-quarter tons at the far end of the farmyard. He leaves his camera in the truck and walks up to join the communion at the roaster-on-wheels. Tottering outbuildings litter the farm grounds. His sister and her betrothed are renting this place for a good price, and everyone has high hopes about it. But Timothy sees failure in the sad conglomeration of outbuildings. He expects to find barnyard animals foraging in the farmyard, looks for a billy goat chained to a tire. It doesn't take a schoolteacher to understand that no one can make a go of dairying on a rented farm. Not in this century. Look at all the farm auctions along these county roads every weekend. No, this farm is doomed, like this union is doomed.

Timothy walks up to the Roast-a-Shoat feeling rather buttoned up in his khakis and oxford. He makes a show of rolling up his sleeves and then extends a hand to his brother, who crushes it.

Look who's here, Cord says. Missed you at the wedding.

The pig is already sizzling. Poor feeder boar picked from the pen by Cord yesterday and destroyed with a small caliber bullet to the brain. Its blackened carcass turns on a homemade rotisserie. Where the apple belongs, an Old Style tallboy tips inward, as if the pig is guzzling it.

My new brother! beams their new brother, to whom his sister was just betrothed at the Sauk County Courthouse. His name is Gust, and he's some fortyish backcountry mashup of trucker, farmer, and cowboy. Amazing thing is he pulls it off. Everyone likes Gust, even the Old Gent. Most surprising is the banker liked him too, enough to finance this sure debacle. Of course, the banker is the farmer's best friend, at least he had better be.

Timothy shakes hands around the Roast-A-Shoat, trying not to grimace at each firm embrace. This is the cast of characters with whom he will celebrate his sister's nuptials. Mostly, they are Cord's friends, area dropouts, not unlike Cord himself, who never packed up and moved away. They're all approaching thirty, like Cord, but they act much younger, spending their time the same way they did a decade ago. Like barnyard animals, they have nicknames given for their dominant physical features—Blaze or Socks—or else some vulgarity related to their surnames. Here stands Skin, who was bald at seventeen, and now wears a beard and a checkered bandanna around his melon. Already in and out of rehab several times, Skin has grown so silent that he's mostly become Cord's nonverbal shadow. And the Nutt brothers, as they are affectionately called. They go by these nicknames: Ballbag, the elder, and Nutsack, the younger. Bag and Sack for short. These aren't names that people call the Nutt brothers behind their backs. These are names the Nutt brothers call themselves. Proud scrotum, Nutsack even has his moniker emblazoned on the hood of his pickup. Of course the rural fad, the nearly ubiquitous tow-hitch scrota that somehow replaced the gun racks and Confederate flags, dangle from the receiver of each Nutt's truck. I exercise my right to bear arms, the rural trucks used to say, or, don't forget I'm a redneck. Now they've given up politics for the cruder message: I've got big balls.

Cord, Skin, and the Nutts are dressed like they're at a pig roast, or a NASCAR rally, maybe church, wherever it is the fuck they go. Denim, plaid, canvas, leather. If they don't sell it at Farm-N-Barn, you don't wear it, goes the Blue River mantra. Gust goes the same except that he's wearing one of those tuxedo T-shirts. Over this he sports a Western plaid with the sleeves hacked off, Marlboro hard pack in one pearl-buttoned pocket and one weed dangling beneath his moustache, gleaming green seed cap sprouting from his head. The sleeveless shirt recalls the names of these men, the extra syllables sawed off, revealing the hard, bare arms of Cord, Gust, Skin, Bag, Sack.

Sack, pour a beer for my little brother, Cord says. Sack reaches for the cups, the tapper. The keg is handy, of course. Timothy wonders if his brother can smell the condescension on him like bad cologne. He almost smells it on himself. He looks down, accepts the beer. Cord is the lead dog here. The Nutts do as they're told. Even Gust is subdued in the presence of Cord. These men are all hulking and strong, but they're also in the early stages of decline, their necks and girths expanding. Not so with Cord. Cord is in his prime, his muscled body sculpted by hard work.

Weed? Gust offers, holding out the hard pack, shaking the box until one little butt-end extends past the others. Yeah, thanks. Timothy's careful in whose company he's seen lighting up. He'll be safe lighting a weed here in the rolling smoke of the pig roaster.

Timothy lights the smoke, drinks some beer. Pilsner, probably Old Style. Beer to be drunk in great quantities.

New guy Timothy doesn't know walks up from behind the roaster and extends a beefy shank from beneath his own sawed-off western. In the other hand he holds a half-empty feed sack by the neck like some choked fowl.

Poach, the man says, as if in introduction.

Say what? says Timothy.

This here's Nicky, Gust offers.

Oh yeah. Sure, Timothy says. Nicky the Poach. This is Gust's dimwit brother, another new member of the family. Joy. Nicky is in his early twenties, about Timothy's age. A wine stain spills across one cheek down onto his thick neck. Timothy realizes now that this creature called Poach is the only other member of his own peer group. Timothy accepts Nicky's gigantic mitt in his own small hand and the big bastard crushes it.

Ouch, goddamn, Timothy says. All you fuckers are the same.

And how did one little fruit fall so far from the tree? Bag says.

Go on, Nicky, and show the boy what you got in the sack, Gust says.

Gust has called him boy.

Nicky grins and holds the sack out to Timothy.

I'll guess it isn't sweet feed, Timothy says, drinking more beer, his hand still smarting.

Wild game for the party, Nicky says. He reaches in the sack and what he pulls out by the feet is feathered—a wild turkey hen. Neck slit, bled out. Timothy holds his breath. He's still careful not to register a reaction, the wrong reaction, but he's afraid he has. Timothy feels the beer working already, and the cigarette. Enough of these and he might just slide down to feel like one of the gang.

Wingshot, Nicky? Cord says.

Naw. Roosting.

Nice hen, says Timothy. Or is it a jake?

You can't tell sometimes, Gust says. Takes an expert.

She's a hen, Nicky says.

Nice hen, then.

Show him what else, Gust says. Each of the men suppresses something. If they were girls, it would be giggles. Guffaws, then. They're not suppressing their guffaws because of the poached fowl and whatever else is in the bag but because they know Timothy disapproves. They're testing him, seeing if he'll take the bait. He's naïve, they think. And these truths about life must be taught to him.

Nicky drops the poached turkey on the gravel and reaches back in the bag. He pulls out a bundle of big green sycamore leaves and unwraps it one corner at a time like a present for Timothy. Timothy catches his breath as the gift is revealed. It's beautiful, a brook trout, not twelve inches long, still damp and fresh, none of the color drained out, the orange halos and red belly catching the sun, the dun back like smoke, eye still alive. This isn't some farm-raised transplant. It's a native brookie, a wild trout.

Nicky holds the fish out toward Timothy. It's as long as his hand.

It's a beauty, Timothy says.

Sure is a beaut, says Nicky.

For a moment, the two men stand mesmerized by the presence of the treasure in Nicky's hands. Then Timothy's certainty that this wild creature was taken without permit, like the turkey, settles in. Timothy frowns, and this gives Gust his opening.

Cord says this one likes fish more than beer. Says he likes fish even more than girls. Gust leans back a little, showing Timothy something. If he had on suspenders, now is when he would hook them with his thumbs. Poach here's got three more in the bag, Gust brags. Poach here knows these cow cricks better than anybody, don't you, Poach? Maybe he'll even take you out. Nicky grins, his wine stain lightening as his skin stretches. Timothy tries to remember what happened to the boy. He heard the story before. Kicked in the head by a Holstein, run over by an Allis-Chalmers, took a header from the silo. One of those things.

Them things. That's what Gust would say. Or Cord would say it too, but not because he didn't know better. He would say it only to win Timothy's disapproval. One of them things.

Looks like your bro poached you a nice wedding gift, Timothy says, trying his best to sound lighthearted, trying to mask his disapproval. That's better than what I got you. Then Timothy chucks Nicky in the arm. You're quite an old poacher, he says, finishing his beer. He holds his empty cup out toward Sack to be refilled.

Get you a grin on, Sack says, and pumps the tap.

Pluck that hen, hey Nicky, Cord says. We'll throw her on the coals with the boar.

Let Timothy pluck her, Skin says. Everyone turns to look at Skin, surprised by his sudden long wind.

What, and mess up them clothes, Bag says.

He can take off his clothes, Sack says.

I'd be afeared to see it, says Gust.

Then Cord turns to Timothy and ends the discussion. You'd better go on to visit the girls, he says. They've been wondering where you been. The girls missed you at the wedding.

This is his brother's invitation to escape. The crowd at the Roast-a-Shoat is unlikely to let up on him once they get started. Difference is like a scab they must worry until it bleeds. Timothy bows out, wondering at this new trait in Cord, this Showing Mercy. Maybe it's just the special occasion.

As Nicky plucks the dead hen, Timothy heads for the house where his sister and the other women fret with what Sack calls the Fixins, the slaw and beans and potatoes and what all that will garnish the pig. Sack doesn't do Fixins, he says. He leaves them—Them Fixins—for the women. He's relieved to be free of the stag party at the Roast-a-Shoat, but not so certain the Fixins crowd will be any friendlier, especially since he skipped the courthouse.

Last year's straw bales hug the limestone foundation of the farmhouse. It's August, mind. Up past the house, the acreage forms a pleasing tableau: high golden hills reaching above the silo top, gnarled burr oaks shading the pastureland. It makes an appealing portrait, sure, but it won't make money, so it won't be permanent. It's a dream, this farm, and what's worse it's a rental. Last tenant on this property tipped his tractor raking hay right on that ridge. The man was crushed beneath the weight of his implement. That was why rent was cheap. One week a funeral and the next a wedding. It was like some made-for-TV Midwest Gothic: Roast-A-Shoat for every occasion.

Arriving at the farmhouse, Timothy's verdict rises like bile for the second time since his arrival: No fucking way this works. Timothy's prescience is what his family calls his cynicism. Old Timmy Frowns-a-Lot, his mother used to say. The question, to Timothy, isn't how he knows failure when he sees it. The question is how his family seems blind to it. Here's his new brother-in-law, forty years old, once bankrupt, twice divorced. And he's got this way of gazing into his beer cup like he's worried where the next beer will come from before he's finished the one in his fist.

Why bank on failure? Timothy had asked his mother when Anita announced the marriage, pointing out the many clear flaws in the arrangement.

Gust is a likeable man, Timothy's mother said.

The world is full of likeable men, Timothy said. Doesn't mean you want to spend the rest of your life with them.

You don't have to, his mother said.

It took this a moment to sink in. She was right, of course. Timothy didn't have to. He didn't even have to be here at the wedding. Sure, it would look bad if he skipped the whole day. He could, however, invent an excuse, some summer school. But something about his family made Timothy come around, despite everything he knew, despite his grim prediction. It wasn't morbidity, or fatalism, the tidal pull one feels to witness a train wreck. He suspects the answer is very nearly the opposite of that. Somehow, against the odds, these people, his family, are happy people. They have some secret wellspring of faith that things will work out for the better, whereas Timothy, well, Timothy is nobody's version of a happy person.

As if to ratify his thought, Timothy hears a whinny rise from behind the barn. A horse laugh all right. That would be Whoa Boy. Whoa Boy is Cord's plug, won in a poker game a few months ago. *I've got the kind of brother who wins a horse in a poker game*, was Timothy's first appraisal of the news. Guy was into him for a grand, and brother-o-mine takes a fucking horse for lucre. Never mind he's got no place to put it. Well, had no place to put it. This doomed union provided Cord pasturage, but the point remains.

It's a two-thousand-dollar horse, Cord had explained when Timothy questioned his judgment. He acted as if the currency could be converted: two U.S. horse to one U.S. dollar. Cord saw the horse as two-thousand-dollars-worth of animal, while Timothy saw the horse for what it was, a useless hay-burner.

It's hard for Timothy to forgive Cord's naïve childishness. He's older by five years, after all, and everyone likes him more. How come Cord can make such a dumb move and no one calls him on it? Probably because his dumb move makes him happy. Also, who doesn't love a man with a horse? Cord's impulsive, but he's quick to love and he's got a big heart for other suckers. So it comes to this. Timothy's the kind of brother who holds his brother's happiness against him. No wonder Cord hates him. For Cord certainly does hate him. There has been a lifetime of beatings and belittlings to prove it. But which kind of brother is worse?

Holding this thought, Timothy steps over the threshold from the porch into the mudroom. It smells stale, sour, a cow barn once removed. The milking bibs are hung on their hooks, the shitty boots all lined up on newspaper that doesn't quite perform its function, the linoleum sprinkled with lime and straw and the ubiquitous little flecks of shit. A cow cane, gentlemanly in aspect, leans into a corner. Perched above, a row of seed caps. Pioneer, Garst, and Timothy's old favorite, DeKalb: the flying corn.

From the mudroom Timothy can see part of the kitchen and what passes for a dining room, but he can't see the business end of the kitchen, where he hears the women at their chores.

Hello the house, Timothy calls. He waits for a feminine reply.

Bless my spectacles. A quavering voice, masculine. It's the Old Gent, Timothy's dad, come through the dining room. In here with the women.

They've been at it all day, he says. I'm just keeping an eye on things.

Keeping an eye on the ball game, comes his mother's voice from across the room.

What's that, Mother? Timothy's dad is growing steadily hard of hearing.

Never mind.

The Old Gent is of an age that he can move easily among the family's factions. He's also of the age that no one expects much of him. He's been relieved of the men's work, put out to pasture so to speak, but he hasn't been asked to take up the women's work. Neither here nor there: Timothy's own family station. The difference is that his father is much beloved. The women dote on him because he was so selfless in raising the family. Whereas with Timothy, no one expects much because he can't provide much.

Some men might balk at their diminished role, feel henpecked. Timothy's dad doesn't mind the soft treatment. At this moment, he's quite content. It is, after all, his only daughter's wedding, even if it is a do-over.

Big day, the Old Gent says. And you're looking a little shaggy. Want me to cut some of that off for you? He makes his cold fingers into scissors on Timothy's neck.

No thanks, Dad, Timothy says.

Starting already? The Old Gent nods at the half-empty beer cup in Timothy's hand.

You know what they say, Timothy says, raising his voice and his cup.

What's that?

Timothy's still standing on the threshold of the mudroom. He steps in now and looks across the kitchen at the row of female backsides. If he only had his camera. They're lined up like bridesmaids from biggest to smallest. His mother; his sister, Anita; Jess—who's Gust's preteen daughter from his first marriage; Gust's mother. What's her name? Lorraine.

How's the Fixins? Timothy calls to the women.

Where have you been? Anita asks. She doesn't turn around. She's wearing her wedding gown yet. It was their mother's gown. Timothy recognizes it from a picture. This hand-me-down wasn't good enough for her first wedding, a regular church affair almost a decade ago.

But for this second wedding, the old dress seems fitting. It's silk, a faded pearl now more yellow than white, with sequins, a train. Her auburn hair hangs in flouncy ringlets over her shoulders. She's lovely in the dress.

Well? she asks.

I was outside with the cave men.

Jess giggles. She's nearly grown, looking more like Anita's sister than her new daughter. She's got her hair done the same way.

You know what I mean. Before. Where were you?

Had to work.

In the summer? That's a new one for you.

Ha, ha.

Would have been nice if someone took pictures. A girl only gets married once or twice you know. Anita's still not looking at him. None of the women are.

You didn't have a photographer?

You're a photographer.

I have a camera is all. I'm sorry. You know I'm not a photographer.

You should be.

Should be a photographer?

Should be sorry. His sister turns to him holding a heavy mushroom-colored casserole in a clear dish. Pyrite, Pyrex, something. She looks beautiful, younger. Her blue eyes sparkle. She's wearing a sassy blue apron that reads, *Yes I Do, But Not With You.*

Here, she says. Carry this to the table. Timothy accepts the heavy dish.

Ow, shit! he says. His sister had been using pot holders. Timothy is bare-handed. Ow, freak. It's scalding. He shoves it back to her and puts his fingers in his mouth.

Oh, you're a wimp, Anita says. She looks at him when she says this. She doesn't smile.

Here, wait, he says, recovering. He reaches under her hands and takes the pot holders, the casserole, everything. There. I've got it.

Put it in the other room, she says. Then put on an apron or clear out.

Timothy carries the casserole to the dining room and adds it to the oil-cloth gathering of other slumgullions—his mother's word—in their unmatched dishes, the green bean casserole, the creamed corn casserole, the potato salad, fifteen beans, the slaw. All these familiar bland dishes together on the table form a united front. His make-do family. Don't expect too much for yourself, the slumgullions warn. Don't put on the dog. Don't be smart. Don't get too big for your britches. You deserve exactly this. This is a plentitude.

Timothy had hoped that dinner might be a sit-down affair, but when Anita calls, Come and Get It, the men come and get it, load it on their paper plates and disperse with it, as if this is just any picnic. Some go back to the roaster, others stroll down to the barn, some join the Old Gent at the TV. All available seats in the house soon fill. New guests wander in, some Timothy recognizes, and some he does not. There is the banker, whom no one seems to know by name, Gust's sister and her litter, a couple of neighbors, and an old redheaded friend of Gust's named Withrow. Timothy had heard about Withrow, the supposed best man, and had expected him earlier. Evidently Timothy isn't the only one who boycotted the wedding.

Cord walks around with a big platter of pork, filling everyone's plates. Behind him, Skin has a pitcher of beer in each fist, refilling the plastic cups. Skin refills Timothy's own cup. This is the problem with drinking from a tapper. You can't keep track of the number of beers you've drunk.

Timothy takes his own plate and beer down to the milk house, where Gust and Withrow eat, their plates perched on the bulk tank. They seem to be discussing something urgent but get quiet when Timothy walks in. Cord follows behind him and forks a roasted trout onto Timothy's plate. The trout is whole and looks perfectly cooked, the charred tail curled, the eyes milk white, the skin crisp and easily

peeled from the flaky pink flesh. Timothy mouths a forkful of the succulent trout, instantly pleased by the smoky flavor and moist, firm
texture.

There, now you're guilty too, his brother says. No more pointing
fingers. Cord looks smug and satisfied. Yes, Sack called it. He has his
grin on.

Timothy wanders with his plate from the milk house. The barn is
freshly whitewashed and the aisles are freshly limed. The corner cob-
webs are frosted white, and even the gutters are white, the barn not
yet defiled by the cows. All the cows are out to pasture. Only Whoa
Boy stands in the cow yard. Timothy steps back to see him through
the barn window and is surprised to see a big red ribbon cinched
around his girth like a belly rope.

So, Cord has made a gift horse of Whoa Boy.

See what your brother give us? Gust yells from the milk house.
You don't have to worry. You can still ride him when you want to.

Maybe Timothy will. Maybe he'll ride the gift horse out to see
the acreage. He takes the last bite of flesh from the poached trout
and drops the skeleton onto the limed aisle. It was a good-tasting
trout.

Timothy explores the barn, climbing up into the hay mow,
breathing heavily from all the drinking, scaring off a few roosting
pigeons. The far end of the mow is stacked with the previous year's
hay, certainly not enough to last the season. Gust will have to buy
more, but where will the money come from? A heavy rope hangs
from the rusted block and tackle, attached to the roof beam in the
center of the barn. With this the farmer hauled in the bales long ago.
It would have been good to grow up here, to have all this mystery to
explore. A boy helping load the hay could stack the bales in such a
way to make tunnels that he could crawl through. These tunnels
could be like a labyrinth with many dead ends, but with a special
entrance to a private sanctuary in the heart of the haystack that only
Timothy could find. The space would be dark and dry and quiet and

smothering, but safe, and each time finding it would be a thrill, and it would be a thrill too thinking about all that weight stacked upon you, yet still you're safe in your hidey hole and no one can find you.

A small band of pigeons flies in the open window up by the peak and startles Timothy. He finishes his beer, puts the cup in his teeth, and climbs down the wooden ladder from the mow.

Midway down the ladder, Timothy can see into the milk house, where Withrow and Gust lean over the bulk tank. They have their backs to him. Are they arguing? Withrow has been holding a big manila envelope, and now he empties the envelope onto the bulk tank. Banded stacks of what looks like Monopoly money spill from the envelope into a pile on the bulk tank. One of the stacks falls to the floor and Withrow bends to retrieve it. He stands and fans the bills. This is not Monopoly money, this is cash. But Timothy's too far away to see the denomination of the bills.

Withrow puts the stack onto the pile with the others and makes a show, like a poker player going all in, of shoving the whole pile toward Gust.

It's all yours, Withrow says. This is what I got saved. Twenty Gs.

I can't take that, Gust says.

Shit, take it. Come with me and it's all yours.

You're drunk, Gust says.

You think I'm drunk.

But I love her.

You love anybody, Withrow says. Fucking drunk. It could be just us, like the old days. Before that bitch. He returns the stacks of bills to the manila envelope one by one.

Timothy tries to read this but he's drunk too. His head swims with questions. What old days? What ridiculous scene is he watching? Is this bum really trying to buy Gust out of his marriage? Have they discussed this before? Isn't it too late now? Don't you have to speak *before* the I Do's? Finally, if Withrow and Timothy both object to the wedding, but for opposite reasons, does this make them allies?

Cord and Skin shuffle back to the barn with more meat and beer, and Withrow secures the manila envelope just in time, sealing the threat inside. Just like that, everyone is drunk and grinning again, and no one sees Timothy on the ladder. The four men walk out into the sunlight, and Timothy climbs down from the mow.

After the wedding feast—for gorging in all corners of a farmyard cannot be construed as a dinner—Gust offers to take everyone who's interested out in the pickup to see the property. So much for riding Whoa Boy. Timothy decides to tag along with the others. Gust has a big blue-and-white Dodge, and the wedding party packs in front and back cheek to jowl. Timothy climbs in the bed. He hopes to sit next to the banker, but the banker rides up front with Gust and the bride. Timothy ends up squeezed between Cord and Nicky. Withrow, too, rides in the back. He's dressed up like it's hunting season with a red-and-black flannel, too heavy for summer. As Gust maneuvers the truck in the farmyard, Skin makes to climb aboard also, but Cord tells him to stay.

You help with the pig, Cord says. Skin looks dejected. He wants to ride along. The truck idles. Gust watches in the side-view. Finally, Cord says, Oh, all right, get in you big baby. Skin climbs aboard and everyone makes room.

The tractor path leading to the back forty is muddy on account of the recent rain, and the ride is rough. The beer and the good scenery, the bodies jostling against one another, somehow put Timothy at ease. This riding out to see the acreage seems like part of a tradition, though Timothy has never taken part in such a ritual before. Gust stops twice while Withrow lumbers out the back and opens a gate, shutting the gate after Gust drives through. The new herd, forty-six Holsteins bought at auction with the bank loan, roams out here somewhere, untrained to the farmer's call. Gust doesn't want his cows wandering back into the overgrown recesses of his farm.

A small creek wends through the property, and Timothy wonders if it holds any fish. Nicky's catch offers the ultimate proof. Timothy can imagine spending some time out here.

Cord and Withrow are talking about Withrow's job in the operator's union. Withrow says he gets paid big money to run the company's largest hydraulic excavator. He brags that he can nudge an egg along the ground with the six-ton bucket of the excavator without breaking the shell. Hell, he says, I could unhitch a woman's bra with my machine if she wore a front loader. Laughs all around. Gust hits another bump and Nicky leans heavily into Timothy. He feels the big man's body against his own, smells his odor of charred pork and sweat. A few tufts of down from the earlier plucking cling to the whiskers on his wine stain like a forgotten smudge of shaving cream. It's sinking in now that this is his brother, one of the family, and that he and Nicky occupy the same low place in the pecking order, the youngest children, adults but not yet real contributors, still free to gather wool and wade streams for fish and show up empty-handed to a wedding. But Nicky did not. No, he did not show up empty-handed at all.

Gust slows down. Cord said something to Withrow and Skin that Timothy has missed, and now he's gesturing to the two of them, motioning in the air, probably about how to build something. He cuts quite a figure against the greenery. Skin looks at Cord adoringly and Withrow nods gravely, tipping his beer. Timothy has already begun to doubt himself and what he saw in the milk house. Maybe it was just the alcohol, the stress of maintaining civility these hours under this pressure. He knows one thing. Withrow is no ally.

The truck stops, and Gust swings out the driver door. Everybody out, he says. Take a gander at the old farmstead.

Gust points to an old fieldstone foundation and the wedding party addresses it. The foundation is perhaps fifteen by twenty, the stones joined by a primitive mortar. The remains of a similar foundation rest a couple dozen yards away. This would have been the barn.

There is no timber left on either of the old foundations. Only the stones and the crumbling mortar remain.

Carry me over the threshold, Gust, Anita says. This is our farm too. She hitches the train of her wedding dress to keep it off the ground. She's made a pledge to wear it all day and then put it away forever. Gust picks her up and carries her over the old threshold, once around the small room, and back out. Everyone watches the little ceremony. Timothy thinks of his mother and the Old Gent. He wonders if the Old Gent performed a similar ceremony. He must have. And his mother in this very dress.

This was the old Knuteson farmstead, the banker says. I've seen the original plat. From the pioneer days. Old Knute—or whatever his name was—reared twelve kids in that modest edifice.

The way he's dressed, this banker might be a farmer too, except there's a certain luster to him the others don't show, his dungarees a little bluer, showing a crease, his farm boots oiled. I'm one of you, the outfit tries to say. Trust me with your money.

Withrow walks over to the second foundation, unzips his pants, and begins pissing.

Jesus, Withrow, Gust says. There's women here. Timothy cannot tell if this is a mock admonishment. Anita is the only woman here.

They've seen it before, he says.

He's a pig, Anita says, with surprising venom. Timothy looks at his sister. He sees something he hadn't seen before, hadn't known about. What about the others? Did they know?

Then Anita says to the banker, I doubt Old Knute did any rearing. Didn't he have an Old Lena?

He had a Lena, the banker responds. Only a couple of their kids lived to tell about it. Epidemics, typhoid, smallpox, what have you. Kids buried around here like animals with no markers. Old Knute perished himself not long after the Civil War.

Poor Old Knute, Withrow says, head down, finishing his job.

Poor Lena, Anita says.

Timothy feels oddly conciliatory, eager to change the subject. He kicks a rusted metal runner lying alongside the foundation. What's this? he asks the banker.

That's from the old sledge, I figure. This whole acreage would have been logged off and cleared with oxen. That farmstead would have been built with hand-hewn tamaracks from these woods.

Cord examines the foundation of the larger structure. This is good workmanship, he says. Imagine building this without electricity or heat or anything. Freezing your ass off in the winter. No power tools.

Fuck that, Withrow says.

It'd be something to rebuild it like it was, Cord says.

I could bury this fucker in fifteen minutes, Withrow says. You could walk over the son of a bitch and not know it was here.

Everyone stops for a moment to finish their beers and consider the two options. Skin and Nicky pick up some of the skull-sized stones that have toppled and stack them by the foundation.

Yep, I'd just bury all of it, Withrow says. You could get another couple acres tilled.

We all know what you'd do with it Withrow, Anita says.

Withrow here is a little anti-history, the banker says.

Just pro-progress, he says.

I might just keep it as it is, Timothy says. It's like a big Danger sign. This is what happens to farmers around here.

We don't own it anyway, Anita says. We're just renters. We can't go around burying things or rebuilding them either.

Still, it's amazing that this old foundation comes with the newer one—itself a relic—at no extra cost. It's like a geologic feature, the layers of history exposed. In the end though, the whole thing tanked. The Knutesons moved out and then the next family moved in. And then they tanked. On and on down the line.

Now it's Cord's turn to piss. He unzips and faces the pickup. Gust follows suit, utilizing a nearby bush. Timothy too. Everyone suddenly needs to open the spigot.

Jesus, Anita says. This is so fucking romantic.

Truly, Cord says. The time has come for more beer.

Everyone piles back in the truck, their seats all rearranged, except Gust, who's still the driver. Timothy rides up front with him, the pickup bouncing along the tractor path toward home, the beer sloshing in his belly and his brain sloshing in his skull. In the side-view mirror he sees that everyone's quiet in the back, holding onto their empty beer cups and onto the rail of the truck bed. Even Withrow seems to have nothing to say. They're like a busload of schoolchildren returning from a field trip, and the teacher has told them to think quietly about what they've learned.

Things do change at a wedding. New unions are formed, that's obvious. Alterations are made. Accommodations. Maybe Timothy will get some photos before it's all over. Make a record. It's a big day, as the Old Gent would say. Of course, he'll say that tomorrow too. Timothy's drunk, and he feels good, and something smells good and it's not the pig. A day does smell different when it's heading away from you. The temperature drops a bare degree and a certain ripeness gets unlocked from the crops and greenery and from the wildflowers. It clings to the air for a while, and you can't get enough of it, until the temperature drops another degree, and then the redolence is gone. New smells indicate evening. Dampnesses and molderings, not ripeness, but rot. Silage and spoiled feed and animal leavings.

Back at the farm, the old folks will be going home now, and the neighbors have their own cows to milk. The ball game is done and the Brewers tanked in the ninth and have slid now into the cellar. The Old Gent says, Wouldn't that frost you, and then nods off in the easy chair. Pretty soon you wonder where everyone has gone. In Timothy's family, a big day shouldn't peter out like a small one. It ought to be capped with a big night. For the serious drinkers it will be time to get serious about the drinking. The evening will turn into night, and for a while it will seem that you have an eternity before midnight, but before you know it you'll be standing around the keg with the other diehards, waiting for the sucker to float.

This is some matter of honor. To polish off a keg. The leftover pig has been wrapped in foil and refrigerated, the coals are dying. The keg certainly looks a bit lopsided in the ice water. The Nutts have gone home. They'll come around for the roaster in the morning. Everyone wonders what happened to Skin, and they go around the farmyard calling him, but no Skin appears. Must've just wandered off. Nicky has headed off into the woods with a spotlight. He's not hunting but tracking. He wants to get his deer before the other hunters foul the woods. Withrow's passed out in his truck with the door open. A dark stain covers his crotch. Either he's pissed himself or spilled his last beer. Now it's just Timothy and Cord, Anita and Gust. Gust had been stabbing the coals with a long stick, but now he's staring into them like he's waiting for the last one to die.

Timothy is beyond drunk now, some second wind the only thing standing him up. He is almost home. He should be in bed already, tucked away somewhere safe in the house, but he's armed with something awful, and there's still the chance he'll use it. He hopes he does not use it. He's watching the lightning bugs flick on and off. Cord, on the other hand, is still going strong, still has his grin on. He's what Anita calls a happy drunk, while Timothy she calls a glum drunk. Glum drunk, she says with a laugh.

Little Timmy Glum-a-Lot, she slurs. She waves her cigarette. She's still wearing her wedding dress, making good on her promise to wear it all day long. She shouldn't wear it outside where it can get wrecked. Someday someone else's wife might want to wear it.

Frowns-a-Lot. Anita's going to keep saying it until he responds.

All right, I've taken enough shit for one wedding day, Timothy says.

You know what they say, Cord says.

What do they say?

You can dish it, but you can't eat it.

Eat shit, Timothy says.

Cord laughs. I used to make you eat plenty.

Anita catches this. There is a little flicker of mischief in her eyes. Timothy can see it. What were some of the names of some of those games? she says.

What games? says Gust. He perks up at the prospect of horseplay and stokes the coals again with his stick.

Don't bring it up, Timothy says. Finish the keg. Leave it be.

What games? says Gust.

You know the ones, Anita says.

Please don't bring it up. Timothy's standing in some of the feathers from Nicky's plucked hen. Little tufts of soft plumage from the hen's breast lift away from his feet when he moves them.

Oh, *those* games, Cord says, pretending it's just come to him. The ones me and Timmy played.

You played, Timothy says. He raises his voice. I didn't play. Please. Can we drop the fucking subject.

Jeez, Gust says. I'm sorry I blew up. The end of his stick is on fire and he uses it to light a smoke. Weed? He says to Timothy, extending the pack.

No. No thanks, I'm done.

Let's Put Mud in Our Orifices, Cord says. That was a good one.

That's funny, Anita says. I remember that one.

Ha, ha, Timothy says. Drop it now. He pushes at Cord with the beer in his hand. Not shoving him, just some physical contact to let his brother know that he hears him, that he disapproves. The cup cracks and some beer spills. Cord just laughs.

Orifices, Gust says. You played Orifices. My gosh.

Whistle or Lose It. Cord's on a roll now. Cry and Tell.

Show us Whistle or Lose It, Gust says. Show us Cry and Tell. He pulls the lit stick out to light Anita's smoke. She puffs on the end of it.

All right, Anita says. He's getting upset.

Oh, *he's* getting upset, Gust says, swirling the firebrand in figure eights in the night air. The flame is followed by its afterimage so it looks as if all the fire is connected. He doesn't worry about you getting upset. About not showing up at his own sister's wedding.

It's silent for a moment, but then Cord continues. How Far Can Our Spit Rope Hang? he says. Above them, as if he's aware of an audience, a lightning bug performs his little show.

Let's drop it, Anita says. He's had enough. It's my fucking wedding. If anybody should have his nose out of joint it's me. I'm sorry I brought it up.

Gust ignores her. Show us Spit Rope, he says.

Cord recalls still another of the childhood games. I'm Put Upon, he says. Who can forget I'm Put Upon. Timothy liked that one.

You won't stop him now, Timothy says.

I'm Put Upon, Gust says. Oh, that's a good one. Let's see I'm Put Upon.

Fuck you, Timothy says. Go fuck yourself, your new horse, whatever.

Oh, Mister Big Shot, Gust says.

Big Words, Cord says. Dirty Words.

Did he call you Words? Gust says. I wouldn't sit still for that. Not if I was a Mister Big Shot. He drops the burning stick into the fire and crosses his arms, his hands tucked in his armpits.

Will you shut the hell up, Gust, Anita says. She drops her butt and stamps out the cherry with her little silver wedding shoe. Have another beer. Finish the keg.

You miss them games, don't you Timmy? Cord says. Let's show them Whistle or Lose It. He grabs at Timothy's shirt. Timothy pushes back, hard this time. Cord stumbles backward and drops his beer.

His brother stands up. Now fill me a new one, he says.

Fill your own.

Cord's grin is all gone now, changed into a grimace. Timothy's seen it happen this way before, the quick change in the weather, but it's been a long time. Timothy thought they had outgrown it. It's too bad one of the Nutts isn't here to put Cord's grin back on.

Easy does it, Gust says. Don't get too excited.

It seems to Timothy that anything could happen now. But it's too late for nothing to happen. I've got one for you, he says. How about, Let's Speak Now, or Forever Hold Our Peace. That's your boyfriend's favorite, hey Gust?

Peace, peace, Gust says, handing Cord a cup. The beer is free.

You should have taken the money, Timothy says.

What's he talking about? Anita says.

Whistle or Lose It, Cord says. You grab him by the titty, and then you keep twisting until he whistles. Once more, Cord lunges for Timothy's shirt. This time Timothy steps back and pushes Cord in the back as he lunges past. His brother falls to a knee and spills his beer again.

What did I tell you? Timothy says. Not to Cord but to Gust and Anita, as if beseeching them to intervene. But he knows it's too late. Without getting off the ground, Cord lunges for Timothy's knees. He tackles Timothy but not to the ground. Somehow, Cord ends up on the ground and Timothy ends up on his back. They're drunk. Who knows how these things happen. Timothy has him in a headlock, not choking, just hanging on. Cord bucks and twists, but Timothy hangs on. Cord is gassed. Timothy should dismount, but this surprise, this coming out on top, is too new, too unforeseen, and he drinks it in.

Let's Ride a Hobbled Horse, Timothy says.

Cord bucks again, but Timothy remains on his brother's back. He can feel the heat in Cord beneath him. In an awkward somersault, Cord unlocks Timothy's grip and throws him to the ground. Timothy lands hard in a pile of feathers.

Looks like he's not broke yet, Timothy says, still on the ground.

And then Cord rises to his feet. Get up, he says.

And then Anita. Don't get up.

And then Timothy. It's a free fucking country.

And then Gust. Big Words.

And finally Cord. Get up.

Timothy stays on the ground. There is a moment when you can see clearly the two courses. You recognize the right course, but you choose the wrong course, perhaps to project some hidden aspect of yourself out into the world, to show the world that it's pegged you wrongly. Or maybe just because you're drunk, and what's beer for if not to make you bolder than you are?

Timothy does as he's told. He rises up to it, and he feels the beer urging him on.

Cord's first full swing comes all the way from his hip and arrives heavily on Timothy's ear. It is an astonishing feeling, not painful, more concussive, the sound in your head a boulder dropped into still water. It stuns Timothy, and he stands there for it. The second blow lands full in his face. He feels the concussion again. He is able to think, This may be the hardest I've ever been hit. Hitten? Hit. Everything blurs, then it unblurs. Fireflies go on and off. Anita attacks Cord, but he swings her easily on his back, and she's a swan up there. He's giving the swan a ride, but then, Uh-oh, there she goes off into the dirt with the old pearl dress. Gust seems stuck to the Roast-a-Shoat.

A big swing floats into the air toward Timothy's head and he waits for the impact, but somehow the impact doesn't arrive. Did he duck? By his own momentum, Cord falls to the ground in front of Timothy. His face is now level with his brother's knee, presenting a golden opportunity for Timothy's boot. Timothy studies the firm set jawline. His boot could put a quick end to this skirmish. But he does not lift his boot. Cord's jawline lingers there, begging to be kicked, but strangely, Timothy does not oblige. Then Cord is back on his feet.

I'm not going to fight you, Timothy says. You're my brother. This is our sister's wedding. Even as he says this he is calculating. He is not taking the moral high ground. Rather, he is daring his brother to hit him again. He can only win by refusing to participate. The bully loses either way. The conscientious objector will appear morally superior, when in truth he is just afraid. The bully may as well get his licks in.

It's her second wedding, Cord says. It don't count anyway. This isn't a Cord line. This is more of a line for Frowns-a-Lot. Now, Cord has turned on everyone. Words are always the more brutal punishment, even Cord knows. Their sister sits in her spoiled dress. Gust is propped up by the Roast-a-Shoat. It seems everyone is in momentary agreement with Cord. In second weddings, someone said, hope trumps experience. Old Gust must be wondering just what he married himself into.

Cord's haymaker is picturesque in its movement, the way it carries its solid freight behind it so effortlessly. There is no feigning or dodging, just as there is no suggestion of some smaller blow concealing the delivery of the big one. It will be the big ones only, from the full windup, from all the way back to roots of his hatred, roots Timothy has never understood. Back when these roots took hold Timothy was just a wee fish, finning in the pickling fluid.

There is eventually a big show of groveling that no one can be much proud of. This is how the games always end. Much bad acting. Timothy is not hurt. Well, he is bleeding, yes, his poor face mashed, but he's not hurt. And he has a secret he'll never reveal.

Timothy peers from the cradle of his arms at Cord, blocking the barn light. His lips meet to blow a kiss toward the big shadow. First there is only breath, like blowing the fluff from a dandelion. Concentrate. The tongue must be held against the bottom incisors and then the lips wet and pursed and the fluff gently blown. Easy to do when there's no pressure. A child can do this. Go back. Just master the tongue. Ignore the antagonist. Become a small bird, a whip-poor-will, a warbler, whistler, whistling.

There's not going to be a honeymoon. Next morning these cows must be milked. This farmer must be fed and given drink. From his cocoon on the living room floor, Timothy hears the lonely moan of the milk pump. Somehow Gust has made it out to the barn to do his thing. The confident footfalls on the stairs can only be Cord's. Timothy curls into his blanket, feigning sleep. Maybe Cord will leave him to lick his wounds in peace. But Cord does not. He nudges Timothy with his foot.

You up? he says.

Timothy plays possum, but the prodding continues. Finally, he rolls onto his back and lifts the blanket. As Cord gauges the damage, Timothy searches for some remorse in his brother's countenance. Instead, he sees a foreman assessing a bad job.

You look like shit, he says.

My head aches, Timothy says.

Head like that ought to ache.

Anita walks through the room ignoring her brothers. She budges up to her own chores in the kitchen, tying the sassy apron around her waist and swinging her hips to it. Timothy's make-do family is supporting cast to her starring role. Fixing coffee, scrambling eggs, making plans to spruce the place up.

Old Gent is out on the porch putting a wire brush to a rusted farm chair. I like these old farm chairs, he says. Just need a fresh coat a paint.

Cord struts into the kitchen. Feed me, he says. More pig. The women ignore him.

Their mother's putting oil cloth down in the cupboards. She says she has some canna bulbs to plant around the goat shed. This won't be so bad, she says. Cannas are cheery.

What's that, Mother? the Old Gent says.

I said, Cannas are cheery.

Fresh coat a paint, the Old Gent says, almost singing it.

Blue Rock Shoot

They meet to settle this thing at a quaint joint called Blue Rock Shoot and choose a seat on the back stoop. The sun shines through the slant-trunked sycamores, glinting the windshields of the deluxe sedans reclined below like bronzed athletes by a pool. They wear gas station sunglasses against the California glare. For dinner they share tuna fish and Chinese chicken salad.

They talk seriously about what a bad idea this is. She's too Left Coast. He's too Middle. Complicated wrinkles will never iron out. They agree. Let's be serious. Let's not be reduced to cliché. They drink dark beer in the sun, toast bad business, and nod gravely. They've learned enough about bliss to be wary of it.

Out on the sun-drenched stoop, the dark beer disappears before the Chinese chicken salad, and somehow, their insincere gravity melts into a judicious flirting, the way, when something good is about to happen, you say that maybe it's not so good. By agreeing that this is not a good thing, they are really saying the opposite. By agreeing that nothing should happen, they agree tacitly that something will. It is exciting maneuvering.

With everything decided, but nothing stated, they leave Blue Rock Shoot by the front door. It's darker out front. The sun sinks on the other side of the hill. More luxe sedans prowl the main drag. It's September, but the trees are lit like Christmas. Well-heeled Saratogans click the sidewalks and valets sniff for a tip.

What next?

He lists the two solid options. There is the Bank next door, where they have a decent pint, and the old bartender knows all the trivia: the annual rainfall of Botswana and the width of a lion's paw. Or they can drive up the hill and take a look at the sun going down.

There is really only one option. Now that his mind is made up, he wants to impress her. If he can show her some things he's learned, well, that might mean something. But she continues the game.

A sunset is not a good idea, she says.

No, he nods gravely, a sunset isn't good.

They stand on the evening sidewalk. The sun goes down every day, she says.

They sit quietly with brown bottles between their thighs driving up the curving mountain road. He loses track counting the curves some-where after forty. Still, they reach the summit in good time. They've finished their beer and the sun isn't yet gone.

He knows a good spot called Goat Rock, where on a clear day you can see clear to the Farallon Islands. To get to Goat Rock they climb over a dry meadow, the dry hills like golden lions' haunches. Finally, they climb to the smooth granite top of Goat Rock, and they are a long way from anything.

The sun has a few feet yet to sink, and the marine layer is rolled out like gauze over the green and golden hillsides. They sit together on the rock outcrop, apart at first, then leaning in, pretending acci-dent, this the first touching. Below, a buzzard catches a thermal, and the green hills turn into blue waves descending past China Grade and out to the sea. They watch as the sun melts into a gilded puddle on the gauze horizon.

Be careful, he says, when she starts to sway.

It happens more swiftly than seems appropriate, and the edge of night rises opposite the sunset. As they move past the accident, he's full of the things he'll tell her: the angle of jet from LAX, the night fishing of the squid boats, and how the moon and the sun are the same size, just as big as a thumb.

They watch the sky change colors. Sure enough, above the twinkling lights of Pacifica, the dark serrations of the Farallons erupt from the fog.

I can't see anything, she says, holding tightly to his shoulder.

No, he says, and closes his eyes. You're right. There's nothing to see.

High Hope
for Fatalists Everywhere

I hear Santa Head sing Ho Ho Ho, so I know someone is at the trailer door. I get up from my recliner to find blind Esther, come round again to ask if the cat trappers have come.

Is that Tootie? she asks when I open the door and set Santa Head off again. Ho Ho Ho. One Ho for each night until Christmas Eve, or until Doom's Eve, as I've been calling it, when my black task must be complete.

No, it's just me, Big Coyote, I say. I can feel Esther's disappointment hang over the threshold like a valley smog. But Tootie's home, I say. Just you wait.

I take her arm in my left arm—I have just the one—and lead her into the trailer. I seat her in her special armchair by the fake tree and wait for Mom to bless us both. I don't tell Esther that I am the cat trapper. Everyone wants the cats dispatched, sure, but who in Phoenix, Arizona, wants to take the executioner by the arm?

Mom, I call, it's Esther. Mom is somewhere in the rear of the Landola folding our clothes.

The feral cats have been plaguing Hacienda de Valencia since we arrived in late September. We had first noticed a few strays last winter after Dad died, but over the summer they multiplied like prickly pears, and by the time the park filled up again this fall, we had a regular epidemic. The cats keep the snowbirds awake all night with their fighting and rumpusing, their noisy loving. The old, dry folks don't want to hear any violent love at night, and who can blame them?

I used to be a mere son of a snowbird, but now I am the special assistant to the manager of Hacienda de Valencia. This is an age-qualified community, but I got an annual age waiver from my boss, Anton, on account of the cat job and because I live with Mom, who used to be a snowbird herself but now foregoes the annual migrations with Dad gone. In September I said good-bye to my boyhood home in a deep Wisconsin coulee and hello to this 1965 Landola Gold Seal single-wide, where I hope to park my rusty carcass until I die. If Mom lives five more years, then I will be fifty-five and can qualify to live in Hacienda on my own. I have a deep yearning to be on my own, yet it is complicated by the love I feel for Mom, who birthed me and suckled me and protected me these fifty years. My independence, which I crave, depends upon her death, which I cannot fathom.

For now I need this annual age waiver—I think of it as a green card—to keep me from being deported. My age waiver expires the first of the year, and Anton says renewal depends on a cat-free Hacienda.

Mom walks through the kitchen, and even before she says a word, blind Esther turns to her like a sunflower turns to face the light. Christmas, to see it. Mom has that effect on people. Once Walt Zummer in 59A—he's one of the rude Canadians—told me how my mother lights up a room. I knew just what he meant. She has this double-wide smile even despite her falsies, and her open generosity makes folks feel alive and worthwhile. I wish I had that. I'm selfish and quiet and glum and don't touch anyone, and no one smiles when the cat killer stalks into the room. Even old Esther, who can't see her hand in front of her nose, who tips protein shakes mixed with blush wine, seems to take Big Coyote for some kind of a bummer.

The old folks here have all taken to calling me Big Coyote on account of my frequent border crossing. At least once a month nowadays I run down to Old Mexico to smuggle in their prescriptions. Down to Naco they got a turnstile at the border and you can park your car in the U.S. of A. and walk right over to Mexico way. The turnstile is too skinny for me, though, and they have to open up the swing gate when Big Coyote comes across. Naco, Mexico, is just crowded with pharmacies, and I go from one to the next to get the best deals on Zedia, Flomax, Accupril, and the like, until I fill my order.

You would think it might make you feel like somebody, exercising your right to come and go at the border turnstile, exploiting the free market. But it don't. It makes you feel ashamed that you can walk across both ways, but for other folks that northbound lane is closed for business. Driving back north through the grass desert with my trunk full of booty, it's not hard to imagine being a real coyote, hiding out there on the landscape with a freight of live cargo. It's a long haul back to Hacienda, anyway, and not much traffic, so you can squander plenty of time thinking. Anton says the old-timers are just making fun. Says they call me Big Coyote on account of I resemble a coyote about as much as a water buffalo. Either way, it's a name I admire.

Good morning, Esther, Mom says. How does the sun shine on O-hi-o this morning? Esther's from Ashtabula, outside Cleveland, and by her smile, the sun is big as pie on O-hi-o. Mom put it there. That's what she does for folks, even without trying. Sometimes the old snowbirds call each other by their hometowns or home states instead of their first names, for endearment and because it's easier to remember hometowns than first names. All these old-fashioned Walts and Millies and Hanks slip the mind, but who can forget a name like Moosejaw or Ladysmith or Thief River Falls.

But when I say, Hello Mississauga—just like I've heard other people do—to Jack Getchel from Ontario, he says, It's Doctor Getchel to you, Big Coyote, even though he's only a horse doctor, and retired. I hold with Ruth Gim from Prairie du Chien that the Canadians fancy themselves a cut above the Americans at Hacienda de Valencia. In any case, the one thing we all have in common here is that we arrived from someplace north, all flown south to recline in the sunshine. Each of us might have brought a little pot of dirt from our home state or province, but mostly we hope to adapt to our new environs. No one was born on the moon after all, and if you can still climb to the top of Camelback and look out over the dried-up Salt River Basin, you see that this place might have been the moon, until the Bureau of Reclamation turned a hose on it.

Mom, who sees the best in everyone, walks right to Esther's chair and gives her a big momma hug. Esther's a brittle stick of woman turning to grass, but Mom's still fat and full of life and unlike the other oldsters seems to get bigger every year. She doesn't coddle the old, frail ones but handles them roughly, reminding them that they're not breakable after all, reminding them of how they used to like to be touched, back when the old river still flowed.

I don't know, Tootie, Esther says from beneath Mom's ample embrace. Those cats kept me awake all night. I didn't think I was going to get up this morning at all.

Esther sings this doom tune most times she comes over. At ninety-three, she should go up on a billboard as High Hope for Fatalists Everywhere. She's right, I suppose. Some morning she won't get up at all, but I wonder how many years she's been saying it. Esther may be going downhill, Mom says, but we can't let her know it. We have to help her think she's as good as she ever was, just like we did with Dad.

Esther calls Mom Tootie. That's Mom's nickname given to her by some relative of ours when she was a baby, and it took. She even signs her name Tootie on the notice board at the Hacienda clubhouse. The *o*'s in Tootie are pronounced just like the *o*'s in foot. Tootie.

Oh, you're doing fine O-hi-o, Mom says. How about some sweet-cake now?

Nothing finishes off an old woman's heart after a rough embrace like sweetcake, my mother seems to know. I have to learn from her. She won't be around to take care of me forever.

Between mouthfuls of sweetcake, Esther complains about the cats. Says she's phoned the Russian again—that's Anton—and even signed the petition. Esther says if the cat trapper don't do his job, he ought to be sacked. Mom says she'll see about it, and she cuts me with a look. She'll place a call to the trapper just as soon as the hour is decent. Esther says the cats don't keep decent hours and any cat trapper worth his trousers would have to ply his trade at night.

Oh Esther, I do ply at night, I want to say. But I keep silent. I excuse myself to go water the citrus. Soon it will be time for me to make my daily rounds, and I want a little peace before I start my work day.

I should be fair and say it's not just the noise that condemns the Hacienda feral cats. I don't want to make the residents of Hacienda seem crueler than they are. These cats gut our songbirds and cause carnage among our quail. They do capital damage to our mobiles. They claw behind our trailer skirts and drop their bastard litters in our floor joists. Soon they've ripped out our insulation and dragged in all manner of dead carcasses to ripen and fester with maggots and fleas. If you remember the childhood odor of the Great Depression like most of these old-timers, chances are you have a small heart for soft furry creatures. Here reside hard pragmatists, even if they are free with a hug, like Mom.

Since it was the cats that led me to this posh special-assistant-to-the-manager gig, I should be thankful for their nuisance. In September, when I first suggested that I trap the cats, Mom laughed. That would be like sending a marshmallow to put out a campfire, she said.

Is my mother cruel to me? Cruel only if you don't know Mom, who knows me and my soft mallow insides better than anyone. It was more than twenty years ago she called me a wimp for complaining over a broken heart. That smarted for a long time, but I now believe she got it right. I am a big softie, just not as sturdy as most people, especially not Mom. That's why she found it so funny when I took this job.

You might wonder how it came to this. What fifty-year-old covets an age waiver to live among the Liver Spots and quiet their nights? I never was cut out for life among my peers, who were always cruel, especially in my youth. Instead of Big Coyote they called me Tractor Path or Just Plain Lard. In Wisconsin, there is a boy in every small town who is rumored to have been kicked in the head by a mad Holstein or had a Farmall run amok over his melon. In Blue River, that unfortunate boy was me.

True story wasn't nothing like that, of course. Yes, I lost my best arm in the PTO of an old Deere, but all my other faculties were intact, Mom said. I wasn't even that slow, just big, and a big body looks to move slower, anybody knows. Sure, I always took my time to answer a question or to make up my mind, but that's just because I was a tad more pondering than your average boy. You could call me slow or you could call me unhurried or even deliberate. Mom said folks always will choose the easy answer first.

Wasn't no big calamities led me here. I just never did find a place apart from my folks, but that's a thing known to happen. A one-armed man ain't exactly cut out for the working life, but I got fairly handy choring around the coulee, thanks to my dad. I knew the love of a woman once, but that didn't take, as they would have said back in Blue River. Not much takes, according to what I've seen, which I admit is not a very great deal.

I made my choices, now I aim to live them out. Took me a few winters in Arizona with my folks to recognize this place as the utopia it's cracked up to be. Anton uses the word to advertise the Hacienda in his flyers. An Egalitarian Paradise, the literature reads, which means that things are pretty much Even Steven around here. Everything gets cooked down to either a single-wide or a double-wide, with a sedan in the carport. It's a sort of reduction for the home stretch. Big ideas like church and class and color and policy don't hold truck against the daily how-do-you-do of goiters and gout and piles and polyps. Even the prickly moral concerns are overlooked here. Often a churchy widow tucks herself into a neighbor's bed but wouldn't dare remarry and lose her dowager's pension. Living in sin, she'll call it, but it's just minor peccadillo this time around.

You can see how this arrangement would suit a man like me, a one-armed hombre with little to show for his life but a well-kept mother. You live alone in the only trailer park in Blue River, well that's about as low to the grass as a body can get. Here folks choose a trailer on purpose. Who's to say Big Coyote didn't make the same choice? Maybe I've got money in the bank and a regular estate back east. No one would know. But even here there are distinctions. The old-timers remind me I am a youngster yet, and not a rightful citizen. You wasn't even born yet when Truman sacked MacArthur, Doc Getchel says to me once. Doc Getchel can lord it over me, but the years have a way of filling themselves in, and I aim to stick. Just get that green card renewed, I tell myself, one stray at a time.

Some days I even allow myself to dream that one of these younger widows will take a shine to Big Coyote and make him a regular fixture in her single-wide. That would solve my residency status. But dreaming is a dangerous occupation, as Dad taught me, and most days I don't allow it.

It was last winter Dad died in the home called Alta Mesa. Every Alzheimer's story you'll ever hear starts the same and ends the same. You can switch out the details. One detail that sticks the most in my dad's Alzheimer's story is the cucumber sandwich, the one that stuck in his throat on the very first visit day at Alta Mesa. They have this rule where if you take your dad to Alta Mesa, you have to leave him there for thirty days before you can visit him. That's just a rule they have. It was day thirty that the sandwich stuck. Mom and me was coming in for lunch, but I was farting around the trailer that morning and put us late. We never saw him. I guess the very last thing my dad forgot was how to swallow his food.

Coming back to Hacienda this fall without Dad to worry over, Mom and me had plenty of time on our hands. For Mom, it was on to the next problem, and she got tough on the cats straight off. She called animal services, and they trapped and dispatched the first cat for free. After cat number one, however, animal services charged a minimum of one hundred dollars to process a feline. What pensioner could afford that, and with the dozens of cats needing processing?

Those animal services are like the chiropractors, Mom said. They sucker you in with their special deals, but they bleed you dry if you come back for seconds.

Hacienda de Valencia had a pair of live-catch traps for resident use, and Mom said she would trap the cats her own self. In Blue River they would open season for such a pest, but Mom reckoned Phoenix, Arizona, was no place for such rifle work.

What will you do when you trap one? I said from my recliner. It had been Dad's recliner, but now I saw fit to claim it as my own.

Club it, I guess, Mom said. Or drown it.

I didn't doubt Mom's steely nerves—I had seen her go to work on pen-raised rabbits and chickens back in the coulee—but how could you club a cat in a wire cage? And how would you drown it?

Good for her word, next day Mom trapped a cat with a bit of tuna bait, a cross-eyed Siamese, the first cross-eyed cat I ever saw. She let it out and tried to club it with a hacked-off sand wedge, but the cross-eyed cat was a quick devil, and she ended up just grazing its hinder parts. She tried again next day with an old, gray tom she snared. This time she had a barbeque fork and intended to skewer it. She stuck that old tom on its haunch, but he must've been all gristle or the barbeque fork wasn't sharp, because Mom couldn't manage to impale the cat, and it squirmed off the fork with just a flesh wound.

Seeing Mom flounder like that reminded me that if I could occupy Dad's recliner, then maybe I could do some of his other jobs, too. His dying and her failing somehow sparked my ambition, first I ever had. That's when I said I would see Anton about taking over the cat trapping, and she made the nasty marshmallow remark.

But I showed her. I showed everyone. It was the first job in a long time I was any good at, and with a wink and nod from Anton, I moved quickly up the ranks—in just these four months—from cat trapper to lawn maintenance, to tree repair, to pool tech, to clubhouse hospitality, to Hacienda Special Assistant to the Manager. I never shed any of my tasks along the way to the top. They all fall under the purview of Hacienda Special Assistant to the Manager, that's me, and for the first time in long years I feel like I have a reason to be. All of us want for a crowd where we both fit in and stand out. I found mine at Hacienda. Anton says he prefers a big leering beef like me to work backstage, so I don't perform much hospitality. He reminds me that all the other jobs are contingent upon the cat job. That's our deal. I figure if I have to trap cats to keep my high station, well, small penalty.

Or so I tell myself each day as I feel my nerve leak away.

I hear Santa Head sing Ho Ho Ho, so I know Esther is making her slow, three-legged way home. I go back into the Landola and tell Mom it's time for me to start my work day. She looks up from the laundry.

Those no-good boys of Esther's, she says. Seems like you can teach a child anything but how to love his mother.

I've heard this before, Mom's tirade against Esther's good-for-nothing boys. Esther won't be able to stay on her own much longer, and her boys, who live just over the border in Henderson, are no help to her. It's known to happen that a child don't love its mother, but it must be a deadly sin. That's one thing I've learned well, and no one can fault me for not loving my own.

Mom puts down her laundry and fixes me with a look so tender I know I could never leave her. At least I have a boy who loves me, she says. I must be the luckiest woman in all of Arizona for that. She reaches to squeeze my remaining arm, and I let her squeeze it. Squeezes so hard, she's liable to squeeze it right off, and I think I would go along and let her do it.

Time to go to work, Mom, I say. Proud. Not a statement I've had to make very often in my life. But along with all the love in Mom's brown eyes, I see a copper speckle of doubt. I know she suspects that I no longer kill the cats. She said Anton finds out I'm soft he's liable to revoke my age waiver, and then where would I go? I told her before that I didn't think I could kill another one.

You show mercy, it will be the end of Big Coyote, she says.

By day Big Coyote can loaf in the shade unless there's a major occasion or other such defugalty. I clean the pool and Jacuzzi when the water starts to scum up or someone complains of hives or a rash. It don't pay to clean the pool too much, Anton says. These old-timers find new ways to dirty the water every day. You can't convince an old-timer who used to cart buckets from the well that a Jacuzzi ain't some giant bubble tub sent from heaven. Some mornings I'll have to scoop out a turd or skim off a crud of razored whiskers. Always some surprise floating in the pool water, yes sir.

Beyond the pool, I mind the horseshoe pits and I wax the shuffleboard. I shovel hot patch and replace a busted sprinkler head now and then. I seem to pick up odd chores along the way, just enough to give a day a nice shape to it. Besides those drug runs to Mexico, I've also been known to change an odd tire, limb a citrus, plumb a ruptured works, or string up Christmas lights, a fair range of one-handed labor. Come spring I might even help Anton keep a little book once the Cactus Leagues start. I always was tolerable with numbers. I see a future solvency that never before graced my horizon, a way to bankroll my eventual independence, and maybe even make me seem valuable to the fairer sex. Anton has a death grip on the manager's suite, but I never was so ambitious, and second gun is high enough gun, if you ask me.

It's the night work I would like to hire out to some assistant to the assistant to the manager. I try to see the trapping as just part of my bigger job. Even a big-shot park manager has to get his hands dirty once in a while—my boss, Anton, notwithstanding, since he's what you would call an absentee manager. It's no trick to trap a cat. Trick is in the disposal, getting that solid body to disappear. Stray cat gets wise to the tuna bait, I switch to fresh carp I reel out of the irrigation canal. Isn't a trailer-park tom alive would turn up his nose at fresh-caught carp. I have to admit to feeling some small thrill when I find a big kitty in one of my traps. You wouldn't think there would be any thrill to it, but I would be lying to say there wasn't. An empty trap has the opposite sort of hollow feeling. Walk out to the mailbox when you're hoping for a special parcel and find the mailbox empty. Now think about all the long hours until tomorrow's delivery, and I expect you'll see what I mean.

It was catching the carp that first gave me the idea of what to do with the cats. So, I started to take my catch out to the canal in the predawn to have a little drink. Something about that time of morning starts the coyotes to lamenting, and I performed my task to their serenade. I needed to finish my work by dawn because there is always an old pensioner who can't sleep and spends his mornings meandering the carp-full canals. What would he say if he witnessed an overgrown hoodlum like me pitching the cage into the canal: the snarl and splash, then the minute of silence and the slow one-handed retrieve as I drew the heavy cage back in on its tether?

Walking back to the Hacienda along the canal with my empty trap, I would often spot a lone coyote loping along hangdog after a long night's industry. I reckon they come in from the desert for the cats themselves, so I felt a natural brotherliness. They hardly seemed afraid of me, just loped by and give me a look like I was a fellow creature. Once a coyote loped by so close I might have reached out and touched its feathered ear if that's what I had a mind to do. I saw him pause and yawn and I heard the little ligaments in his jaw kittle and churr when he did so, I was that close to him.

Communing with the wildlife aside, it was no more than a couple dozen strays and I could no longer stomach the canal work: the lifting of the dead cat by the tail and the swinging into the hydrangeas, the sad dull thud when the wet body hit hard dirt. I'm just not the man for it. You wouldn't think a fellow would operate this way. A man gets callused the more hard work he does, that's a known fact. But for me it seemed to work the opposite, and I would dread a canal visit more and more each time. I won't even mention what I done with the kittens. There's no explaining. I guess if I was like most men, I wouldn't be swinging cats to begin with.

I decided then to take the cats for a drive about town. Nights I would head to some other trailer park on some other side of town. I would stop at Dreamland Villas or Fairway Vista or Saguaro Heights and put the cage to the gate and open the latch. The cat would squirt through the bars and into some other old pensioner's nightmares. I looked for parks that took kids, of course, because old pensioners have hearts of purest granite. But family-friendly trailer parks are a rare commodity here in Geritol Valley.

During these night sojourns, I would see other cat killers, dirty workers, and petty hoodlums about. Sometimes a helicopter fluttered over, answering to another violent felony. The crime out here on the desert is rampant—there's still an Old Westness about the place—but the swath of mobile homes and big box outfits is too vast for a law-man to traverse in a cruiser any longer. More and more the Arizona law flies in a chopper. Two weeks ago, I found myself in the spotlight of one of those police choppers, just as I was about to unload a prisoner onto the unsuspecting streets of Alta Mesa. It was one of my favorite drop-off spots, on account of what they did to my dad. I stood and put my hand up, but they weren't looking for me, an overweight, one-armed hombre in a mechanic's jumpsuit. I'm gray enough up top, maybe they thought I was just another oldster fell out of his rocker. The chopper headed out for some other territory and I finished my deed. But I knew then there must be another place to make my deliveries. So long, green card, if a midnight cat trader makes the news.

Since my scrape with the law, I've been taking my quarry into the desert proper. It seems the most natural place. I have a special feeling for the Sonoran Desert, even the winding drive through Apache Junction with the Superstition Mountains looming over the twinkling metropolis. I like to think of an old lost Dutchman, still swinging his pickaxe for a vein of gold. Out there the air is clean, and you don't taste the exhaust of all those thousands of rolling coffins. It feels as though I'm liberating the cats when I open the cage door and they scram into the clear, dry darkness. But the coyotes sing a different song, their voices echoing the rock walls, shaped like caved stomachs and clawing hands. I know I am just delivering a more brutal death. If I'm not dispatching the cats to the mouths of coyotes, certainly I am sentencing them to starve or die of thirst out here on the rock moonscape. An executioner with a soft touch is no good to anyone, least of all his victims.

After I loose a cat I always linger a bit by the trailhead, waiting for some sign, some thankful meow sent by the cat to tell me he appreciates my kindness. No meow ever comes, just the hungry coyote cantos. I know the desert work is no good because I never feel good after it. But what alternative do I have? I make my decisions alone. There's not exactly a union where stiffs like me can discuss a better business. Sure would be nice to round them up and fence them in like they do with the old folks. Ideas like that it's no wonder I'm in this jam. I feel sick and empty driving back to the Hacienda with the empty traps, back to Mom, who always sleeps in the chair by the door until I return from my errand.

Christmas Eve brings me home late like some shot Santa with an empty sack, all his presents delivered. A job done. Coming home again empty-handed, the empty traps in the trunk of my mother's Buick, I acknowledge a truth that perhaps even Anton suspects. There is no end to the feral cats in Geritol Valley. The old folks' trailer parks replicate themselves endlessly across the valley floor, and every few blocks you see the same pharmacy outlet, quick lube, and storage joint, on and on down the line. On the wide boulevards are others like me, foisting their nuisance off on the other parks at night. The big fences and the gates can't keep the cats out, can't protect the old from the feral young who just breed too damned fast.

Before I pull into Mom's carport at 89B I take a slow troll around Hacienda, observing the 10 mph speed limit. I roll up Calle Leon and across Calle de Oro and back down Calle Verde. It brings me a smile to think of the old-timers calling the streets Cally this and Cally the other. Almost every lot has some bit of decoration out for the season, and many of those colored lights I strung myself. No small sense of accomplishment now to find the streets quiet and cat-free. I hope Esther sleeps good tonight, deep and dreamless.

Cat season is never a dry season, though, and they'll be on the prowl sooner or later. Anton will be here tomorrow or the next day for holiday inspection, and he'll either find Hacienda cat-free or cat-full. I will have met Anton's objective or failed it. The age waiver will be mine for another year, or it will be lost. Either way, I know I have trapped my last cat, and I know life is hard and lonesome outside these gates.

I take a slow spin past the clubhouse to see if anyone's swimming naked in the pool, another little pipe dream I sometimes allow. But the Hacienda pool curfew is 9 p.m. and everyone obeys. This is a law-abiding community, after all.

Rolling up to the wrought iron gate, I'm surprised to see a stooped oldster crabbing along sideways toward the pool. Must be an old lost one, gone astray after midnight bingo or out searching for a lost child. I shine the headlights on the old bird to see if I can ID her. Looks like a ghost, like some bathrobe left hung on a branch without a body inside at all. Ghost glances up toward the light and her wall-eye gives her away. It's Esther. I should have recognized that bathrobe. What's she doing out here?

Esther, I say, opening the Buick door for her. It's me, Big Coyote. Tootie's boy. Get in, I'll take you home. Are you lost, Esther?

There's a nuisance at the pool, she says. Kept me awake all night. Dear Esther, who must have the best ears for nuisance in all of Arizona.

Leaving the car, I take Esther in my arm and lead her toward the pool to see what's the nuisance. She's not exactly a willing partner, and I wonder if some feline odor still clings to me. It's OK, Esther, I say. I've got you.

Sure enough, a splashing sound comes from the pool, and I hear a faint whimper. I think for a moment about my skinny-dipping fantasy. Perhaps I'm not the only age waiver at Hacienda. Perhaps some fiftiesh Madonna has come to sit with her mother, as I've come to sit with mine.

The pool is dark, so I lead Esther into the even darker Jacuzzi room to find the light switch. In the damp warmth of the Jacuzzi room I feel her tremble, and a little tremor of shame runs along where my other arm used to hang. I have to let go of the old girl to grope for the lights, so I tell her to hold on tight. Esther and me are joined in our blindness, and I feel a chilling premonition.

The splashing from the pool has abated. I realize with sudden sureness that a body has drowned out there. Graveyard shift at the canal renders me expert in this diagnosis. My hand shoots back to the light board and finds the switch that turns on the underwater pool lights. Looking to the pool, I see what Esther cannot, a dark shape afloat in the deep middle.

Esther, stay here, I say. There's been an accident. I lumber toward the water, picking up speed. I flounder into the shallow end and wallow toward the deep middle, my blue jumpsuit heavy with water, its empty sleeve unrolling. Looking out at the shape, even with all my splashing, I see that this is no human body. It is only a dog, some old fleabag escaped its master and tipped into the pool while getting himself a drink. Maybe even a suicide, a thing known to happen. Yes, I feel relief, but this water seems too familiar.

I reach for the animal, grabbing its full tail, and make for the shallow end, kicking hard and flailing my stump. Finally I feel the smooth pool bottom rise to my feet, and I stop thrashing to catch my breath. It's not dead, this dog. Life announces itself in the form of teeth clenched on my wrist. A weak bite, but startling. I let out a yowl. Goddamn animal bites you whether you mean to drown it or rescue it. No dog, I see now. This is a wild creature, a coyote.

It lets go of my wrist, and its head lolls back in the water. Last bite. Surely it is about dead. How did this coyote get by the gate and into the pool? No wonder the cats are hiding tonight.

I drag it toward the pool edge and heft its wet form in my arms, not even mindful of its jaws. Esther, I call. Here's a coyote, Esther. It's still alive.

While I brood over the half-drowned animal, Esther arrives at my side. She offers her robe, which I use to towel the coyote's head and back. It claws at me and tries to bite, but so weak now it seems almost playful. Esther makes a little chirrup sound with her mouth and even puts out a hand to pat its head and ruff it a bit. The coyote mouths her hand as a pet would. We take our time drying the animal, together with our hands rubbing some warmth into its bones. I get out of my jumpsuit, so I'm just in my drawers, but there's no one to see. Our underclothes are soaked and the coyote coughs like an old man getting the phlegm up. In a moment I'll load this animal in my trunk for a later delivery.

All is quiet at the clubhouse, and the soft blue light comes from underwater. I hear a helicopter wing by and pause overhead, but its searchlight doesn't find us. The picture we must make, these bodies so frail, and me with all this girth, enough to go around a couple of times. So this is what it's like to be a lifeguard.

You would figure a wild creature like that could save its own self, Esther says.

I hear Santa Head sing a dismal Ho . . . Ho . . . Ho . . . announcing my own arrival with the dumps. I've still got Esther on my arm, and she's snuggled into my bare chest to get warm. Batteries are running low on Santa Head, and he sounds like Santa with emphysema who must catch a breath between every dejected Ho. I guess he's just survived the season.

From the porch I see Mom's ample belly filling the Landola window. She's parked in her recliner with her feet up, lit by the Christmas lights, not stirring. Older you get, more fearful you are to see a body asleep. But I see a little pitch and fall in Mom's housedress. Relieved, and sort of emptied out, I have the urge to sit with Esther on the porch a while. Esther's mobile is just three lots down. We passed it on the way here. Hers is a Fleetwood, not quite as posh as our Landola, but the same vintage, and it sets on a prettier lot.

We sit for a while, a safe distance from the door. I wrap Esther in a towel Mom had drying on the railing. Only racket is my big stomach, growling something fierce. I could use a nightcap maybe, or even a cigarette, old cravings I thought I quieted long ago.

Esther's feeling talky, and she doesn't want to complain about cats, which is a relief. Her new story is an Ohio story. That's more like it. In Arizona, all the best stories happen someplace else. Esther tells me that when she was a girl in Ashtabula, she was a regular eagle eye. She remembers seeing clean across Lake Erie to the wooded shores of Ontario, fifty miles away. Other people never believed her, but she saw the far shore a dozen times if she saw it once. When the weather and the wind were just right, she said, them big Canada firs stood up like they was planted just across the street. It felt like something, Esther says, to see clean across the water to a foreign land, like there was no distance at all.

I don't know what made me think of that now, Esther says.

I don't know either, but I know if you hear one person share a story about her little days, it makes you want to tell your own. Some reason I think about the fog, reaching its arms around that tilted little shack in the coulee and settling there like a quilt. I had forgotten about that. When I came back from the hospital after the accident, that's how I saw it. I tell Esther how, for a while, Dad was determined to show me a one-armed boy was the most natural thing in Blue River. Dad had a milk route back then, and after work he would swing down from the milk truck with one arm slipped inside his shirt, as if it had been like that all day long. Then we would chore around the coulee one-handed, hoeing in the garden, mowing some grass, spraying out the bulk tank on Dad's route truck. Dinner was a one-handed fork clattering, and even Mom played along, her arm stuffed inside her apron. Later on, Dad put me to bed one-handed, and in the morning when he woke me up, his arm was still tucked inside his shirt. It went on for quite a while like that. We were a happy one-armed family.

Esther sighs when I finish my story. It's been a long time since I heard a girl sigh like that.

I don't want Esther to catch a cold, so I usher her inside while Santa Head hangs there spent. I look at him crossly. Funny I never noticed it before, but Santa Head looks a little like Anton. I doubt I'll be able to look at him the same after this.

Mom startles, seeing me come home late with a girl on my arm.

Where's your clothes? Mom says.

Oh, we've had quite a night, I say.

I lead Esther to her armchair next to the fake tree. She squeezes my arm and doesn't seem to want to let go. Tootie seems confused. She leaves her feet propped up on the footrest.

Big Coyote went for a splash in the pool, Esther says. You should have seen him. She laughs. It's a joke, sure, but there's something in the way she says my name. No mockery there. I had hoped to trade the other way, for a younger widow, but if there's one thing I know it's filling a need.

I got the one more delivery to make, and first light's not very far off, but I can see that Esther wants to tell the story of my rescue, so I sit and listen to how she remembers it.

The Bush Robin Sings

Any luck with the fish, you lads?

No, I don't expect it. Not many fish left in Rotoroa. Or in them rivers. Eels, now. Eels we have aplenty. Eels from here to the ground. But not trout. The DOC would be happy if there weren't a trout finning anywhere in New Zealand. But I don't want to hear anything about the DOC.

Just arrived, have ye? That's Department of Conservation. Responsible, among other things, for the total destruction of all introduced game animals and the blind conservation of everything that was here before the Europeans set bloody foot. That's your DOC.

Bugger the sand flies. I can't abide them. I don't prefer to wander meself out there in the wilderness amongst the sand flies. Bloody sand fly heaven, this. I cast me line around that bend after dark, after the sand flies have gone and went to bed.

Scotland, yes. Sure. I never could lose me accent, though it's softened a wee bit. They said if you came on the boat when you were school-aged you could lose it, but I came when I was eighteen and all through with school. Nearly sixty years in this country and I'm a Scotsman as soon as I open me mouth.

There used to be trout. Oh yes. Uncountable numbers of huge fish. If you asked me to count them, I couldn't count them. They swum by in shoals. Shoals of nine- and eleven-pounders over here, there a shoal of the fours and sixes, and then another shoal of little beggars over there. The water clear as gin and so inundated with beautiful fish you couldn't count them even if they asked you to.

DOC sent their first officer up here in '66, ten years after I came. Said, Look up Scotty and he'll teach you how to cast. I was nifty with a fly rod as a lad, understand, but I didn't have much use for it here with all the deer to shoot. Beggar looked me up, and I taught the lad to cast. Had an old cane pole belonged to his granddad. I taught him for a day, and he could still only cast from here to that sign. That was one day before the season opened, and he said he was counting fish, but I think he was looking to write tickets for fishing out of season.

The next day I swapped him some venison for some trout.

By God, Scotty, he says to me. I never seen such trout. I caught a dozen. Maybe more. If you asked me to count how many I hooked, I couldn't say. So many trout. Huge trout. Broke me off and swum upstream, or else they swum downstream.

Didn't matter that he could only cast from here to that sign. The trout were there to be had, even for a learner with no business catching them.

Who's a native and who's been introduced? That's the question the little people squabble about. They're German browns, and the DOC won't stock a one. The hidebound buzzards would be happy if the last one disappeared. Which is a fine thing when they're luring the tourists here with visions of trout as big as your holiday, pardon my speech.

See a trout in the Sabine Gorge did ye? Ay, that trout has lived there for a decade, maybe more. He's what you might call the poster fish for the Nelson Lakes. Only feeds at midnight on rainy nights during a full moon of a mayfly hatch. Good luck with that trout, lads.

Yes, yes, we have our native trout. Sure we do. Little beggars.

Only yea long. I was with me friend Rennie, fellow culler, and we decided to shoot one, have a taste of the native fruit if you know what I mean. By God, it was like cutting through wool that was inundated with bones. Just inundated. And when you got to the meat after a fortnight of cutting, it tasted of possum, I swear to you.

That's the wee trout we have native, and to protect the useless beggars, the DOC won't stock another brown. But don't ask me about the DOC.

You care to smoke?

Oh, quitter are ye? I don't want to know about it.

I used to smoke a pipe meself. I loved a pipe. By God. I never let it burn out. It felt good to smoke a pipe, and it looked good too. It is a handsome thing to hold a sturdy pipe in yer teeth. Ay. That American pipe tobacco tastes so good you could just eat it. I could smoke a pipe in me sleep. But you can't afford it. These little rollies, you use less tobacco.

No, gentlemen. You just can't afford the pipe.

What is it you say you do for a living? Ay, you didn't say, did ye. I'm a nosey beggar. I won't say I'm not. I find people here to talk to every day. Waiting for the shuttle like you, or looking for a place to pop their tents. German, Israeli, Czech Republic, American. I'll take them back to my house to pitch a tent under me clothesline before I'll recommend they camp on that miserable stretch of grass the DOC provideth. So many lads over the years you can't count 'em. And some of them real gentlemen too. Some keep in touch still via the mails. I met an Israeli girl who was trying to cook tea in the campground there, and the sand flies were absolutely murdering her. I says to her, Come to me house and cook yer tea, lass. And she jumped right at the idea. Didn't even stop to wonder if she should trust a stranger. The sand flies were just murdering the poor lass. Bloody insatiable beasts.

Stayed two weeks, that one. A real gentleman. She keeps in touch through the mails yet. That was twenty years ago.

History, say? I'm a big fan of U.S. history. Anything from the Revolution until the Civil War you can ask me about. I'm just mad about anything to do with yer Kentucky black powder muskets.

They ran a special on the history of the American West here on the New Zealand telly. It ran six or seven nights. A regular miniseries. It was done by Spielberg. They showed it at two thirty in the morning, and it ran for two hours, but I was so keen I didn't miss an episode. Two thirty in the morning they showed it. Beggars. They'll do that sort of thing to you here in New Zealand.

Yes, I know they have their modern black powder rifles. But I don't want to hear anything about a muzzleloader that don't look like a muzzleloader.

For years I wrote letters to the president of the Muzzleloaders Association in the U.S. Up until he died two years ago. His name was Miles Standish. True descendant of the militia man if you can believe it. I was lucky enough to know him and to get one meself when I hung up me deer gun, a black powder musket, .50 caliber with the flint lock and curly maple stock. Oh, she was a lovely creature. Shoot as straight as a rifle. And very dear. Would have cost me $1,800 New Zealand. But Mr. Standish found me a deal for $200.

Ay, Mr. Standish would send me this delicious American tobacco, right through the mails. By God, I can still taste it. The Prince Arthur and the Larsen's Pure Kentucky Gold. Our tobacco doesn't hold a candle, but we didn't know better because we were brung up on it. I sent letters to him me whole life. He had a keen interest in deer culling, and I had a keen interest in U.S. history, so you could say we were natural pen pals. I would send him stories of life in the bush, and he would send me literature on the black powder muskets. Mr. Standish loved his tobacco too, he did. And coffee. He drank it black as the devil's heart. Black coffee and that gorgeous American tobacco. My God.

You can get anything you want in the U.S. Rennie and me used to scour the American magazines, just amazed at what you could buy. My God, we'd say. You can buy that? And then we'd turn the page and say it again.

Do you know I'm seventy-six years old? I don't feel seventy-six. By God. Until I go to take in the washing or have a go at the garden. Then I get tired and realize I'm seventy-six years old. Or I see a picture of meself and I think, Who's the old dodger in the photograph?

I used to have a friend back in Scotland. Les was his name. He's long gone now. He was older than me by a stretch. Maybe he was thirty and I was seventeen. We were mad about gunning. Mostly pheasant and grouse, but also stalking deer. Les had the antlers of a trophy stag he shot in the highlands mounted above his stove in the parlor. One night I was at his house for tea and he's leaning over a paper, making a big secret about it.

And I says, Let's have a wee look, lad.

And he pushes the paper at me and says, Yes, have a wee look at this, Scotty.

I read the paper, just astonished. Do you believe it? I says.

The paper was a color advertisement calling for sharpshooters in New Zealand. You could get paid by the government to shoot the red deer off the land. The acclimatization society called the deer the red menace on account of they ate the native flora, beech seedlings and such.

Do you reckon it's legitimate? I says.

And Les says to me, Says right here in English it is.

According to the advertisement, the program was begun in the 1930s and still growing. It had to be legitimate. There was already a bloody history to it.

My God, I says. It was like a dream sent down from heaven above.

And he says, My God.

And we had a wee nip and just let the possibility settle into us. Nobody says anything.

Then he says to me, says, If I were you, Scotty, a man of your age and not tied down with woman and child, I'd get out now. I'd go to

New Zealand. Poor Les had two girls and a missuz, and it was hopeless for him to go anywhere but down the lane.

I decided right then at the table that's what I'd do. It was no contest really. I could follow me father into the bloody mines, or ship off to exotic climes and live from the fruit of the land.

I walked home in the dark just brimming with it. And in the morning I told me folks I was bound for New Zealand.

New Zealand, they said. Bosh, Scotty. Eat yer porridge, lad.

And I said, It's settled. I'm going to sling me Daniel, Father.

And he said, Think it over, lad.

And I said, I've thought of nothing else, sir.

And in six weeks, seven at the most, I had me berth on the Castel Felice, and here I've been ever since.

Yes, it was legitimate, I wrote to Les. True as the Queen of England. I signed on as Hunter Second Grade. The bottom of the staircase. That was me livelihood, gentlemen.

I've shot thousands of deer. Tens of thousands. Stags the rich Brits may only dream of. Too many to count, though back then we had to count them. The DOC has always been big accountants. At first we had to hide the animals and cart the hides back from the bush with us. Until the DOC realized that was holding up the killing. Then we just cut the bloody tails off and brought them to the office to collect our payment.

Of course we had a quota. Twenty deer per month or find a new line of employment, lads. It wasn't the quota that drove most lads off. It was the hard yakka in the bush they couldn't tolerate. The cold and the rain. Snow even in the summer. Rough as guts, it was. The wasps and the bloody sand flies and nary a flat patch of earth to pitch yer tent. Not to mention the lonesomeness.

We cut the backstraps for tea and left the carcasses to rot in the bush. Which was a bloody shame, and I don't like to talk about it. But we was two, maybe three weeks back in the wop-wops sometimes, and you couldn't haul the carcasses out with ye. No sir.

Well, let's just say it wasn't too hard hauling me paycheck home with me. Let's just leave it at that.

I wrote to Mr. Standish about it. He said he was going to make a chronicle of me life, but I don't think he ever did. I told him of the exploits of a deer culler, fair and foul. My God, lads, I could tell you stories.

I started on the north island in the Tararuas. The trout were as plenteous as they were here. And the deer were so common you could shoot them from camp. Back then no one cared about fishing except the rich Brits, and you wouldn't find them wanderin' far from the lodge. We'd be living up in the bush, miles from anything. Just me and Rennie. He was me partner for the duration. We worked in twos like that. Part of a bigger group of sixes sent off by the DOC, but it was always just the two of us. We'd get tired of eating venison, and we'd walk down to the river for trout. I'd get in the river up to me knees, and Rennie'd be up on the bank with his deer rifle, and he'd say, Are ye ready, Scotty?

And I'd shout out, Ready lad, and he'd fire his rifle at one. The water was as clear as gin and you could see them swimming in the pools just as big as life. By God. You didn't have to hit the beggars, just hit close by and you'd stun them, and they'd float belly up down-stream like a loaf of bread into me acceptin' arms.

And we had this gorgeous trout for dinner that night instead of venison. Those were the days, lord.

It was me elder boy hooked me back into fishing years later. Legal fishing, not with a rifle. Returned to the old country that one. A rare visitor. And me younger lad's a city lad now. Lives in Christchurch.

Yes, I met me wife here in the south when I was thirty. Had a couple of kids later on, and that put a crimp in me hunting, you could say. Big changes coming, but I was bloody hopeless against it. The culler's life was hard on the marriage, I see now. Three or four weeks stalking deer and then a week at home. Though at the time it seemed like a beautiful arrangement, I'll confess to ye. To save the lot, I had to hang up my rifle and pick up a pencil, which was a bloody shame. I was never much use with the pencil. I worked in the DOC office, filing the reports, playing wet nurse to the new recruits. It wasn't the same as being a freelancer. I was a clerk. I wasn't me own man.

Rennie, he stayed in the field. New partner. A good, keen man, that one. He stayed in touch with me all those years. He was a better man than me, I'll wager.

Me elder boy used to go out fishing at night, after the sand flies had went to bed, and I'd be sitting at home thinking, I hope he doesn't catch any. For you know who was the one would have to clean them. But home he'd come with three or four trout as long as yer arm, and I'd clean them, and by God they tasted fine.

The roar was over for me by then lads, if you know what I mean. I was in me forties then, and it was a calm stretch of water. Had the house here in Rotorua and a little hut we built in the woods. Time for me hobbies like the black powder musket and yer histories on the subject. The wife and me younger lad were keen on the flora, and I'd take me elder boy out into the woods to shoot. It was a satisfactory arrangement. Yes, lads, me forties was a lovely stretch. I don't recall that the sand flies was as wicked in those years, but you could say that memory is yer best repellant.

Eel! Don't touch a bloody eel, lads. They're native. Protected by the DOC. You can go out and murder an old lady or commit some heinous felony against yer fellow creature, but don't harm the hair of a bloody eel or you'll be imprisoned for it. The lake is just inundated with eel. You could eat them back in the days, but I never cared to handle an eel meself. Slimy beggars.

I read an article in an American magazine once about the eels in Bulgaria. There was a village where the people lived to be a hundred on the average, and they sent government scientists over to account for the miracle.

Well, they studied everything. The air and the water and the color of the soils. They couldn't come up with a defining theory. Finally they came to the conclusion that your layman could spot his first day in town. Of course, that wouldn't have been a study then, would it? One thing all these centenarians had in common was the eels. They ate the bloody river eels breakfast, lunch, and dinner. And they lived to be a hundred and some change. Eels themselves have longevity in their bones.

I'll never see a hundred. Set me sights on seventy-seven. By God.

The DOC could open season for the eels, and I doubt I'd eat one. Of course I smoke too, and that knocks the years off the end, or so they say.

That's a bush robin. Friendly creature. Tame as chooks, some of them.

I can make the whistle.

Listen.

Well, I used to be able to make the whistle.

Put your walking stick up like yea, and he'll come and perch on it.

You could say that. You could say he's just looking for a handout. Other experts say he follows the trampers and catches the insects they stir up. Parasitic behavior, I read. That don't account for it if you ask me. I think he's just a friendly creature. I think he just likes people. Which is a fine thing considering he belongs to the bush. No doubt yer government scientist would see it a different way.

When me and Rennie was in the bush, the robins would just move in with us. At first they seemed a nuisance, but after a while we saw they was a blessing. They would sit on yer shoulder and tell you a song or they'd peck at yer hand, and the next day you'd find a little bruise and wonder where it come from, until it dawned on you that's where the wee bush robin sat a pecking. You'd never know he left a mark until the next day.

It was so lonesome out in the bush sometime, me tramping up one river valley and Rennie in another. Cutting through bush as thick as wool, going insane from the sand flies, just hoping to make the quota while yer wife is home in the warm bed and yer sons they barely know ye. Then a bush robin appears like a wee miracle out of the cabbage and perches on yer gun barrel like it's a beech limb. He seems to count himself fortunate for finding ye.

Yes, you needed a friend in the bush. Years Rennie brought his dog named Black. Good mix of sheepdog, Black. He would prefer to hunt pigs than deer, but he was a fair companion. Twice Black got into the possum bait and Rennie had to cut off his ear to bleed him.

You think I'm joking, do ye? Yer a skeptical lot. It's a good thing Black only found the 1080 poison twice, because he only had the two ears. The bleeding made his heart pump faster and kept the poison from killing him. It was an old bush remedy. We come across another culler in the bush, and he'd look at Old Black with the ears lopped off and say, Got into the possum bait, did he?

That was the best cure, and everybody knew about it.

You know there was a time when the acclimatization society had the possum on its protected list. Hard to believe. Big celebration when they was released. Schoolchildren got the day off school for it. On the protected list one year and then a mortal menace the next. Same thing with the red deer. That was the acclimatization society for ye. Fledgling version of your DOC. Both about as native as yer common hedgehog and with the same cockadoodle theories.

Rennie, he was a good, keen man. Ay, he was a character. A man of vigour, reality, laughter, and with a total disdain for the stupidity and constipation of government departments. He died five years ago. Rest his soul.

We were whitebaiting in the West Country beyond them mountains. On the Hokitika upstream of the old quay. I had my stretch of bank and he had his stretch downstream aways. I came downriver to see how he made out, and he was nowhere to be found. Just disappeared off the bank. Me life's friend.

We found him later facedown in a pool like he was having a rest. He died with his boots on, which is how he would have wanted it. Maybe his knees just give out after all those years of tramping. Who can tell? Speedboaters were out that day making waves on the bank. Bloody hoons.

Is the smoke affecting ye?

I won't hover about if the smoke affects ye.

You still like the smell, hey?

Well, yer some kind gentlemen. Bless ye.

You know we went through sixteen pairs of boots in a season? By God. That's how rugged the country was and just murder on yer feet. The DOC provideth the boots. That's one thing I'll give them.

Yes, I know you've heard of the helicopter culling, but don't ask me about it. We went to the bush on foot. No free rides for the Scottish lads, we said. We went so far back in the wop-wops no other human animal had walked there but a fellow culler. And a generation before us did the same. Was the cullers who made those tracks ye been walking on these past days. And cullers built the huts. You could say we was the Kiwi version of your American frontiersman, yer Daniel Boones and the lot. But we was two centuries later, of course.

In the winter when the stags was off the roar and the sand flies had gone to bed, the DOC sent us out to build huts and do our shooting on the side. A culler could stay longer in the bush in a hut and wouldn't have to carry his tent and such accoutrements. Now, there is nothing says a good hunter will be a competent builder, but Rennie and me built many a fine hut.

One hut we built in the Ruahines in '59 everybody knows about. It wasn't the prettiest hut, but it might be the most famous. We were instructed to build a hut up at Mokai Patea. Well, there wasn't a stag in the vicinity, and we still had a quota to fill even though the hut was priority number one. I was cutting timbers while Rennie was out stalking. There I was, feeling like the first pioneer of the land, and do you know what I found nestling amongst the kidney ferns? You'll never guess, it was a tube of red lipstick! Who knows how it got there. By God. Laid by a rare bird maybe, or dropped from the planet Venus.

Rennie come back empty-handed and said it would be a miracle if anyone shot a deer on this godforsaken mountain. I showed him the lipstick, and he said, By God that explains it! Well, we had a long laugh. We got our quota in the end. And we built our hut. We christened the place Miracle Hut, and scrawled the name in red lipstick over the door when we finished her.

The name stuck, and you can read about it in yer lore and literature on the subject.

I was interviewed by the BBC once after I hung up my rifle. For their documentary on the deer cullers. They called it *Good, Keen Men* after the book with the same title. I told them about the Miracle Hut and about how one time I killed four hinds with a single bullet. This was a Remington .222, mind. Yer triple deuce. A small caliber for a deer rifle. Not like the .303s the old-timers used. But it was light and accurate, and you could carry more ammunition. It was the favored rifle of the deer cullers of me day. Of course, it's practically obsolete today.

Beware the man who owns only the one rifle, we used to say. He probably knows how to use it.

Rennie and me had pushed a herd up the Travers Valley toward the saddle. Pretty soon one herd amassed into three or four. Let's just say there was a mess of deer moving up that valley. You can see Mount Hopeless there, capped in snow, and Mount Travers is just beyond it. Well, we just kept pushing them up the valley, and the whole lot stuck together, stags, hinds, and fawns. Normally a clever stag would split off and lead some animals to circle back behind ye. But these animals just kept going up and up. Pretty soon they hit the snow line. It was hopeless to get any higher, but they didn't have the brains to turn back. They just pawed at the snow and fell over one another. Rennie and me was behind them watching, just amazed. We found a comfortable spot in the rocks so we could do it sitting down. I fired the first shot into the herd and four hinds come tumbling down the mountain. I couldn't believe me eyes.

Rennie and me culled two hundred deer in an hour. We'd set our rifles in the snow to cool them after every few clips. We shot every last one of them. We counted them later, cutting tails. Most of the animals were still alive, but we had no more ammunition. We got kicked to bits cutting tails. It was a deadly afternoon and tough as guts. While we were shooting it was like we went mad, just brimming with it. Couldn't reload fast enough. But then after, we didn't feel so beautiful. We just prayed for snow or an avalanche to cover them carcasses.

It's a grisly story, and I hate to tell it to ye.

The BBC got it all down, but they just saved the wee bit about the four hinds with the single bullet. I was a good, keen man, if I was to understand it right. Most of the real old-time cullers were gone by then. I told them to go and interview Rennie if they wanted the genuine article. They tried to ring him up too, but Rennie didn't want to hear about the BBC.

I miss Rennie. He was a Hunter First Grade and then a Head Man. I never made Head Man meself, but it wouldn't have cost the DOC much flint to lend me the title. A couple of years I led the seasonal tally for the whole South Island. And I always made me quota. After that I gave them two decades of desk work. Trained scores of lads to do what I learned on my own. You'd think you could pry the DOC loose of a little credit for a life's work. But you'd be wrong. It would be nice. A thank you, sir, and we see you're not completely without talent or native intelligence. Instead you get pushed out the door for a newer model who shoots his deer from a helicopter over a cup of tea.

Don't ask me about it.

Excuse me while I enjoy a cigarette. Smoke keeps the bloody sand flies away at the very least. They've been known to drive a body stark raving insane. I've seen a woman screeching blue murder right there in the car park. Her bloke had gone off fishing or shooting in the woods and left her with the kids. A fine thing. They were being absolutely bloody destroyed by the sand flies.

The bush robin again. Hear him? And that wee beggar's a fantail. Another friendly sort of chap.

Yes, I've heard about it. To listen to the DOC we have more birds now than ever in the last century, with the 1080 poison and the trapping for possums and stoats. Don't ask me about the 1080 poison. Kills everything, not just the wasps and the possums and the stoats. It kills the birds too, and the deer. They drop it from helicopters just like they did your latter-day cullers.

For the DOC, the deer is just a possum on stilts. The 1080 does beautiful things to a deer. Too beautiful to talk about.

Ask anyone who's lived here for a while, they're not too keen on the DOC. That's a certainty. The conservationist and the recreationist are warring breeds, it's a known fact. They say the deer eviscerate the bush, but the moa, he had an appetite for bush plants too. You know the moa. Hunted to extinction by the Maori. Yer kiwi is a creature relative to the moa. Of course he'd be extinct if it weren't for the 1080 poison. So sayeth the DOC.

There's a certain logic in it, but I'll take a sportsman over a righteous protector of the earth any day. Yer sportsman, he sees the value in all the creatures.

No, that's not a hawk. That's a falcon. Falco Novae-see-lan-diae, if you want to be scientific about it. Now, he's a native. Enemy to your friendly native songbirds, but protected. They say the New Zealand Falcon brooks no rival in his own domain. Will chase the Harris hawk out of his sky, hunt the shepherd's collies back to his master's heels and attack even the master himself.

The Harris hawk, now, is imported, though that don't make it a less noble creature. You can shoot him out of the sky if you have a notion and a decent eye. Don't ask me about it.

Bloody rollie is a poor replacement for a pipe. By God. And extinction is a fine conversation topic for a holiday. Forgive me, gentlemen. I'm an endangered breed meself. Last culler stalked a deer in 1987. We'll be an artifact before you know it. By God. Hung up for show like the triple deuce. Maybe the DOC will put us on their list. Read about it in the histories and the literature.

But let's change the subject, shall we? I see you're itching to go. Or is that the bleeding sand flies got you on your toes.

The shuttle will be along soon, lads. You'll see a van will have *Shuttle* painted on the side. You can go up to the backpackers for a wee coffee. If the driver don't find you here, he'll know where to look for ye.

Oh, I'd take your bags along with ye. Nice rucksack like that, some bloke might come along and decide he'd like to have it for his own. That's a myth what they say about New Zealand is a safe and friendly place. Of course, it used to be so.

I'll just walk along to the backpackers with ye, show you where to find it. Not that you'll need help to find it, but I've got no hurry. The wife's at the flower show in Christchurch with me youngest lad. International event. It's not my cup of tea, but she enjoys it. She's always off someplace.

I'll just travel along with ye. Seems I was going that way anyway.

Three Ps

All American photogs have flown home and I am left alone. Stresa, pearl of Lago Maggiore, opens to me wide and crude. I want to see it through my little hole again. But my Leica is gone. The conference was another constriction. And now that is over. Time and space again seem to me unbounded.

The Trattoria Inferno, where I left my camera last night, opens at 11 a.m. Until eleven, I window-shop. I look in the fine shops for fine things to buy for Liz and old Hugh. But what to buy among all that? Silks and porcelain? I'm afraid to go into the shops. I just look in the windows until I catch the paranoid eye of the store clerk, readying his inquisition.

May I help you? These scarves are handmade. The finest Como silk. What price range were you considering? For whom are you buying? Sir, if I may. What's her color?

The scenario makes my blood pressure rise. How do I explain I have no sense of taste, a man like me? I don't know colors, fabrics, materials, styles. The words themselves make me itch. There is a purple silk scarf with a pattern of yellow butterflies and elaborate marble columns. It is pretty, I think. But is it pretty? I cannot discern. Would Liz wear it? Would Hugh?

What do I have to complain about, alone in Italy in the sun. I'll go and buy some pasta. A gift of food. I can pick colorful pasta or plain pasta. I can buy a jar of red sauce or white sauce. The choices are finite. If I don't want to choose, I can buy some of each color, a pasta mélange.

I make my way toward the Trattoria Inferno. I walk slowly, so not to arrive early. The streets here are nice—cool and cobbled, freshly washed. The terraces spill geraniums and foliage down toward the street and all the shutters are open. Laundry hangs out like decoration, smelling fresh. All streets lead to the lake, where the fine old hotels repose over the clear water. I walk by them, up the cobbled streets, then down.

If I find my camera, I will embark for Switzerland. I have never been to Switzerland—have only seen it from a distance. Surely I will find something in Switzerland to photograph. One travels, after all, to come home and flaunt it. One makes pictures to recover the daily loss of beauty, halt life's minute-by-minute decay. All photographs are elegies.

And so on, and so forth. Conference theoretics still linger. *Am I an eye or a finger?* I long for all things practical. To do, to see, not to say . . . But I need my Leica. Yesterday I had it with me, out in the countryside taking pictures: valley fog low in the grasses. The camera is gone for sure, and there goes Switzerland too. I won't go unless I can shoot it.

At eleven the doors of the trattoria open and I walk in. There isn't much suspense. The young waiter recognizes me immediately. His eyes dilate and he practically dives behind the bar and comes up holding my camera. I am relieved to see the old thing, having begun to say good-bye to it in my mind. Now I feel somewhat guilty. Were I to find a camera at a bar without the owner I would keep the camera. Well, maybe not now. I accept the camera, and utter an embarrassed grazie. Then, Mille grazie, mille grazie. I bow and back away. Prego, he says, a caricature of himself for me.

The young waiter is handsome. I hadn't noticed last night, though I recognize him as the same waiter. It's amazing the things that are lost on one sometimes, especially if you try to be one on whom nothing is lost. If that's your job. I walk out holding my camera, embarrassed, still partially resigned to its being lost. I'm lucky to have it still. I look back and the waiter is standing in the opening of the doorway, framed by a canvas awning. I wave to him, and he waves back, smiling. I shoot a picture of him, just for the hell of it. He doesn't stop smiling.

Thoughtless! I should have given him a tip. But now it's too late. I can't walk back and take money out of my wallet and thrust it toward him. He would be too embarrassed to take the money, though he would want it. The waiters here are professionals. They don't assault you with their sob stories of how they're saving for law school in order to get more of a tip from you. I haven't the expected sympathy for American waiters with their constant clawing-to-get-somewhere American-ness. You work in a profession for its own sake, not as a way to get somewhere else. No, my waiter wouldn't expect to be compensated. He would like to be, though, surely. That wanting but not expecting made me want to do it for him. The camera is worth probably four hundred dollars, yet it would cost me several times that to replace it. Perhaps I could not replace it.

I resolve then to go back for a late lunch, have a large lunch, and leave a very large tip. That will express my gratitude and reward my waiter appropriately.

In the two hours before lunch I buy the pasta, a bottle of the honey grappa—gifts enough—then make my reservations for that evening's ferry. Switzerland is salvageable after all. A five-hour round-trip, it will kill this last night. I can have dinner on board the ferry. I go to the lake and dip my feet. It is a hot day. The lake is still but for the waves from the ferry boats lapping at my feet, barely cool. Several large carp school near shore. They've come up from the depths, sucking the surface of the water for algae or air. I shoot the carp, where the water laps at their backs.

Liz left two days ago, when the conference ended. I stayed on with no special plans but to use up my vacation and try to see some things. Liz was the whole reason I came to Italy to begin with. She's art editor at *Cabin Life*, the magazine where we work. She wrote a grant to come to this conference, the American Photographers' Association. She belongs. I told her I didn't want to go, but she said it wasn't a question of wanting. Liz had been speaking with the managing editor. It seems that my photographs hadn't inspired much enthusiasm in the ten months I had been there, and my probation was nearly up. My work was stagnant. Liz wanted it *frizzante*, like the water, she said. This conference was a way to catch up with what was new in my profession. Liz was always trying to sniff the zeitgeist. I told her I had no interest in fashion.

But in truth this was my third magazine in five years. I was running out of magazines. Also, a deductible trip to Europe. I could gain some cultural currency.

The conference had been a wash, more or less. So many black suits and so much theoretical cant. The conference theme was aptly opaque. The Three Ps of Photography, whatever they were. The point seemed less to penetrate to the core of the medium than to make it seem impenetrable through convolution. I hadn't learned anything. I hadn't met but one interesting person, and sharing a hotel room with Liz for seven days had probably done more damage to my position at the magazine than my loggy photography. By the time she left I could hardly breathe.

Either you travel alone and are lonely or you travel with someone and fight, those the words of Hugh Feller, the one genuine character in the whole morass. Liz liked Hugh as well. You wait your whole life to describe someone with the word lugubrious, and then you meet Hugh Feller, those the words of Liz. Hugh's wife divorced him. He was traveling alone. I'm not sure if there was anything divorceable about Hugh. Probably there wasn't anything particularly marriageable, either, but what divorceable? He was big and gentle with big soft hands and he carried a fine Italian leather purse when we met him, on the last afternoon of the conference, aboard the funicular to the Mottarone, high above Stresa. Hugh's purse wasn't a European unisex handbag; it was a woman's purse.

Hugh still wore his conference name tag, so we knew he was one of us. He was reserved at first. He evidently did his work and didn't need to palaver, fine by me. Liz was good at meeting people and she asked him directly about the purse, a comment that made me blush.

My pockets were full, and my hands, Hugh said, holding them up. I realized I couldn't carry any more. I looked up and saw a window full of these.

As the funicular went up you could see things. The two islands off Stresa, an entire unforeseen arm of the lake. I introduced myself to Hugh, then asked how one went about buying a purse.

I just picked one out of the window and put it on the counter, he said.

I asked, But how did you choose?

Liz said the purse was good quality, that she would have chosen a similar purse. Was it expensive? she asked.

The funicular went up. Now you could see the lay of the country out beyond the lakes. The high country stepped down and spread out to the plain of Milan.

I just put it on the counter, Hugh said. When you get to be my age, you don't ask how much things cost or anything. You put it on the counter and pay what they ask you to pay.

At the end of the line, we climbed out onto a wooden platform and walked toward the top of the Mottarone. At 1,500 meters the air was thin enough that we breathed heavily and didn't say much. Hugh carried his purse. Liz held my arm. We rose up slowly. Atop the Mottarone, we saw the snowcapped peaks of Switzerland, where

I would go when Liz left, I decided then. One could always escape to Switzerland, its neutrality. The map showed an imaginary line that zigzagged across the mountains and through the lake. This line separated the two countries. There was an obelisk at the peak with a brass plaque engraved in Italian. Liz asked Hugh what the plaque said.

It reads, Happy 4th of July, he said, grinning. We had forgotten all about the American holiday. To celebrate, we agreed to have dinner, up high, at the chalet near the terminus of the funicular.

We sat inside near a window with a big view of the lake. We drank an aperitif and talked a little shop. I almost always avoid such talks; they give me the sort of high-blood-pressure feeling I get from the store clerks. Liz asked Hugh why he was a photog and he responded that he photographed to find out what something would look like photographed. He was probably quoting someone. I agreed, though, that it was always a surprise, no matter what you saw through the little hole.

Liz said people go through life mostly asleep, and in her photos she strove to shock them awake. Very nice, I said, photography as pig prod. I said her view was pornographic. She said my photos lacked a *punctum*—that which penetrates—that my work put people back to sleep. She was showing off her new vocabulary. I was sure glad Hugh was there. Shoptalk gave way to gossip soon enough when the food and wine came. Photographers are natural voyeurs, Liz said, during the meal. She finally asked Hugh the question I was afraid she would ask him.

Are you gay, Hugh? Women can ask men that question, evidently. Liz and I were drinking plenty of wine and Hugh practically none. Since his divorce he didn't drink much. One of the things that distinguished Hugh was that he was never glib. He pondered your questions and answered them all with equal earnestness. He didn't seem surprised by Liz's frank question.

I was married thirty years, Hugh said. Then he paused for a while. He put a big hand in his hair, all gone to gray. I think I am sexless. What is the word, androgynous.

The word was not androgynous, but who was I to say. The word was asexual, which is how I might have described Hugh, or perhaps *un*-sexual. I felt ashamed to think such of a man I hardly knew, and whom I liked. But it seemed right; he could have worn an old wives' apron or a silk scarf and he would have been the same old Hugh.

Liz surprised me, then, when she turned the question on me.

No one has ever asked me that before, I said. I guess I don't look the type, whatever the type is. I felt for the stem of my wine glass. I was speaking to Hugh. I said, since he mentioned it, I believed I had an androgynous childhood. Two overbearing older siblings. I was like a little girl. They did everything for me. But since I could remember I've always desired women. I've never imagined sleeping with a man.

Liz broke in about how she slept with a woman when she was in college, just for the fresh perspective. Since then she only slept with men. She had been married too, before. Now, she only had lovers.

You seem very sexual, Hugh told her.

It was a mistake to get married, Liz said.

If my marriage were a mistake, then my children would be mistakes, Hugh said. Poor little mistakes grown up to big ones now.

It was getting dark. Out the window the lakefront towns lit up, and the little hamlets on the dark hillsides. The lake was all gone dark, no boats, but you could see its shady outline yawning beneath the glistening eyelets.

Hugh looked at me. You're a good-natured fellow, he said, grasping my shoulder.

We rode the funicular back down the mountain. It was the last night. Liz and Hugh were to fly out in the morning. When we left him, late, Hugh walked home alone to his hotel, and we turned to walk to ours. I looked back. There went Hugh, slump-shouldered, lugubrious, his figure lost before long in the shadows.

Back in the hotel room I didn't have much choice. It was a long time coming, I guess. I wasn't nice to her and she didn't mind. She was randy as a goat, she said, after. I said, For Christ's sake. She talked excitedly about it while I was falling asleep. She figured she had done me a favor, that it was good to sleep with your superior. Sex restored the power imbalance that encumbered true learning. In J-school she slept with her photography professor, she said. Yes, this was just what I needed, she was sure.

Liz was always sure, when it came to me. It was probably that sureness that killed it.

The Trattoria Inferno is empty, but my waiter's working, and I know he'll come to wait on me. I sit on the terrace in the shade of the grapevines, the same seat as last night. Someone else takes my drink order. I order a carafe of the *vino bianco*, aerified wine, somewhere near champagne. I don't have to choose this wine. It is the house wine and I've had it before. Everything seems to be happening as if it were supposed to happen. All the discomfort from the shopping windows is gone. I sip the cool wine.

Then he comes out. We both know what I'm doing there. I tell him, Buon giorno, and he hands me a menu. Please, he says. His eyes are lowered. He wears a silver chain on one wrist and a loose silver watch on the other. Please, he says, evidently his only English. He comes back in a moment with the bread. I order the *penne al salmone*, an easy choice, a type of salad. I try to work out the cost right so I can pay with a fifty-euro note. The meal should be less than thirty euros.

Prego, he says when I order.

Grazie, I say.

He walks away. He is muscular, this young man. His black-and-white waiter's uniform doesn't conceal his build, but he is shy. He keeps his eyes lowered, as if this transaction required that. The lowered eyes become him, I catch myself noticing, and I am pleased with the quality of my noticing, so often lacking, especially without my camera. Without my little hole I am blue collar, merely pedestrian.

I think now about Hugh. Large, ambitionless, androgynous Hugh. Old carp, he keeps rising in my consciousness. Certainly Hugh didn't care, any longer, if the world saw itself through his aperture. But did this mean he didn't care about himself, or that he didn't care about the world? I've risen above my station, far enough. Liz, talentless younger woman, is my boss, my lover? My collar is white now, but I am at the bottom of my profession. I have somehow lost a sense of the genuine. More conference claptrap, perhaps, but something important has been eroded, to be sure. Liz is correct in that. I am thirty-eight years old and earn the same as I earned when I was thirty. The value of what I do lessens each year, though I do more work, perhaps better work. I cannot discern. This, perhaps, is the root. All potential is gone now. I am a known commodity. Either a thing grows or it is a dead thing, Liz, ambitious industrialist, says. I see myself in a dozen years: large, lugubrious, alone. So.

I have often wondered how people come to realize, or even think that, perhaps, if it were to come to it, they might be gay. Now I begin to think I know. That's not true. I've thought it before. But now the idea comes a little more in focus.

Please, my waiter says, when I catch his attention to ask for more wine. I only want to watch him come and go. The whole of himself is developing with each trip to my table. He wears a white tank top under his white button-down. Surely he is conscious of his physique. He smiles easily, is shy, but eager to please. I will give him a very large tip.

The dinner is fine. I am alone on the terrace and so occupy myself solely with my food, and of course with thoughts of him. When one is traveling alone and there is time to kill, one can always safely eat. An

American couple comes by along the sidewalk, and she asks me if I speak English. I shake my head. She continues in English anyway all the while gesturing and pointing.

Restaurante? Il Punto? You know where is? Dove is Il Punto?

No parlo Inglese, I say, enjoying my little fraud. My waiter comes out and smiles complicitly as he watches me. I wink at him. The couple leaves finally, and I am finished eating. I motion to my new friend and he comes carrying my bill on a small silver tray. Please, he says. He leaves it. I have done well. The dinner is twenty-six euros. I retrieve a fifty from my wallet and put it on the tray. I consider it. I realize it is up to me if anything else is to happen. It is a thrill to consider that something else might happen. Nothing else ever happens. But why shouldn't it? Liz is gone. I have no obligation. I am a stranger here. It is that sense of being a stranger that makes me what I am. If any place to do this, it is here. And so I watch myself tear off a piece of the white napkin and write on the napkin, Hotel Splendide, 11 p.m. Please.

With something to anticipate back in Stresa, I just want to get Switzerland done with. The ferry leaves at four and returns at nine. I sit up on the open top deck at first. The boat is very big, and the top deck so high up I can't even feel the motion of the water. This is what a cruise ship must feel like. You can say you were out on the water without the discomforting feeling of the waves. Taking a cruise must be like looking at a photograph of a cruise.

I go down and spend the rest of the outward trip on the deck with the crew near the water. Down here, the water sprays onto the deck. The boat must make passport checks at certain ports. The boat cruises into shore, and the crewmen stand ready to cast ropes to the dockhands. But if no carabinieri are on the dock, the crewmen just cast the heavy ropes into the water and pull them in. They call out to their friends on the docks. They seem happy to be crewmen. At the last Italian port the dockhand is a woman, and all the crewmen shout to her. Her name is Susie. It makes the men happy to see Susie and to shout Susie's name. Susie is the highlight of their trip to Switzerland. The crewmen cast the ropes into the water and drag them back in, laughing and shouting.

After the feigned passport check at Susie's port, the ferry motors back out. We cross the imaginary line into Switzerland and dock at Brissago, a small village that was a smuggling port a century ago, though illicit activity has been replaced by tourism. A steward explains this in Italian over the loudspeaker. Most of it I don't understand. My map shows a valley leading out of the town with a small road winding up into the Alps. We have fifteen minutes to potter about town, but I don't feel like mixing with that crush of people, all randy to accumulate photographs. I go up to the upper deck and take out my Leica and portable tripod. The upper deck is empty. I shoot several delayed exposures of Switzerland: the green descent of the hills into the green water. One full second seems like a lifetime compared with one two-hundred-fiftieth.

For the return, I have a table to myself, looking out over the lake. Out in the distance there are other boats, small craft artfully obscured by the fog. These must be the local fishermen, hauling their living from the evening lake. Most of the return trip is devoted to the meal. The food keeps coming in various small courses, and all the wine you can drink. Soon it is dark and the windows reflect only the dinner scene. The smartly dressed waiters bring food without your having to choose from a menu. They put the food in front of you and you eat the food. I am afraid each course will be the last, but there always seems to be another course after that.

I don't have time to get nervous about seeing my waiter, whether he will come or not, and what if he does. I keep busy, eating and drinking. My waiter. He smiled when I gave him the fifty and waived off his gesture to get change. Was the tip enough? Did he see the note? Probably he did. It is nice, anyway, not to be sure.

The ferry docks back in Stresa. I disembark and walk up the cobbled street to my hotel, my one-star at the top of town. I take time to get ready. Because I am leaving in the morning, and because the room is so small, I pack. I leave my camera out on the small table by the bed. I walk back down to the Hotel Splendide on the water.

This hotel has five stars. I didn't know a hotel could have so many stars. Many famous people have evidently stayed here. There is a singer with a piano accompaniment. All the people are suited and tied. I hear one American exclaim to another that the big chandelier is Murano glass. I sit in the lounge and drink a brandy. I drink it very fast and order another. When I finish it, if he doesn't show, I will leave. There is a big grandfather clock. I look at the big hands. It is nearly eleven and then it is eleven and then a little after eleven. I finish with the small brandy and get up to leave.

He shows. I sit back down on the overstuffed sofa. The clock, and everything, disappears. He isn't wearing his waiter's uniform. He has on tight black jeans and a type of boot. His belt buckle is silver and seems very big. His shirt is silver, silk perhaps. It shines, anyway. Is it attractive? I'm not sure. Perhaps the outfit, as a composition, would be considered garish by someone who knew. Despite myself I focus on the belt buckle—the *punctum*. It arrests me. What do I have on? My usual attire. I have no imagination: khakis, a rumpled blue shirt. We sit together on the big sofa. We order a drink from the waiter, a lemon liqueur, local specialty, his suggestion.

We sit for quite a while over the lemon drinks. From my vantage point, his body is backlit by the famous chandelier. In a photograph, I can't help but think, the chandelier would be growing from his head. He catches me staring. He grasps my hand and returns my gaze, causing me to blush. Now we're both uncomfortable, though neither of us moves. I wonder if he feels as if he owes me this, for the tip, the way I felt I owed him for saving my camera. Here we are, anyway. When we finish our drinks, he lets me pay. It occurs to me for the first time, oddly enough, that he is probably experienced at this sort of thing, my shy waiter.

We walk up to my hotel, anyway, my suggestion. The light on the nighttime streets is attractive, but the streets stink now. All the freshness of the morning is gone. All the laundry has been hauled in and the shutters are shut tight.

I can see he is disappointed this is my hotel. We tread up the dark steps and down the dark hall. In the room, though, there isn't much else that can happen. It is a small room, spare, and the bed is a single bed. The toilet is down the hall, the sink is here. We can't talk to each other. There is nowhere to sit but the bed. We stand there facing each other. We embrace, first, in the dark room. Not sure what to do, I try to kiss him. Then he turns the light on. I see his tongue come out and pass over his lip. A piercing on his tongue glints in the light. I can't imagine anymore how he was as my waiter. He pushes me backward on the bed and turns me. I am a much bigger man than he, but he is stronger, and I let him handle me. The bed is next to the wall, more a workbench than a bed. The room is only thirty euros per night. What happens next, I don't see. He works my khakis down. I hear him taking his belt off. A long time seems to pass as he does something back there. I feel the belt buckle cold against my thigh. The Leica sits poised on the nightstand.

He fucks me. There is no other way to say it. It hurts me, very much, but I do experience pleasure. Everything that happens, happens from behind, so I don't see any of it, which, strangely, I like. He holds me by the neck some of the time. We are noiseless. Before very long he is lying down hard on top of me, breathing into my ear. His breathing flattens. A picture of us both comes into my mind. A black-and-white I seem to recognize. Perhaps a Mapplethorpe. Hugh, were he here, might comment on the staging, the meanness of the sink, the degree of openness of the subject's hand. But the *punctum* is in the interlocked bodies, too big for the bed. Liz said, casually, she would rather be fucked. So this is what it's like.

We make some half-hearted attempt at romance, but he is falling asleep. I'm glad he can't speak English so he can't say anything to me about sharing his soul. You could say we cradled each other.

Early in the morning and he is gone already. My camera, too, is gone, and the precious film. Did he take it, or did I give it to him? Lost and now lost again.

On the ferry back to Varenna to catch my train to Milano, plane home, the boat passes right between the two islands, Isola Bella and Isola dei Pescatori. The locals joke that these two islands are the testicles of Stresa, though they're placed more like ovaries. The water is like mercury, reflecting everything. On Isola Bella there is a grand villa where Napoleon and Josephine once stayed, and where Mussolini was held prisoner, captured trying to escape across the lake into Switzerland. One whole end of the island is given over to a formal garden with manicured lawns and clipped vegetation from every continent. White peacocks strut among the faux Roman sculpture lining the terraces.

On Isola dei Pescatori, Fishermen's Island, a line of colorful old dilapidated houses hunker over the lake, their façades reflecting back at them. This is the island for me. The houses look like old fisher wives, mending the fishing nets. The old fishermen, out late last night, must still be asleep. I recall then that I had wanted to be a fisherman. That was the idea, at one time. I would have a charter boat on one of the Great Lakes. I would know the lake to its depths, and I would take people out to the spots where the fish were—places that only I knew—and catch them all their limit of fish. As long as I produce the beautiful fish, my patrons do not question me. They revere me, my secret knowledge, and pay me for it. I think for a moment of the Great Lakes: Huron, Ontario, Michigan, Erie . . . There are others, but I have been gone a long while. Which one had I wanted to be a fisherman on?

Cubness

I always believed that being a Cubs fan built strong character. It taught a person that if you try hard enough and long enough, you'll still lose. And that's the story of life.

Mike Royko

Where we're from we have this saying, Happiness is Chicago in the rearview mirror. Each of us has been heard saying this. We like to make fun of the people of Chicago and call them citiots because they can't change their own oil or plumb their own sinks. Of course when our friend from Chicago invites us to the city, we're the first to go. And we always take cash out of the bank in big bills, and in Chicago we appear to spend it freely because we don't want to look like cheap hicks to the people of Chicago. But it hurts us. Each twenty peeled from our rolls and blown in the windy city of Chicago hurts us, though we don't make it known.

The reason we go to Chicago is to see the Chicago Cubs play baseball in Wrigley Field. Somehow the Cubs belong to us, even though we don't belong to Chicago, and all the things that we revile about Chicago do not apply to the Chicago Cubs. We usually go twice per year, once in the spring when the season is full of hope, and once in late summer when the season has been pissed away and all hope is lost.

Most of us don't think about a Chicago Cubs game as a thing we would like to do. None of us would put a Cubs game on the calendar, and none of us would get on StubHub and pay eighty dollars for a ticket. But when our friend from Chicago calls in August, like he does every August, and says he has extra tickets, and he got them free so don't worry, we're the first to accept. After we accept, we think of the misery of driving to Chicago and finding a place to park and then forking over fifty dollars just for the parking spot. We think about the awful crowds and the bodies crammed into small spaces. Granted we think about the beautiful bodies of women we'll see who are somehow baseball fans. But we think more about hundred-dollar bills shrinking into twenty-dollar bills, and we can see ourselves peeling those from our rolls and handing them out like singles for rounds of beer and for soft pretzels, and later for cab rides and more rounds of beer and a burrito as big as our heads. We can actually picture the twenties peeling off like that and our rolls diminished. It makes us sick to think that we'll act bigger than we are, and that we'll come home poorer than we were.

We think about that whole day gone and what we'll be trading it for and will it be worth it. We think about how much beer we'll consume and how we'll feel the next day. We think we would rather get the boat out, or maybe catch up on yard work, or stay in bed all morning for once with our wives, or get the woodpile where it needs to be. But we accept the tickets because we feel the pull of Chicago as a place we should want to be, even though we were smart never to have been suckered into living there. Chicago is a death sentence we have, until this fateful summer in the year of our Lord—Jesus Christ, 2006— avoided.

After we accept the tickets for next weekend's game, we spend the week regretting our decision. We complain to our wives, and when our wives say, Just stay home if you're going to hate it so much, we get angry that our wives don't understand us and never even seem to want to try. We love our wives, we do. But we tell ourselves that a day in Chicago away from our wives is just what we need, if they're going to treat us this way. And so we go to Wrigley Field, twice per year we go, and we've been going for two decades now and would probably continue to go if it weren't for the events of this upcoming game.

Some of us hold a vague hope that something will happen at Wrigley Field, something improbable and memorable enough to talk about at work on Monday, or maybe even at future Cubs games. Others of us think the key to happiness is never to expect anything to happen, ever. None of us in our small hayfield brains can begin to fathom the events that will occur later that drunken afternoon just beyond the friendly confines of Wrigley Field.

We are farmers and contractors and small-business owners and one of us is even a teacher and one of us is a union slug. One of us was the valedictorian of our class, and one of us flunked out but later got an advanced degree. One of us is a veteran of the Iraq campaigns and has just been discharged after two decades in the military. This game, in fact, is a celebration of TK's discharge, or it happens to coincide with his discharge. Whichever. In high school, we were teammates on the best baseball team in recent school history. Yes, we led our team to the state playoffs for the first time in decades, where we were eliminated in round one. For that reason, our names are still uttered around town, even by the younger generations. At school our pictures still grace the trophy case along with a grass-stained baseball with all of our tiny signatures. We remain heroes of sorts, something for the younger generations to aspire to. And that responsibility binds us. When one of us shows up to a high school baseball game in our own it's like Ernie Banks at Wrigley Field. Something like that.

We're Lutheran or we used to be, though one of us is Catholic but he had to go to church in the next town. We're white, each of us, though our friend who works for ComEd is some part Mexican and his nickname, Babosa, is Mexican for slug. We're approaching middle age, or we've already arrived, though none of us can quite understand what that means. As younger men we thought of middle age as the pathetic end of natural life, but now that we're knocking on the door of middle age we don't feel completely dead. We're all straight, though some of us have experimented and may continue to experiment, though none of us knows which one of us that might be, though we have our suspicions. If we talked about it, which we don't, our opinions would differ on whether occasionally sleeping with another man makes you gay. Our friend with the tickets is Jewish, though none of us knew any Jews growing up, and we knew exactly one black person, who is now in prison, which some of us say just goes to show. Though we have a Jewish friend, we still don't know a single Muslim. TK, who fought in Desert Storm, has unified our low opinion of Muhammad's people.

Each of us inherited the Cubs from our parents, who were also fans, and each of us understands, some of us more clearly than others, that childhood allegiances—to friends, to sports teams, to religions, or to implement manufacturers—are the biggest predictor of adult-hood allegiances. We're also beginning to understand that lifelong allegiances can fray under pressure, or they can simply molder from disuse and inattention.

With game day approaching, none of us wants to drive, though each of us has an SUV big enough for the five of us. Except for the teacher, whose name is Jody, who of course drives a rice burner. One of us finally agrees to drive if he doesn't have to supply the beer for the ride. Agreed, we say. It is the same one of us who always agrees to drive. It is Delavan, who owns a small business selling ag byproducts no one has ever heard of. Delavan is also a farmer, though that's just so he can collect the subsidies, we tease.

Delavan drives to pick us up at our houses on Saturday morning, and we pick up TK last, on account of his house is furthest east. TK we find standing at the end of his gravel drive like a boy waiting for the school bus. His school uniform is digital camo and Cubbie blue, and his lunch bucket is an outsized red beer cooler. Some of us wonder why TK continues to wear the military issue, though none of us mentions it.

S'up n-words, TK says when he boards the bus.

My n-word, Babosa says, taking the cooler from his hands.

You can't say that, Jody says and accepts a beer from the cooler. TK passes beers all around and Delavan points the SUV toward Chicago. The five of us ride together to the game just as we did to our high school games, and the seating chart is even the same. Delavan at the helm and Mike Bell at his right hand. Mike Bell is a contractor who is really more of a roofer. In the back, TK and Babosa are separated by Jody, who is the closest thing we've got to a female, and who therefore always rides bitch.

At the game we attended in May it was decided that this was the year for the Cubs, though by June it was decided it might be next year. In July the Cubs fired their skipper and started dumping contracts. Now it's August and the Chicago Cubs have the worst record in all of baseball. Still, Wrigley Field promises to be sold out today.

We always drink beers on our biannual sojourns to Wrigley Field. We remind ourselves about the old high school covenant: The D the D, or, The Driver's the Drunkest, and we drink beers one after the other for the duration of the two-hour ride into Wrigleyville. We drink so much beer that we must stop at the Belvidere tollway oasis and then the Des Plaines Oasis to use the toilet. By the time we get to the Des Plaines Oasis we're bleary and grinning. One of us says he's hungry for a Longaberger basket. Another of us says, Des Plaines, Des Plaines, as if enjoying the taste of the words in his mouth. We load back into the SUV and pass out fresh beers and drive. The D the D, yo, one of us puts out, and gets fist bumps in return.

The trust we have in our driver is unimpeachable, like a child's trust in his father. None of us suspects that our friend will careen off the interstate and manslaughter us or some other motorist, and indeed he does not. Our drunken savior Delavan keeps us safe, for now.

We are one unit as we hurdle in our SUV through the tollway corridor, past exits for towns that have become in our lifetime the exurbs, then past the western suburbs and into the near-western suburbs. We are veterans of many campaigns to Wrigley Field. On the tollway other SUVs and pickups full of men and boys head to Wrigley Field. The closer we get, the more the vehicles on the tollway seem like a convoy headed for a rendezvous. As we near our destination, the mood in the SUV becomes somber. The tightly wound orbit in which we travel is beginning to fray. It frays so gradually none of us even knows it's happening.

This year one of our wives will be born again.

One of us will give his father his final shave.

One of our daughters is pulling out all her hair.

One of us will find his brother hanging from a barn rafter.

One of our wives is about to invite a friend into the bedroom.

On the Kennedy Expressway there are so many lanes of traffic one of us tries to count them and has to start over. Each of us stares in wonder as the Chicago skyline reveals itself. Now we can see the skyscrapers. There's the Standard Oil building, one of us thinks, or maybe that's not it. There's the Sears Tower. Each of us is certain about that. On our fourth-grade field trip each of us went to the top of the Sears Tower, and none of us has been back since. Each of us is grateful to see the West Addison Street exit for Wrigley Field, for each of us again has to piss.

If Wrigley Field is known as the confines, then what do we call the myriad streets and alleys radiating away from the old edifice? One of us is reminded of an old European quarter, what with the narrow passages and the rows of merchandise and the hawkers and pushers, some holding fistfuls of money as they make confusing transactions with the hordes. Mike Bell peels a hundred from his roll to pay for the slim gap in the alley where Delavan somehow squeezes his SUV. And though the slot is so narrow we can barely open our doors, we each manage to piss right there between the telephone poles and old garages of Wrigleyville. The old Polish woman who sells us the spot looks like a character from a fairy tale with her brown sweater and plaid headscarf. She makes change for Mike Bell even while Mike Bell has one hand on his dick. We drain our beers and enter the mighty current that pulls us toward the ballpark.

Arriving at Clark and Addison at the main Wrigley gate, some of us are surprised, even after so many arrivals, to see that the place exists in color, for we grew up watching the Cubs on black-and-white sets, and in our first thousand views of this fabled place, the shapely marquee that reads, *Wrigley Field, Home of the Chicago Cubs*, was not brilliant red but monochrome. One of us imagines the marquee as an alluring set of feminine lips. We stand before it with a few extra minutes on our hands. Still time, thanks to Delavan's good driving, to dip into the Cubby Bear, where Jody breaks his first C-note on a quick round of tallboys.

In the Cubby Bear our attention is captured by a dazzling twenty-something couple. The man wears an orange track suit and aviator glasses, and the blonde beauty on his arm looks like an advertisement for this place. Her tight Cubs T-shirt looks painted on, and the bear cub in the logo of her snug team shorts seems to nuzzle the succulent cup of her buttocks. Her blonde hair she wears in a bun under a Cubs visor. There is little to suggest she belongs to the same species we do. The smear of eye black she wears under each eye is the proverbial frosting on the cake.

Tell me a chick with eye black is not the sexiest thing you've ever seen, one of us says. We watch in amazement as Orange Track Suit guides the Cub Model into the men's john, past the line of men who are in fact waiting for the john. None of us can believe it when the door shuts behind them. Did you see that? we say to one another, and we answer with the same question, Did you see that?

In the time it takes us to finish our tallboys, the door opens again and the couple walks out, the line of waiting men parting for them. The Cub Model's eye black looks streakier now, which is somehow even sexier, and her blonde bun looks mussed. Are we imagining this? Did Orange Track Suit just wink at another dude in the line? Chicago is a difficult city to understand, we all agree, and the transactions that occur here mystify us. In our town, we would invite Orange Track Suit to taste our pavement outside our local bar. In Chicago, he gets to eff the hottest number in the place while everyone stands around imagining it. Anything, it appears, is possible within the radiant halo of Wrigley Field.

Back in the sunlit intersection of Clark and Addison, in the confusion and mayhem, the cabs honk and eddy. One nearly mows us down as we jaywalk across Addison. The cabbie is dark and turbanned and yells something at us in a language we cannot fathom, the sounds like bringing up phlegm from deep within and expelling the moistness toward us. One of us slaps the rear fender of the yellow beast as it rushes past. We barely register the calamity we just avoided before we pass beneath the glistening red marquee, and Wrigley Field swallows us.

The sun always shines on the left-field bleachers at Wrigley Field, and it is shining hotly this day as we emerge from the stadium's bowels to search for our seats. The game is already underway, and one of us asks, The fuck are the Cubs playing anyway? and one of us answers, The lowly Pads. We have, gentlemen, a puncher's chance.

Of the five of us, only Babosa is worth a shit at reading the tickets. As we wait, one of us licks a finger, holds it up, and announces the wind is indeed blowing out. Babosa is triumphant, and he finds the five empty seats in the middle of a row. There is our ticket patron, Simon, waving to us, and before we can even sit down next to him, the closest vendor yells, Beer Here! TK peels a Franklin from his roll, hands it down the line, and five tallboys come back down the line toward our accepting arms.

Thanks for the tickets, hey Simon, one of us says. Free tickets and they're still a ripoff.

Up yours, Simon says, giving us the finger. Then Simon says, Hey look who I found. At his right is a golden-haired young man in a camo Angels' jersey smiling like he knows us. He's the only person in the bleachers not wearing blue.

It takes us a moment, but we finally recognize him as one of our own. Yes, he's from our town. Nice kid, Gin Phillips's little cousin Henry. A good ballplayer too, we remember.

Hey Henry, we all say.

TK fucked you, Henry, another of us says, meaning Henry was shorted a beer.

Henry, we remember, was like a dozen years behind us in school. Gin was in our class, though he rode the pine on our winning team. We give high fives to Simon and Henry. One of us went to college with Simon, and now he's our adopted Jewish citiot, an honorary member of our hometown who works at the Mercantile Exchange. He comes to our town in the fall and shoots our deer from our shelter-belts and carries back with him our venison and good oak firewood. In return, he furnishes these bleacher seats and stock tips we rarely use. We are glad to have our own private citiot, Simon.

We settle back and take in the expanse of the confines: the green, green perfection of the outfield grass, the impeccably raked diamond infield, the tight rows of box seats rising like the galleries of a ship, up to the air-conditioned skyboxes where those rich pricks sit and palm their highballs. Down below us, the miniature ballplayers punch their gloves and hurl the pearl around the horn. Here is the oldest yard in the majors, bar one, and we bush-league pals are among the thousands who brine the rim of it. Already we're drunker—more drunk—than we've been in many weeks and it's still the first inning and first blood has not yet been scratched by either team. One of us imagines Wrigley as a giant ark cradling the last of our kind. Another of us is thinking about the brick outfield walls cloaked in ivy, which makes Wrigley seem more like a coliseum than a ballpark, home to sport's most ancient rivalries. An old place, like Wrigley, is better than a new place, all of us would agree. Len Kasper announces a sell-out crowd of 41,072 souls. Announces Armed Forces Day, and we all yell, Hooray. TK tips his digital camo hat and takes applause from the bleacher fans around us. He's assured not to buy another beer for the duration, and one of us thinks the lucky SOB will get home with his roll intact.

In the bottom of the second the Cubs mount a threat, but the inning ends with our guys stranded at first and third. The Padres starter worked his ass out of a jam and is now liable to settle down. Maddux is pitching for our guys. Yes, crafty old Maddux is back in Chi-town for a swan song and tossing two-seamers at like eighty-two.

Please don't let this be a pitcher's duel, one of us says.

The bleachers refuel between innings, and we take in the spectacle, arguing whether or not these are the same seats we had last year, or the year before that. Some of us remember our dads talking about paying a quarter for bleacher seats after the war. Talking about how, in those days, women could come to the games free. Our dads, some of them dead now, may have sat in these very seats next to dames who got in for nothing. Now, a bleacher seat set you back the same as a field box, and the bleachers are the more coveted. We come to watch baseball, sure, but we also come to watch the Young and the Beautiful, for most everyone in the bleacher seats these days seems cast for the show. Looking out over the sea of young fans, one of us thinks of a saying he heard one time. What was it? Youth is the only thing worth having.

In the top of the third, the Pads nick Maddux for a run on a bunt single, a stolen base, and a couple of groundouts. In the bottom of the inning the Padres starter sets the Cubs down in order. Christ, one of us says, let's at least see a fly ball. The game is indeed shaping up to be a pitcher's duel despite the favorable wind. The outfielders for both teams blow bubbles and stretch their legs.

With nothing much to see on the ballfield, we concern ourselves with rounds of beer and trips to the head. We catch up with Henry and Simon. After high school, Henry did a hitch in the Navy, he tells us, but never left San Diego, what they called Operation Desert Vacation. Now he's back, living in Chicago, running trades on the floor of the Merc—where he met Simon—and taking law classes nights on the GI Bill.

Henry is a version of us a dozen years newer. Here's a home-owner making a go of it in the city, though he is no citiot. Henry belongs in these bleachers in ways we do not. He's one of the Young and the Beautiful, sure, but he's one of ours, too. He looks into our eyes when he talks to us and asks each of us about our wives and families. When Henry takes out his roll to pay for a round, one of us says, Put that away, and we all say, Yes, put that away, Henry.

Henry is a handsome boy, one of us thinks, though in your middle twenties are you still a boy? Each of us finds himself wondering about Henry, the shiny new member of the team. What makes Henry so charming, one of us thinks, is that he shows us a devotion we didn't earn. Henry saw our pictures in the trophy case every day at school. We were the boys Henry grew up wanting to be. Do you ever out-grow that devotion? Most of Henry's attention seems directed at TK, which makes sense since they share the military. Still, at least one of us wishes the seats were rearranged.

Beer here! calls the vendor. True to the spirit of Armed Forces Day, the rounds keep coming for TK. Drunken bleacher bums can't seem to thank him enough for his service to our country. Two or three Cubs models ask to take selfies with TK, and we suddenly realize why he isn't wearing civvies. Henry could cash in on this Support-Our-Troops Lovefest, but he does not, even though he's sitting right beside TK talking about his discharge.

We don't yet know the nature of his discharge. We tell ourselves that it's honorable, but we confess to our wives that we're not sure.

By the fourth inning the beer doesn't even want to loiter in our bladders before demanding release. One of us leans forward, unzips, and fills the very cup he just emptied. Behind our sunglasses some of us close our eyes and nod off in the sun. We stir only when we hear the crack of a bat, and we stand and cheer, or else we boo. Behind our sunglasses our heads swim and our moods turn sour. In between cracks of the bat and trips to the head we dwell on the Cubs' sad state of being, what some of us think of as Cubness. It's not like us to dwell, but this is a battle of cellar-dwellers after all, and a pitcher's duel to boot.

Each year our Cubs find new and unexpected ways to flounder. They start each season with foolproof plans to win, yet lose. They win the sweepstakes for the bona fide star but the bona fide star fades in Cubby blue and bloats with the contract. They nurture a blue chipper through four years on the farm, only to see the blue chipper's ulnar collateral rupture into spaghetti. They bring in an old vet to unify the clubhouse. They hire a new skipper. Invest in Latin America. They make the investments, but the investments don't pan out. Each investment seemed sound at the time but in the August sun of the bleacher seats seems glaringly bad. There are limitless ways to lose, each of us knows. Promise leads to disappointment leads to Waveland Avenue. Seventy-five losses on the year thus far. One hundred losses is within our reach.

Every decade or so the hibernating Cubs arise from the cellar to threaten a run, but then they tucker and collapse and settle back in the cellar where they seem most comfortable. Still, 41,072 souls arrive to see the spectacle.

This is what it means to be middle-aged, we begin to fathom. It's August in the major leagues. All potential is gone, the cake of our mediocrity baked.

Why do we drive all this way? one of us says.

It's like asking why we live in a hick town in a hayfield where the weather is the only thing that blows.

Next year we'll go see the Brew Crew, one of us says.

Word up, one of us comes back.

But none of us can really imagine it. Our dads didn't root for the Brew Crew, after all. It's not as if you can simply choose for whom to root. If you could, the citiots would surely go elsewhere. They have their brownstones in Bucktown or Roscoe Village that doubled in value just last year. Any night of the week they might take a cab to Division Street and bring home a willing bedfellow. Like ours, their dads too must have taken these seats for a quarter, and so they're stuck here with us, in the only place that could bring us together, rooting for a team that will never win.

No fan from anywhere else can quite understand what it's like to reside in these bleachers. This is Cubness. Here we are and we don't quite understand it ourselves. If you root for another team you can always console yourself by thinking back to the glory days when your team brought home the World Series trophy. With the Cubs that was generations ago. Our dads weren't even alive back in that day. Our granddads and their dads were born into this ancient losing streak.

In the fifth inning it's still 1–0 and Maddux is dealing like the Maddux of old, nibbling at the corners, changing speeds just percep-ibly. Maddux is a pitcher our fathers deeply admired, a bridge of our generations. That old fucker still owns the plate, one of us says. Dela-van breaks a C-note for a round. Henry is still chatting with TK, all smiles and gestures suggest he's telling TK a happy story. It's strange to have Henry out here with us. These biannual trips and this stupefying drunkenness are routine, but Henry is a newness we didn't expect.

In the bottom of the fifth, or maybe it's the sixth, the Pads scotch another Cubs rally. Cubs' next white hope Murton K's on a hanging slider to end the threat.

Sosa would have gone yard on that pitch, one of us says.

This declaration leads us to recount the names of bygone Cubs, something we often do to pass the time and cheer ourselves. We say the litany of usuals. We say Banks and we say Santo and we say Williams and Jenkins and Sandberg, and we do say Sosa, in spite of the bad things he did. One of us reaches way back and brings forth Mordecai Three Fingers Brown, but none of us is a historian of the game. Three Fingers Brown is like Honest Abe Lincoln or some other dead president from days of yore that you can name, but you can't ever know. We shun history, which we don't understand, for the deep cuts of our youth, naming players who were our personal favorites, or perhaps the Cubs who disappointed us the most.

Kingman, one of us says.

Kingman, another of us repeats. If you can say Kingman I can say Ron Cey.

Bobby Dernier, one of us says, as if changing the subject.

Grace, one of us says.

Word, one of us replies.

Recall Rick Reuschel, another of us says.

Another of us says another Rick. Sutcliffe.

Fucking Sutcliffe.

How about Dunston?

How about Bowa?

Jo-dy, Jo-dy Davis, sings Jody, and we all laugh out loud.

It takes quite a while for one of us to summon the nerve to say Buckner, who always gets said last.

William Joseph Buckner, one of us replies. Jesus Christ.

His Cubness. Billy Buck.

Beer here! yells the vendor, and Mike Bell digs out his roll.

As the game drags on each of us gets lost in the daydreamy innings of the August afternoon. Our minds follow tangents like flyballs from our youth that we lost in the sun. The game seems like it will never end, yet at the same time we know that when the end does come, it will seem too soon.

One of us thinks about shagging flies with his dad on a summer afternoon. They popped flies in the fenced pasture between the horse barn and the line of trees. That expanse once seemed like all the space you would ever need. The father stood, barn as a backstop, lofting flies over the horse pasture with the electrified fence. The son tried to snag the flies without touching the fence. Can of corn, the father called out when the son gloved a ball. Once in a while the father unleashed his potential and sent a Ruthian clout sailing over the trees. That one's in orbit, the father said, and the son believed him.

One of us thinks of gluttony: 41,072 bodies consuming and then expelling beer and bratwurst and peanuts and mustard and pretzel dough and tobacco juice, and add a cupful of bodily pearlescence to wash it down into the soil under Wrigley, where surely it must moisten and weaken the century-old footings upon which our collective weight depends.

Another of us thinks about that ripe young peach two rows up and the asshole next to her. How did he rate her? Maybe she's just another cooze with cum dripping down her leg from what happened in the john before the game. Everything gets taken to its logical conclusion. In the john before the game. Under the bleachers between innings. On the cab ride home. Or maybe they make it all the way to her friend's efficiency under the L and her friend says, Sure, I'll step out for a bit, feel free to use the futon. It's happened already or it's going to happen. It's just not going to happen to one of us, unless we run a batch off in the stall with ten guys waiting to use it.

Another of us thinks of Henry. Here was Henry who still had a chance. Henry seemed to grow more radiant as the game went on. There was something youthful and hopeful about him. And something physically inviting. The delicate sunburned skin on his neck, the promise of salt on his skin, and the full healthiness of his hair. The mismatched jersey in a sea of blue. Henry was no joiner. Henry made his own way.

Another of us can't stop dwelling on Buckner, the epitome of all the Cubs' hope and failing. Buckner spent years building an argument for the Hall of Fame and had that future stolen on a slow roller. How was that fair? How could a ground ball define a career? Had that grounder found the web of Buckner's glove, he would be a cinch for the Hall. Open up your legs, Cooperstown, here comes Billy Buck, sliding home head first. But it was not to be, as everyone knows. That dribbler Mookie hit was like a grenade lobbed toward first. It exploded everything. What remains is this viral mental image of a broken-down Buckner stooped over, out beyond first bag. Everyone knows what's coming to him. Bent over out there in those ridiculous high tops. Bent over so many thousands of times the ankles gone and can't bend over good when it counts.

It's better just to imagine Buckner on his big ranch in Idaho. That's better. Buckner's just in from shooting grouse, and he cracks a beer and doesn't think about baseball at all. Buckner's ranch has like a hundred solid-wood, six-panel doors. His baseball career is behind one of them. It's a door Buckner never opens anymore. Buckner only opens the doors that lead to good places.

A most thunderous, deafening boom interrupts our musings and we follow the eyes of our bleacher mates skyward. It's not so far past 9/11 that some of us don't still get nervous in a crowd in our major cities. Especially when three fighter jets shatter the sound barrier just above our heads. There go the three Tomcats, or whatever they are. They've just buzzed our bleachers. What the hell?

No, we are not being attacked. We are being invited to stretch, and to salute the members of our armed forces. It's the middle of the seventh, and there's John Fogerty hanging out of the announcer's box to sing with us. Uh-one, uh-two, uh-three . . .

We do sing. The bleachers are a sea of sloppy drunks, beer sloshed from the sonic boom, mascara running, buttons sprung, cleavages and crotches ripening in the sun. We're sodden and slurring and we spill more beer and embrace each other and we sing. One of us sings the lyrics from the forgotten verse. *There isn't anyone else like me / Maybe I'll go down in his-tory* . . . We're triumphant and blissful and none of us thinks about anything else at all until we finish the song, and then we exhale, and we give some skin to our neighbors and settle back into our collective stupor.

During the stretch TK gets more attention. Fans fall over themselves to shake his hand. Thank you for keeping us safe, the fans say, and then ask for a selfie. Yes, everyone seems to want to suck TK's dick, especially the men.

We're surprised that Henry tells us that after the stretch he has to go.

Go in a cup, yo, one of us says. Fist bumps. More skin.

Duty calls, Henry tells us. He's got class tonight and he has to go home to study.

Sure, Henry you'll go home and study, we think. We can all imagine what Henry has waiting in his apartment for him. It isn't a book. . . . But it does have a spine! Booh-yeah, Henry! We cheer Henry in our minds. Here's one of us who conquered the city. Here's one who deserves what's coming to him. Here's our boy, Henry!

So long, Henry, each of us says. We bro-hug him and give him skin and tell him we'll buy him a beer at the Best Shot next time he's in town. Yes, Henry could hold his own with the citiots, and he could run the table back home too. The Cubs might lose a hundred games, but not our Henry.

I'd like to get to know that kid better, more than one of us thinks.

When he gets to the aisle, Henry looks back and gives us a big sweeping wave and a smile. He shoots TK a salute, and TK says, Cubs suck.

Hey, anyone can have a bad century, Henry comes back. It sounds like he's quoting someone. One of his old naval officers, or maybe some Cubs legend of yore. We can't tell if he's serious or full of shit. In any case, those are his last words, and that's the last we ever see of him. None of us will ever get to know Henry any better than we already know him.

The seventh inning is to a baseball game what early August is to summer. By the time August rolls around you can kiss the summer good-bye and likewise the ball game. After the stretch, everything rushes toward conclusion and you had better drink up, yo, because they stop watering the bleachers in the middle of the eighth.

Last call! shouts the vendor, and Jody peels two more twenties from his roll. Let these be the last, he thinks, and they are.

In the ninth the Cubs muster one last gasp. With two gone and the bases empty Ramirez sends a moon shot deep to left. The bleachers rise as one to accept the ball. The Pads' left fielder backs to the warning track and readies his leap into the ivy. This will be close. From our vantage point we lose the ball, and for a moment no one is sure what happened. Then a deep cheer erupts from Wrigley and we know. It is. A home run.

Some bleacher bum from a generation ago holds the ball aloft in a landing net. He's got no shirt and a big red *U* painted on his fat gut. His friends' midsections spell the rest of the home team. Those old fuckers might be happier than they've ever been, one of us thinks. Ramirez rounds the bases with his fist in the air. Wrigley rocks. The stadium really does seem to pitch and heel. We can barely maintain our balance. Here it is. Vindication. Ramirez's two-out home run is our home run. His success against the odds is the unlikely success of each fan still in attendance. At Wrigley Field you get what you pay for after all. We've won. Or at least we've forestalled losing, which might be the same thing. Our exaltation, complete for several moments, fades just perceptibly at the prospects of facing extra innings without beer. Too bad Henry didn't stay for the finale, one of us says. Henry would have loved to see this.

But wait a minute, the umpires are gathered in the infield. Something has gone awry. Dusty Baker trots out of the dugout and confronts the umps. The conference continues with Baker pointing to the sky and then shaking his fist at the left-field bleachers, like he's scolding us. Finally, the umps point to the dugout and Ramirez comes limp-trotting back out into the infield with his head hung low. The umps assign him to second base, and they toss a defiant Baker just for good measure. The home run has been ruled a double. Wrigley Field groans to its buttresses. It is a groan that unleashes a century's worth of groans stored in the grain of this old architecture. It appears as if the fat schmuck with the *U* belly has gone Bartman and interfered with the outfielder. We deserve each other, one of us thinks. Our Cubs and their fans. Cruel, cruel life. Two security guards await the sorry-ass fan in the aisle. Here's another loser that will be defined by a moment, one of us thinks, and this one not even original. That was a live one lobbed his way and he should know better than to touch it.

You can't make this shit up anymore, one of us says. Let's go home.

As if he hears our friend's voice in his ear, Theriot, the little pussy, nubs a weak comebacker to the mound to end the game. Even with the conclusion we expect, there is still a sharp intestinal ache at the final verdict. That's us down there in the batter's box failing to extend the game. Each of us feels it. Final score: One-zip. Zilch. Nil. Nulla. Cubs lose. Cubs lose. Cubs lose.

We start at Murphy's Bleachers and then head to Guthrie's Tavern. One of us wonders if Cubs fans drink more after a win or after a loss. Once you've drunken yourself sober, it takes more work to get your grin back on. It becomes clear that we will not leave until our rolls have been depleted. It would be a deadly sin to leave Chicago with a single bill in our rolls, we seem to agree.

Night has fallen without our wherewithal. Simon decides to head back to his condo in Wicker Park. We say good-bye to Simon and say thanks for the good times. Say hey to Henry when you see him, we say. Now it's just the hometown crew. Most of the Cubs fans seem to have gone home, and regular people trickle into the bar, people on dates, or people just starting for the night, ready to take over our shift. We're like the last hangers on at a party the host can't convince to leave. TK's gone silent, one of us notices. Another of us has pissed himself and spends too long in the john with the hand dryer. And yet another round arrives and departs like the last.

One of us finally insists we go to the Billy Goat on Michigan. The Billy Goat is the appropriate place to say good-bye. But the Billy Goat means a cab ride, so we check our rolls to see who's paying, and guess what? Our rolls are exhausted. Nothing to spend means no more to drink means time to go home. We stumble out of the tavern to search for our SUV among the ancient back alleys of Wrigleyville.

Most of us pass out in the SUV on the Kennedy before we even get to see Chicago in the rearview mirror. Delavan is a machine, bless him. He passes beneath the Des Plaines Oasis. The radio is now his copilot. Stone Temple Pilot. He drives and drives. The SUV is a blaring hearse hauling the four bodies back to their families.

All bad news awakens us from a slumber. In the morning it's our wives handing us the phone.

Henry's gone.

Fuck you.

No, man. It's true. Listen.

Delavan speaks now into our ears and we obey, sobering and quiet. Delavan himself got the news in a series of predawn texts and phone calls from Simon. Henry had evidently hailed a cab on Addison after he left us in the bleachers. When a cabbie stopped for the fare, Henry refused the ride. The cabbie would have been a Muslim, and Henry passed no commerce with Muslims. That was a rule he had

Who knows where he came up with it. Maybe that was his way of honoring TK and others in the brotherhood, or who knows, maybe he had a private feud we didn't understand.

You couldn't have a rule like that, even we knew.

Henry lived long enough to tell part of his story in the ER. Simon was there. Henry was awake and alive to the world. But then a brain aneurysm and massive hemorrhage finished Henry's story for him.

We can imagine how it happened. Henry and the cabbie exchanged words. That much we know. There wouldn't have been too many words. In our town, you don't spend much time telling your rival what you're about to do to him. Henry would have gotten his licks in.

Henry was half-in, half-out of the cab. When the cabbie peeled out, Henry was still hanging on. After that, we don't know. When they found Henry, his body was badly mangled and ruptured. One witness later said the cabbie backed up and ran him over again, but another witness said, no, it didn't happen that way. The cabbie escaped. It doesn't matter. Henry, his beautiful body alive and among us just hours ago, is now cold.

Stupid and half-awake, helpless now in our dumb beds, we don't know what to think: The outcome you hope for is never the one that comes to you? There is no justice in the world?

In the days and weeks after the accident, or the murder as some of us call it, the whole town is abuzz. More than one of us believe there is some kind of conspiracy going on in the city of Chicago and elsewhere in the country. You tell me, one of us says, if the tables were turned, and one of us was driving that cab, and it was a Christian killed a Muslim. You tell me things wouldn't be different.

Some of us agree. Yes, if the tables were turned, things would be different. One of the witnesses said the cabbie wasn't a Muslim at all, but a Sikh.

That cabbie is still in Chicago taking fares, which is one reason we don't go anymore to Wrigley Field. We don't see each other as much around town either. A thing like that. Who can say? Your sentence could be delivered to you from any quarter, each of us knows. Something always comes up. One of us is too busy at work, or one of us is home with the kid. It's always something. Or another thing: TK's discharge was not honorable, we learn. Something with a private. Something not very honorable at all.

Henry didn't have any kids at least, but his parents were still living. And he had a younger sister, we learned. Our whole town turned out for his memorial, which they had at the town park, on the same stage where one of us was once crowned Homecoming King so many years ago. Each of us loved that park, where the hundred-year-old sugar maples made one big canopy. During the service the five of us stood together. It was only natural that we did. At one point Henry's kid sister noticed us, but then she looked away. Later during the service the wind came up, and the old maples sent down their squadrons of helicopters onto the heads of the grievers.

≡

First One Out

Cunningham awoke to the high-pitched drone of an outboard motor. He savored the sound, eyes shut tight. He could imagine the flat, glass lake, colored greenish from the weed spawn. He watched himself ski behind the fiberglass boat, natural as a pendulum, cutting walls of water on each side of the wake, muscles straining, ears ringing from the Mercury's whine and the perceptible cut of the wooden slalom on the veneer, the backspray filleting his calf. Cunningham could ski, boy. In his mind's eye, he could see it. He could bring his shoulder down near the veneer on his cuts and lay himself flat like that, defying gravity, his spray fanning out colorful in the sunlight, a peacock tail.

Cunningham opened his eyes and saw his flowered bedroom curtains. The alarm was buzzing beside the bed and the numbers on the clock shone redly. Cunningham awoke to the high-pitched drone of his alarm clock. He was in some city, far away from home. The windows were shut tight behind their curtains, and no seaweed breeze tickled his nostrils. Those days were long past, and these days were clichés. Cunningham hit snooze.

There was reason to fling oneself from bed, rush barefoot lake-
ward, haul off the boat canvas, and prime the black rubber egg until
it was hard and hurt your forearms to squeeze and your nose to smell
the squirting 50:1. The reason was loveliness. A boy wants nothing
more than to destroy the lovely. And the lake at 9 a.m. before boating
hours and the morning breeze that ruined it is lovely, a lovely that
has everything to do with evanescence and nothing to do with sticking
around for people who hit snooze. Cunningham could wreck it, and
only in wrecking it achieve his own adolescent, acrobatic human
loveliness. There is no use in skiing, in perfecting a motion, and the
expense is high. But in Cunningham's mind the trade-off was square.
He would take no shine from the hunchback fishermen in their beat-
up dinghies who cursed his waves, boy.

The alarm droned again. Twelve minutes had disappeared.
There was no reason to hoard minutes these days, no reason to get
up at all. Why move from bed to car to chair to car to couch to bed?
Why not stay in bed? A smoker, an overeater, Cunningham figured
he did himself a favor by sleeping extra. By sleeping more, he killed
himself less. *I am saving my life*, Cunningham thought. His overweight
fist shot out and hit the snooze. But the ringing was still there, waves
rippling the lake.

Minutes counted back then, boy, seconds. At ten to nine the lake
was fair game, and often as not there were other boys like Cunningham around the lake prodding their dads, begging that they be the
first one out. And those days are what count now, each one with its
loveliness simultaneously wrecked and made: blankness filled with
the boyish cursive of waves.

As long as they are your waves and not the waves of some other
undeserving rummy. Get out early, Cunningham. Be the first one.
Stand ready at the gate, one foot in ski, the other on wooden dock,
quivering, ready to jump, hit water, sink, and then careen to the
surface, skiing. Put your thumb up then and yell, *Faster! Can't this old
tub move any faster!* Wreck it all quickly, without remorse. Wreck it

especially for those who come after you. Leave a wake for them. And drench the sadass naysaying fishermen in their wingding boats on your way past. What are they waiting for anyway, some nibble?

There is no date on Cunningham's clock. The day bleeds on, becomes the next day, or the next, even. Cunningham remains in bed, corpse-like, saving his life. Somewhere in the house, a bell rings and rings, and rings, until the very sound of it begins to collect dust. If you added up all the growing-up, summertime lake stories in all the Middle West, you would have a sadass stringer full of bottom-feeders as long as this. Fact is you grow up, get tired, and hit snooze. To get a story like this right, you would have to start with Cunningham lighting a firecracker, no, a cherry bomb. Boom. Perfect red ball explodes into, say it, smithereens. Perfection begs destruction. And Cunningham gets the novel idea then that everything in the world has already been made at least once, so wouldn't it be better just to shoot it all to hell.

After the explosion comes the love scene, a sad one of course, starring some tow-headed girl named Rhonda with her feet a little too big, which is, of course, what makes her as lovely as she is. Cunningham tells Rhonda how one day, his best day maybe, he slingshot a midair swallow. Just a piece of gravel. And how the dipsy-diving swallow dropped, splish, dead, and floated there in the lake like an iridescent bobber. How all the lice onboard the swallow clambered for the top of her when they felt their ship begin to pitch and heel. How that beautiful gliding bird had become just a raft for a bunch of cotton-picking lice. How Cunningham had turned that perfect bird into an obscene floater. And how his big brother had seen him drop the midair swallow, which had never been done before, and how Cunningham was a confused hero for a while.

Isn't that some kind of story, he tells Rhonda, reminiscing with her about his little days. These stories about Cunningham's little days bore the shit out of Rhonda, leaving her vulnerable.

And along comes Cunningham's big brother, who knows all about busting cherries and who doesn't give a shit about Tuesday when it's Wednesday out. The story unravels from here, and Cunningham, wounded, wants to fill that dent Rhonda made. For some reason his mind fixes on the two old fishermen. Don't they run on the same gas mix after all? Maybe it's their steadfastness that hooks him. Cunningham tries to understand what it's like to be those old fishermen in their boat, bobber fishing, regular as seagulls. The futility begins here. There can be no commiseration because there is no meaning in the word *empathy*. You don't know what it feels like, old fishermen, to be Cunningham, so don't say you know. You can't even remember what it was like to be you, yesterday, what that felt like.

When a moment is gone, it is replaced immediately with the false memory of a moment. The sublime feeling of catching a fish is resurrected only when there's another tug on the line. In between exists only a stagnant deadness. A cherry bomb bursting, that longed-for destructive creation, becomes only the sterile ringing in the ears. This ringing is not noise but its very absence. Only the next damaging explosion offers some manner of relief.

A swallow's purple dive. A fish's silver leap. Beauty. Entirely useless, but beautiful nonetheless. As arc and acrobatics. Even a myopic old fisherman can notice, That was a nice one, and look forward yet: to something more, or at least *else*. But not you, Cunningham, tackle box of body parts. Get back into your mind and ski, boy. That lake upstairs is waiting for your pathetic ripples.

Lazy *B*

The hair-and-nails place next door looks open, but the barbershop looks shut. The blinds are drawn and the red-and-white barber pole sits frozen. You try the door anyway. You're long overdue for a haircut, and tomorrow is a special occasion. You find the door locked but rattle it again. Two fingers split the blinds, a lock clicks, and the glass front door swings open.

The barber squints against the sun. Danny, where you been? he says. Come on in.

You stand on the threshold. Over your shoulder on the busy expressway the cars reflect the slanting sunlight. Inside, Alex has a bald old man in his chair and behind him a father-son tandem in matching palomino cowboy hats.

Sure you can fit me in?

The barber is all smiles. You know me. I can't turn out a good man.

You return Alex's friendly smile and step into the barbershop. You shut the door behind you and Alex locks it. I have a big job for you then, you say, glancing down to the small mess of gray hair on the checkered floor.

You nod to the old man in the red barber chair. His bald head looks like some globe—Jupiter maybe—ringed with thin white hair and marred by an angry melanoma. You choose the spare red barber chair opposite the row of short red seats where the cowboy and his son sit. The little cowboy, perhaps he is eight, gazes up at Alex's legion of model cars. Two walls are lined with a double row of wooden shelves up high, featuring die-cast models in clear plastic boxes. The big cowboy looks at a magazine. Above him, an imitation antique sign reads: *This **is** your father's barbershop.*

You pick from the stack of vintage nudie magazines on the side counter. You heft the magazine then open it, flipping the glossy pages, settling into the barber chair.

There are two barber chairs here, but Alex is the only barber. One time on a slow day you found Alex himself enthroned in the extra chair, chin up, perusing one of the vintage magazines. You've only been in this barbershop a half-dozen times. On your second visit, Alex called you by your first name when you walked in, as if you were old friends. Actually, Alex knows you only by Danny—the name you go by—but Daniel is your Christian name. It's pronounced Danielle, like a girl's. You're half Polish and half Mexican, but no one would know that. An old friend of yours once said that the Polish and the Mexican canceled each other out. Your skin might be a shade darker than white, but this is California, after all.

Tomorrow, when she visits California for the first time, your mother will dust off that old name. Daniel, she'll say, cupping your face. Look at you. Your father would be so happy with your haircut.

After your last visit to Alex's barbershop, you disappeared for six months to England on assignment with your aerospace company. This is the same company that brought you to California from Wisconsin four years ago. Here in California, the locals call your aerospace company the Lazy *L* because of its ranch-like setting along the 101, and also because it's a gravy job: union benefits and government contracts. Everything used to be a ranch out here at one time, evidently.

Now you sit comfortably in the spare barber chair waiting your turn. The old nudie magazine smiles up at you from every page. It's nice that Alex has remembered you after six months, showing his care and familiarity.

Alex and Jupiter number the country's problems, part of the barbershop routine. Actually, Alex numbers the problems, and Jupiter nods his bald head in time. Jupiter looks old enough to be Alex's father. And Alex, in turn, could be your father. From this angle, you can't quite see Jupiter's eyes. His neck is bent. Could be he's nodding off. Alex's voice rises, either for Jupiter's benefit or because he needs convincing himself. A man will speak louder sometimes to convince himself, the bold sound of his own voice urging him on.

In the five minutes you've been waiting, the barber has numbered the old problem of taxes and the old problem of gasoline prices. To Alex's view, the skyrocketing cost of gasoline had mostly to do with the liberals and their string of lawyers who forbid searching for resources on our own soils.

You tell me how they get nearly four dollars for a cotton-picking gallon of gasoline? Alex says.

In the barbershop this is an old record that spins again and again. Some people avoid barbershops because of these routines, but you find it familiar to be face-to-face with Alex's assurance. Most of the men who work at the Lazy *L* are similarly self-confident. After all, they make good money. And they work for the best company—the Lazy *L*—in the best state—California—in the best country in the world. Throw in a defined benefit pension plan and the promise of even greener pastures in the Lazy Hereafter, and it's no surprise why everyone is so self-satisfied.

Yes, here in the barbershop you feel right at home. A barber is just a barber, harmless as a haircut. Here, the contracts are uncomplicated, and you can see the whole place from one chair. And so you return, every three months or so, because given a choice, you would rather come back to an old place than go someplace new.

You let the barber's bold, ignorant arguments comfort rather than rile you. Now Alex has settled on the country's number one mother of a problem. He's been finished with Jupiter's hair for some time, but he's putting the finishing touches on with the straight razor. Alex loves the finishing touches. The old men in his chair don't mind paying for a haircut, so long as Alex doesn't finish them off too quickly. In theory, Alex says, waving the razor, you can link most of our problems right now to illegal immigration. All these illegals come flooding into the country and take up our jobs and suck up our taxes. You take our hospitals. L.A. alone had twenty thousand illegal Mexicans born last year.

Alex touches the straight razor to the strop then spins Jupiter in his chair to look at himself in the mirror. Did we get her? Alex asks. Jupiter nods approval and Alex wipes the blade. He undoes the drop cloth, spilling a meager palmful of Jupiter's gray clippings onto the black-and-white tiles. That's brown babies paid for by you and me, Alex says. Now tell me we don't got a problem right there.

You put down your magazine and consider. I'm a Mexican, Alex. Did you know that about me? My dad was a Mexican and a veteran of a foreign war. This is what you want to say. But you say nothing. This is what you get for passing. Talk that should happen behind your back happens in front of your face. It's happened a hundred times, yet still it cuts. You'll spend the next hours wishing you would have said something hard and decisive instead of sitting mute and compliant.

Jupiter unbends himself and retrieves his wallet. Sounds like you have it all down square, Alex, he says. I can't argue with you there. He moves around toward the door. What's that come to now?

That comes to eighteen, Alex says. He stands behind the chair. Above him, next to his framed barbering license, a black-and-white placard reads, *Standard hairstyles for men and boys*. There are several illustrations, all subtle variations on the *fade*, the *flat top*, and the *high and tight*.

Eighteen, Jupiter says. He pauses, seeming to mull over the questionable figure. His fresh haircut, something like a *low and tight*, isn't on the chart. He says, The first haircut you gave me cost four dollars right here, what, twenty-five years ago? Jupiter looks over to you and gives you a wink. The amount of hair I got, the price ought to go down, not up.

Well, you got the cost of living to consider, Alex protests, until he sees the old man smile and place a twenty on the counter.

You can make up the difference next time, Jupiter says, and moves toward the door.

I'll be here. You know me . . . , Alex calls after him.

When Jupiter lets himself out, the barber locks the door behind him, finishes dusting the chair, then turns to the two on the short red seats. Next victim, he says to the boy. The boy looks down, his face disappearing behind the palomino hat, and moves in closer to his father.

This is his first real haircut, the cowboy says. I been cutting it myself at home till now. Till now that's been all right, but the wife thinks Little Man ought to have a real haircut. You feel a twinge of sympathy for the boy. His father has a shaggy handlebar mustache. He seems good-natured enough—a cowboy like in those movies, the one you're supposed to root for.

Let's step up to the chute then, Little Man, Alex says. He spreads the drop cloth like a cape. I promise to go easy on you since it's your first time through. The boy doesn't look up, so the barber walks toward him. From his shirt pocket peer two silver curves, the tops of his scissors. The barber makes a little show of stepping over the black tiles and pausing on the white ones, trying to capture the boy's downcast gaze. But Little Man isn't having any. He crams onto his father's lap, burying his face in his father's denim shirt. Cowboy tries to peel him off, and when he does, you catch a glimpse of the boy's face. He's a pale, tow-headed boy, but his face has reddened now, a shade lighter than the chairs. He doesn't appear to be breathing.

The barber gives the boy some ground. Let's see what I have to put Little Man more at ease, he says. He walks over to the shelves lining the walls, still stepping over the black tiles. He begins to finger some of the dozens of model cars, each in clear plastic boxes, each the size of a good-sized hand. I've got every make of car ever manufactured on American soils, he says, handling a red, late-fifties T-Bird. The boy casts a look up from under his hat, up to his father, then up further yet to the barber and the line of boxed cars. Alex seems to be searching for just the right car. He handles others the same vintage as the T-Bird, then moves along the shelf toward the present day. The boy watches him fully now. He breathes a small gulp of air.

Looking at the barber from behind, with his head tilted back, you can see that Alex is blessed with a full head of hair—no tell-tale thinning in the center of his scalp. He has deep black hair yet—probably dyed. He seems more Italian in the pictures taped along the mirror, of himself as a confident young soldier. Somehow the Italianness of the older man standing here fussing over the model cars has receded. Neither the barber's age nor his ethnicity is evident. You know he's a Vietnam veteran, which means he has to be in his sixties. But he could pass for a decade younger. In the picture, he made a fine-looking soldier. Except for the uniform, he could have been a soldier in any of our wars.

The barber's fingers settle on a box and lift it gently, like a trophy. This, Little Man, is a '66 Ford Mustang ragtop. I bought this vehicle when I got back from the service. She's got two hundred wild ponies under the hood. He kneels close to Little Man, leaning in, leading with the clear plastic box. The other hand he's got against his thigh, palming the scissors. Somehow he made the switch. Little Man shows two rows of straight white teeth. In his fist, the barber's scissors glint.

The barber holds the box closer now. Inside the box the Mustang is sky blue. The barber talks softly, expertly, coaxing the boy. Look at the chrome ornament on the grille, he says. It's a chrome pony, just like a real pony. I used to polish the chrome pony before I took her out. Alex looks up at Cowboy smiling and then back to the Little Man. Go on. Take her out, he says. He pushes the box toward the boy and the boy reaches to accept.

The barber is poised to jerk back the offering and seize the boy's thin wrists. But of course he does not. Of course he hands the box over. Little Man slides his tiny fingers under the lid of clear plastic, loosening it. The lid falls open. The boy tilts the box, and the sky-blue Mustang hesitates, then rolls out.

She's a beaut, Little Man says. The barber stands up then, steps back, and crosses his strong bare arms. He still holds the scissors in one fist. For a moment, it's quiet and still in the barbershop.

Why don't you go on ahead, Cowboy says to you. We're in no hurry, and this thing might take a while. You go on first.

The cowboy's offering startles you. You've been watching the scene over the nude pictures in the magazine, and you realize you've been holding your breath. Something has just been narrowly averted. The pages feel slick and vulgar in your fingers. You replace the glossy magazine on the stack, arise from the comfortable chair, somewhat dizzily, and approach the barber.

Back at his station, Alex makes his ceremonious preparations with the neck cloth and drop cloth. Short haircut, Danny?

Yes, short haircut, but don't go above the ears. Tomorrow my mother visits from Wisconsin, and that's the way she likes it.

Special haircut for Mom, then, Alex says, and spins you around to face the mirror. He won't cut your hair in this position—he'll face you away from the mirror. He doesn't like you to watch him while he cuts your hair. You yourself would rather not watch. On the counter by the mirror sits a wide-mouthed jar filled with blue liquid and various combs and scissors. All these scissors remind you of an article you read about how, historically, barbers kept the sharpest and most sterile instruments in town. For this reason, they were not only barbers but also doctors and veterinarians. The red-and-white swirl of the barber pole signaled to townsfolk, and to passersby, that blood-letting occurred here.

Alex dedicates some attention to the natural cowlick in your hair, massaging in some sort of product. Alex's face is directly above your face in the mirror. Looking at the two of you in the mirror, you see that you could be Alex's *hijo*. The word comes to you in Spanish, surprising you. You never went to the barbershop as a boy. Your father, career military, did all the barbering.

Alex has selected the appropriate attachment for his clippers, and now he spins the chair smoothly back around and begins to cut. The clippers buzz deeply in your skull and teeth, and the barber's strong fingers hold your temples. Alex cuts expertly and quickly during this part of the operation. Generally speaking, he worked quickly over a head of hair until he got to the finish work, the short clipping of the individual hairs and the shaping and shaving of the short hairs around the ears and neck.

Now, Alex is unusually quiet. The strong, unmistakably male fingers work on your scalp. You would rather have your hair cut by a man. When a beautician runs her fingers through your hair, brushing you with her pelvis and chest, you feel the weight of her hope and regret. With a man, the contract has no hidden dangers. Yes, it's better to have a man. The question of preference is solved easily enough by recalling simply that your father had cut your hair, not your mother. Your earliest associations with this shearing ritual were male associations.

The barber pauses for a moment and walks to the window. He twists the thin plastic stick that opens the blinds, and blush evening light floods the barbershop, fitting everything in the room with low-slung shadows. Outside, the cars flow down the expressway. The barber walks back to his station. You squint, glancing down at Alex's watch. His watch is set to military time, not California time. It's six o'clock California time. No rest for the wicked, Alex says. I'll have to phone I'll be late for supper.

Outside, the red-and-white barber pole is spinning. When you walked in, it was still.

That thing just goes berserk, Alex says.

In the ruddy light, the red swirls of the barber pole appear black. Just then a tight group of four Latino boys walks by the front of Alex's shop. They seem to be coming from the hair-and-nails place next door. They loiter about awhile outside laughing and talking in Spanish until the barber waves them off with both arms. Go on, he says. We're closed.

Three of the four wear dark, hooded sweatshirts with Greek letters on the front. They wear their hoods up. You noticed this before, a trend from your childhood come back round. You used to wear your own sweatshirt hood up, to hide your shaved head.

What goes on there next door? you ask. Cowboy looks up, also interested. Alex is through with the clippers for now. He scissors rapidly at the sides of your scalp. The hair falls in thick, dark clumps on the drop cloth.

Don't get me started on next door, Alex says. Mexican woman runs the place. She don't own a license. I warned her the inspector's past due. It's none of my business. Hair, nails, massage. Who knows, maybe she's hooking too. It's none of my business if she's hooking, but the inspector is liable to show up.

Alex pushes your head forward gently, yet firmly. He's working on the back of your head now. From this awkward angle, you see the shelves along the barber chair with various products for sale: shampoo, talc, motor oil, hair gel, bug killer. A thin layer of dust coats the products. The barber has never tried to hawk these items. On the side of the shelf facing the corner, in clear plastic packages, hang what appear to be WWII-vintage gas masks. You've never noticed these before. There are two of them, olive drab. They hang from heavy nails. There is no dust on the packaging. Alex abruptly lifts your chin.

How are things down at the Lazy *L*? he says. Are you gearing up for the troop surge?

The room spins a little. Cowboy looks up from his magazine at the mention of the Lazy *L*. Little Man has moved off the chair, and he's taking the Mustang in figure eights between the different-colored tiles, idling low in his throat. Behind them, behind the legion of die-cast cars on the top shelf, a framed picture of a capital letter *B* is tipped on its side. *B* is for Barbershop. Or maybe Alex's last name begins with a *B*, who knows. The *B* is a blocked letter, just a big black letter *B* with a white background, except that, sideways, the two curved bulges of the *B* bulge upward like bellies.

Well? Alex asks.

Your company has been in the news each day, the wall of protesters and their picket signs about murdering and war profiteering. Working at the Lazy *L* these last months, you feel like an abortionist. You want to tell Alex you're just a GM worker with a bigger paycheck. Instead you say, The usual, you know how it is. Just sucking clock.

At this moment two successive percussions explode from the front window. Like two birds have dive-bombed the glass, one after the other. The glass pulsates, but it doesn't shatter. Everyone in the barbershop is stunned.

Sons of bitches, Alex says. Think they can terrorize me in my own place. He makes a move toward the door, then stops. A voice calls from outside—La puta que te parió!—followed by two more explosions.

Eggs. Those boys have egged the barbershop window.

Cowboy snaps his magazine shut. We under attack here? he says. Little Man is still spread-eagle on the floor, but he's frozen. His turn is coming, he seems to know. Get up out of the dirt, Cowboy says. He pulls his son up by a rear belt loop, jackknifing him and sending the Mustang flying. Little Man comes easily but his hat falls off, loosening his straw hair. The Mustang winds up overturned on a white square. Seeing this, Little Man's bottom lip curls. You can see he's fighting it, but he can't hold back the waterworks any longer.

Alex inspects the damage at the storefront, which is a mess. Gelatinous egg matter runs like snot down the entire façade. Ahh, he groans, like he's injured. I'll clean that up later. He picks up the Mustang and returns to the barber chair, but he's unsteady. He puts the Mustang on the counter by the blue jar and picks up the clippers. Everything happens quickly. You feel the clippers make a nick in your hair, just above your ear. The barber lets out a breath. Damnit, he says. I'll have to fix that. You can't see. You're still facing away from the mirror. Cowboy's got his arm around his boy's neck, whispering to him, but the boy seems inconsolable. He sobs intermittently.

Goddamnit, the barber says. He's made another mistake.

Cowboy gathers up his son, finally. It's not too late for Little Man. The crying boy can still go home to his mother. Looks like we're not gonna make it through this, he says and moves toward the door with his son. He holds Little Man's hat. The boy is glued to his father's leg. No chance he shows his face. We're sorry about your business, Cowboy says. He unlocks the door, and the two disappear past the damaged storefront and into the red glare. The door swings shut.

Let them go, the barber says. Cut my losses. He brings out the clippers again, but stops. Listen, the haircut's not too good. I got the jitters, I guess. Jesus, your mom won't be so happy. Sons of bitches. I've got one hell of a mess.

The barber stands behind you, his fingers at your temples. You're facing away, waiting. You have the upper hand here. How should you play it? You can further punish the barber. It dawns on you that Alex has ratted out his neighbor. The old bigot, of course he did. Now the neighbors will be at war until the end. Who knows how the end will look, except ugly. You can get up out of the chair, walk out the door after the cowboys and toward your own people.

Instead you relent. It's OK, Alex. I'm used to a nick here and there. You tell him the story of how your old man used to cut your hair, with just the clippers. He would set you down on the toilet seat and drape an apron over your neck. Your mother always told him not to go too high, but he said a boy needed a crewcut. Your dad won that argument every time. You were thirteen and he was still going high and tight.

Your dad a soldier? the barber asks.

He was a soldier. Killed in Action. I grew my hair out when he went overseas. Of course, he never had a chance to see.

Jesus, I'm sorry to hear that, the barber says. Which theater?

First Gulf War. He could have retired in a year, but he got blown to pieces.

Send an angel to sustain us, Alex says, and together you have a moment of silence.

You know I botched this, he says. I'll have to go all the way up.

You're the barber, you say. Do what needs to be done.

Alex pushes your head forward. You close your eyes and feel the clippers dig in. When it's over, the buzzing in your ears continues, only softer. From somewhere, from the other room, you hear the agitated chattering of women's voices.

Alex spins the chair back around so you're facing the mirror again. Did we get her? he asks.

You open your eyes. In the mirror the whiteness of your own scalp surprises you. You no longer resemble the man behind you holding the clippers. Now you're like the boy in the ad for the high and tight, just another in a long line of crew-cut boys.

Strings

Harry Lutz, auto dealer, home in Mount Horeb visiting his aged and ailing father, was shopping for soap-on-a-rope. The clerk at this, his third stop, seemed to mock his search. He would find no such item in the summertime. Soap-on-a-rope was a Christmastime gift.

Though it was none of the clerk's business, Harry explained that the gift was for his father, who had been in a terrible accident. Early one morning, after his daily jog, Harry's dad was standing at his mailbox checking the newspaper headlines when a hit-and-run driver plowed him down. He was badly broken and ruptured. Now, after six months, he was home from the hospital, and he could finally bathe himself. But, even with the shower seat, the soap gave him troubles. His father's fine motor skills had deteriorated, and his shattered femur prevented him from bending to retrieve the bar soap when dropped. The slippery soap lay there by the drain and mocked him. His father cursed the goddamn soap, and then Harry or his mother would have to go and pick it up. But his father couldn't hold the soap. It just kept squirting from his hands.

The clerk said he was sorry to hear about the accident. Liquid soap, in many colorful varieties, could be found in aisle 10.

Perhaps soap-on-a-rope was a lame idea, but Harry, who hadn't visited all throughout his father's squalid convalescence, was eager now to make a familial contribution before heading back west to Denver. He had spent most of his week-long visit home to Mount Horeb at the faltering freeway outlets, shopping, buying things he thought his parents could use. Soap-on-a-rope was a beautiful idea, his mother had said, praising Harry for his thoughtfulness.

When Harry stepped empty-handed from the drug store and into the sunlight, a new shopping opportunity presented itself. Next door to the drugstore was a runners' store, the Fast Foot. A big foot with an angelic wing sprouting from the heel was emblazoned on the glass door. Something about the winged foot made Harry feel as if he had been here before. These look-alike strip malls! He hadn't even noticed the Fast Foot when he entered the drugstore. Yet here it was, bigger than life. He went into the store now, to buy his dad new running shoes.

Here was a gift that might bolster his father's spirits, or here was a gift that might depress him further: running shoes for a man who couldn't walk. Harry's father had always been a runner, who knows why. He spent hours upon hours running around the country blocks outside Mount Horeb, running away from home one direction, running back toward home from the other. Mount Horeb was ironically named, Harry thought. It was a comparatively flat place with no mountains to prop it up. Harry himself had no such patience for running or the Wisconsin countryside. He was his mother's boy, and when he was a child, he and his mother often watched comfortably from the kitchen window while his father came galloping down the gravel road in all kinds of weather. Now, Harry thought nostalgically about his father's running, and he hated to think that the old man couldn't do it anymore.

Harry took the chance and bought some expensive running shoes for his dad. He bought a running shirt too, just to be safe. Maybe his father could put the shoes on and appreciate their cushion and traction and think once more about all the running he had done in the old days. Such thoughts might make Harry's dad happy, as they made Harry happy now.

Harry left the Fast Foot with a big white bag in his arms. Back out in the sun, he noticed the vastness of the parking lot, with just a few cars crowded into the close-in spots. Nothing unsettled Harry Lutz like an empty parking lot. The adjacent building had been a large department store, but it was all boarded up now. The parking lot, with its hundreds of empty spots, and the boarded-up building, reminded Harry of a cemetery. It would be all right, though. A new big-box store was going in across the road, and soon all the cars could park there. This was a good place for a shoe store, anyway. The blacktop stretched out before Harry like an asphalt playground.

Something about buying shoes! Harry felt a childish excitement. Even though he was no runner, and even though these were a little big for him, he felt the urge to try on his dad's new shoes and take them for a spin around the lot.

He walked toward the cars, easily picking out his folks' boxy sedan. Just as he passed the handicapped stalls, he heard a shriek. He turned to see a boy and his mother. They were attached at the wrist by a leash of some kind. Was that normal?

Then the reason for the shriek, which had been one of genuine terror or surprise, revealed itself. The boy was waving his free hand at a royal blue helium balloon, which had escaped him. The balloon seemed to drift toward Harry out of a dream, and he reached out slowly to catch the string, affixed to a small plastic fish, a weight to prevent just this sort of accident. As Harry reached casually for the string, a slight updraft caught the balloon, lifting the too-small fish just beyond his outstretched hand.

Harry gestured to the boy and mother. It would be all right. The balloon would come down now, Harry would see to that. The boy, maybe he was five or six, was tugging at the leash. He was a fat little boy, and he reminded Harry of himself at that age. Harry took a few nonchalant steps toward the balloon and reached to grab it. This time a major updraft caught the balloon and sent it scudding across the empty parking lot, until it luffed again, some dozen yards away. Amused, Harry broke into a trot. He caught up with the balloon and reached for it, casually grabbing for the small blue fish. The prize seemed easily within his grasp, yet Harry miscalculated, and once more the slippery fish squirted away. The wind was hard to judge, and Harry had tried to move quickly without appearing to expend effort. He wanted to impress the boy and his mother.

Now, though, intending to be certain, he ran after the balloon. His feet, encased in sloppy loafers, slapped the asphalt, the big bag banging his thighs. Sure enough, though, he was gaining on the balloon.

But when Harry dropped the bag to lighten his load, the wind came up and the balloon skated even faster along the parking lot. He looked back at the mother and son. They were hurrying toward him, or, rather, the mother was dragging the boy by the leash. The boy was crying. Don't worry, Harry wanted to say. He was doing his best. He would catch the balloon. Harry had run about a hundred yards now. He was out of breath. The parking lot was like a huge landing strip. Jesus, the cars you could fit in a lot this size! He might not catch the balloon, after all. It might elude him.

Harry's early loafing was a tragic mistake, and now he must make up for it. But he was not fast enough to make up for it. He was not fast, period. He had never been fast. When Harry was in grade school he had convinced his mother to buy him new shoes for Track and Field Day. The shoes were called Zips, and the TV commercial showed a boy wearing Zips easily vaulting a healthy green hedge row. When the boy began to run, the Zips left only a blurry afterimage of a red Z across the TV screen—he was that fast. Harry's mother bought him the Zips, but the Zips did Harry no good. During the race, when he saw that he would finish nowhere near the leader, he eased up, jogging toward the finish. Harry finished seventh in the fifty-yard dash. Two girls had beaten him.

Harry's father was in the bleachers that day. He had taken the day off work to see his boy run. The little grandstand was full of parents waving and shaking their fists to urge their children on. Not Harry's dad. Harry's dad sat quietly in the grandstand.

Harry had forgotten all of this. He had forgotten he was so slow, such a faker. In races, as a boy, Harry would watch the fast boys closely to catch the secret of their swiftness. One of the fast boys kept his fingers together and his hands flat and straight, cutting the wind as he ran. Harry tried this aerodynamic technique, but it didn't work for him. Another of the fast boys knotted his hands into fists and pumped them like pistons, but Harry's pumping fists did not propel him toward the finish line any faster. It wasn't fair. Oh, how Harry suffered his slowness all those childhood years.

Luckily for Harry, the trait that was all-important in his youth had little consequence in adulthood. Back home in Denver, Harry drove a big Chrysler with eight cylinders. He had learned to conceal his lack of talent and natural ability in the accoutrements of prosperity. He was not an athletic child, to be sure, but he was a clever student, and he had become a reasonably successful adult. Until now. Because he had been a slow boy, he felt the need to fake nonchalance as a man, and it cost him. After all these years, seventh place still hurt him. And it hurt his dad, Harry's need to act as if he didn't care, as if he weren't trying.

Forget the brat and his mother. Harry wanted that fish, hung by a string beneath the fat balloon. He wanted it for himself, and for his dad. It was the blue ribbon he failed to deliver before. Harry ran panicked, sprinting with all his ability. He felt his dad's car keys jangling in his pocket, and he felt the wind, generated by his own speed, whipping his hair, and Harry heard the cars on the freeway rush by like the sound of cheers. One of Harry's sloppy loafers flopped off his foot and spun along the asphalt behind him. Harry was cooking now, boy, if only his dad could see him run!

But he was too late. The balloon lifted up several stories dangling its fish mockingly as it winked in the sun. It drifted toward a stand of trees at the border of the buzzing freeway. Harry had missed his chance. No amount of effort would rescue him now. He slowed down, and the balloon gained ground. He continued to jog but without hope. He ran only because there was space to run, the landing strip reaching out yet in front of him.

At the limit of the landing strip, the stand of trees waved in the wind. The trees were a buffer against the freeway. Looking closer, Harry saw they were aspens. A gust of wind turned the bright-green aspen leaves backward to their pale sides: a thousand pale fists shook at him.

Harry stopped running. The balloon was gone into the sky. He had run a long way, but for no use. He hadn't done anyone any good. He turned and headed back toward the Fast Foot, where everything had started. His shoe lay on the asphalt like a dropped baton. He saw the boy and his mother. They were small across the vast lot. Harry squinted into the sun. The mother was still dragging the boy, but this time away, back toward the cluster of cars. In her other hand she carried a big white shopping bag.

Hey! Harry yelled. Stop! He wanted to tell the mother and son that he had done his best. He could explain everything: his loafing, his tragic lack of speed.

There was something else he wanted to account for now. Harry wanted to tell the boy and his mother that his father was a good man. No matter what happened. He went about his own business, nurturing his own small talent faithfully and without claptrap even into his autumn years. No one really knew Dennis Lutz, least of all Harry or his mother, but there wasn't a soul who would say a bad word against him. No sir. Dennis Lutz had never chiseled, swindled, nor borne false witness. He was neither selfish nor conceited.

How about you, Harry? Next to his father Harry knew he was no kind of man.

Stop! he yelled again. But no one could hear, and he was too tired to run. The mother and son climbed into their getaway car, a foreign model Harry couldn't ID, and raced breakneck across the empty parking spots toward the exit. What was Mount Horeb coming to where such a thing would happen in broad daylight? Those criminals. They had taken away his father's gift.

Birds of Paradise

They trod along the old oxcart path to see the famed strand of emerald sand that necklaced the southern limit of the island. Burgess had read about the beach in his Baedeker and had convinced Blyth to come here after their visit to the volcanoes. Now, yoked with daypacks, they traipsed along the ancient dirt trail, the fine red dust rising from their feet enveloping them. The travelers linked hands over the deep rut cloven by the oxen hooves, while on either side ran the thinner grooves cleft by the wagon wheels. These furrows sprawled out over the rolling land in cursive toward the uneven eastern horizon. To the south was the expanse of the ocean. They had already hiked much further than the two miles suggested in the Baedeker.

This is like the Oregon Trail, Burgess offered. I feel like we're headed for the Willamite Valley. A new beginning.

Willamette, Blyth returned. It's the Willamette Valley and this is an island. It appears our destiny is not so brilliantly manifest. How much longer? Blyth repositioned her canvas backpack and groaned. Her back was already soaked where the backpack rested. She let go of Burgess's hand, and now the chasm created by the rumbling of the oxen was unspanned between them.

It's just over this next rise, Burgess said. They say this is the only green sand beach in the world. The grains of sand glisten like emeralds. And there is a dramatic precipice. We won't miss it.

Well I think we've passed it up, said Blyth. She gestured toward the ocean. That sand over there looks green. Anyway, the world is full of beaches.

Blyth had wanted to spend the entire day at the volcanoes. You'll get bored with the volcanoes, he had told her as they drove the rental along the highway that girdled the island. You've said so yourself. We don't actually get to see the eruptions. It's all underground. Most of those things have been dormant for years. You have to be lucky to see any fireworks. That's what the guidebook says anyway. And you've been there already. Besides, a swim afterward will be refreshing. And the sand will be green. Can you imagine?

Blyth bent. After all, this was Burgess's trip. His first from the mainland, and such a long way from Blue River, Wisconsin. Sure it was their first trip together, but this was really for Burgess. So he would have some common ground with her. So he could be where she had been so much and understand. But Burgess was a difficult student. He was always professing textbook knowledge about things she knew from experience. Always trying to come across as more sophisticated than he was. They had spent the day arguing about the goddess of volcanoes.

The natives give her gin so she won't get angry, Burgess had said, reading his Baedeker as they walked across the barren charcoal surface of a crater. It's part of their religion. Look at this picture. It's Gordon's gin. I wouldn't bribe a goddess with cheap gin.

They don't give her gin to placate her, Blyth had responded. They give it as a gift to honor her. There's a difference between placating someone and giving someone a gift to honor her.

And so it went that they could agree on almost nothing—neither the tint and texture of the exotic birds of paradise growing abundantly on the island nor the name and origin of the tiny green lizards that wriggled loose of their tails when Burgess managed to grab one.

They're geckos, said Blyth.

They're axolotls, said Burgess. Plumed serpents. Keepers of the Aztec spirit. They are venerated here.

There are no Aztecs on this island, you ass. People like geckos because they eat flies.

Blyth led Burgess through the last of the volcano craters and upward toward the car. Looking back, Burgess remarked that the sundry crater beds gave the impression of a minefield.

Wait, he said, unloading his expensive camera. One last picture.

When they finally got to the ocean after a two-hour drive southward, it was a new set of circumstances.

Look at those waves, Burgess exclaimed, gesturing toward the surf. Those must be six-footers.

Those are two-footers, Blyth replied. You always think they're bigger than they really are.

And now they had been hiking for more than an hour and still no green sand.

You and your guidebook, said Blyth. I told you those distances couldn't be trusted. Did you pack the sun lotion? We're getting burned.

Burgess reached over his shoulder into his backpack for the lotion. It was next to the bottle of wine he had packed secretly for after their swim. For a surprise. He handed the lotion over the crevasse and Blyth accepted. When their fingers touched, Burgess felt the touch. It came down to that. She applied the lotion to the back of her reddening forehead, face, and neck. As she did so, the tops of her ears folded perceptibly under her massaging fingers. My word, she was lovely. He longed to touch her there, to feel the flexible cartilage ebb and flow beneath the pressure of his fingers.

Well lo and behold. Blyth's voice brought him back to the surface. Rounding a bend they recognized the view they had both seen in the guidebook. It was indeed impressive. Carved granite swept out from the red dirt and sparse grass toward the promise of the ocean. The headland was frozen there like a motionless tidal wave, never to reach the blue. Below would be the promised jeweled beach.

And there it was. Not quite so green as the obviously retouched photo in the guidebook. Certainly not emerald. More aged copper bathed in black. But it stood out against the crystalline blue ocean and the black relief of the precipice above. Jesus, Blyth, it's beautiful. Burgess dropped his pack and wrestled his camera out. Looking through the viewfinder, he carefully cropped out the other sunbathers who weren't supposed to be there. He snapped one photo and changed the angle. He snapped another and another, including one with Blyth in the foreground, a gust of wind removing a shock of blonde from an ear-top. He could already see the photo framed in cherry on his living room wall. That's the green sand beach Blyth and I visited, he could hear himself telling his visitors. It's the only one in the world. I swam there.

And so the promise of fulfilling the photograph pushed Burgess down the steep incline toward the beach. He pulled Blyth along after.

On the green sand at last, Burgess changed into his suit under his beach towel and waited for Blyth to follow. His bare white feet sparkled greenish.

I'm not going to swim, she said. It's not hot enough. Go on. I'll watch.

Save me, he said, if the waves pearl me. He grinned, using the new word she had taught him. Then he added, Those must be six-footers, and ran to the surf. Rather than gingerly wetting his toes, Burgess dived in head first. He played in the surf for a while, and the biggest waves he had ever seen sent him ass over teakettle. Why couldn't Blyth get in and enjoy this also, to frolic and splash, and to forget everything. Out here! he called, waving. But she wasn't coming.

She sat splendidly on the beach, now in her bikini, her face tilted toward the sun. She was inscrutable.

Burgess wanted to impress her. This whole trip he had wanted to impress her and show her he wasn't, as she said, provincial. He tried to know things. But that came off bad. And now here he was acting like a kid in the waves, thrilled about something that for her was mundane. For her, a bird of paradise was just a dandelion.

He swam out past the surf. Blyth had been giving him lessons, and he would impress her with his open-water swimming. He swam toward the mouth of the bay, intending to climb out at the foot of the black precipice. He would climb up a span and then dive off. He could dive. And so he floated southward toward the open ocean, the waves coming in series to stymie his progress. He turned to see Blyth on the beach and got doused by a wave.

At the foot of the outcrop the waves dashed. The outcrop was black volcanic rock, sharp and uneven. This whole island was probably volcanic. He certainly wasn't going to climb onto these rocks without getting cut up, perhaps crushed. There was no foothold, and the waves were too strong. He would swim back, and he wouldn't mention to Blyth that he had meant to climb up. He had just gone for a nice ocean swim. Did she notice his stroke?

Burgess turned back toward the beach, and suddenly Blyth seemed farther away than she had ever been. He had read in his Baedeker that the currents were so treacherous on this side of the island that an unwary swimmer would get an express trip to Antarctica if he ventured too far out—the currents swept that way. Fishermen here used to tie themselves to shore after so many had been lost.

Can you imagine? Burgess had wondered aloud, repeating the subject he had broached before. Rowing and rowing out there and all the time getting farther and farther from shore? Rowing harder and drifting farther. At what point would you give up?

You'd never give up, said Blyth. You can't read a forgone conclusion.

Burgess remembered the conversation. Luckily, he was still in the protected waters of the cove. Wasn't he? His swimming was coming along, Blyth had said so herself. He took perhaps two dozen freestyle strokes, rolling his body like Blyth taught him, stretching, trying to relax. When he looked again toward the beach, Blyth remained a glinting statue. He hadn't gotten any closer.

Suddenly it dawned on Burgess that he would drown. The feeling came over him as surely as a wave, nauseating. The ocean was a thing apart from the land. It had an appetite that was unimaginable from shore. There was no land anywhere beneath Burgess now, only a depth of mystery that could cause such green. The six-foot waves swept in to the beach, but out here beyond the surf there was only a turmoil of frenzied currents. Each time a wave swelled, his vision of the beach was obscured, and he was alone in the world.

He switched to a steady breaststroke. He knew Blyth was watching him. He knew if he flailed she would take notice. When working as a lifeguard she said she watched the strokes swimmers took. She knew if they sped up, became erratic, that they could be in trouble. Burgess tried to measure his stroke, but he began to tire.

What was Blyth thinking as she sat there on the beach? How can I rescue him, she would wonder, without injuring his manhood? She was gracious like that, concerned with an intact manhood. She could pretend she was just cooling off. Burgess was all done worrying about his manhood. All he wanted was to be saved by his Blyth. He wanted to be on the beach, the beautiful green-sand beach, and he wanted to be stuck to her like a thousand tiny emerald grains of sand, to put his head in her lap and keep it there always.

Can you imagine? Burgess thought. He composed himself. If he wasn't getting closer, at least he wasn't getting farther away. Was he? He stopped swimming and began to tread water. Blyth moved from her reclining position. Had she come to rescue him at last? What a lovely picture she made against the verdant sand. Burgess drifted with the swell and ebb of the ocean tide. Afloat there, he began to imagine in islands, each thought untethered from the next. Could she even see him from the beach? His head bobbed above the surface, like a seagull perhaps, or some piece of wrapper that had blown away from a happy beachgoer.

Trollway

Your mother, bless her heart, told you no secrets survive a honeymoon. She didn't say anything about an eruption. You joke at first that maybe you're allergic to marriage. Your new husband smiles and says that's a good one. But as the days throb along and the rash worsens, you both begin secretly to believe your joke. You're newlyweds after all. If you have an allergic reaction to your husband on your honeymoon, what hope?

For the first week everything is appropriately paradisiacal. You've a month together in San Sebastián on Spain's north coast. You've an apartment in the Parte Vieja, the old city, overlooking the picturesque harbor, the old shrimping fleet, and the Bay of Biscay. Your apartment is nicely furnished: a tiled kitchen and a big bed with mirrors. No Wi-Fi, but who needs it on a honeymoon. The Parte Vieja is like a small town nestled in a larger seafront city. It's traffic free, and the cobbled streets are lined with tapas bars, *bocadillo* shops, and an occasional ancient cathedral. The streets are cool and dark, narrow and labyrinthine. It's easy to become disoriented, but if you walk far enough in any direction, you emerge into the light and a view of the ocean and your choice in nice sand beaches.

Your husband, Ricky, is a newly minted U.S. Foreign Serviceman, and you've coordinated your honeymoon with his language training. Ricky has to work on this trip, but only for a few hours, a few days a week. He could have had his language training in a number of places, including Madison, Wisconsin, just down the road from your hometown of Mount Horeb. Ricky wanted to stay at home—considering that you would be moving away to your foreign post after language training—but you wanted a clean break. You decided on San Sebastián, in Spain's Basque country. You speak enough Spanish to get along, but not enough so that you have to engage in conversation. You congratulate yourself on your choice of honeymoon. Here no one knows the dreary circumstances you've traded for these happy ones: the dying mother you've exchanged for a lively husband, the predictable future you've exchanged for a chance to begin again somewhere, anywhere, else. Shortly after she witnessed your marriage at the Sauk County courthouse, your mother had her final emergency, and Ricky kept his promise and swept you away.

Now here you are enjoying this anonymous freedom: the city, the beach, the kitchen, the mirrors. You spend your alone time lounging in cafés, nibbling on exotic tapas, shopping on the street markets, and buying interesting local foods to prepare for dinner. You wander into gothic cathedrals and watch the pigeons flutter among the grisly old relics and colorful mosaics. When Ricky comes home from language training, early in the afternoons, you go straight to bed. Afterward, you go to the beach and watch the pounding surf and the nudist sunbathers, or else you take short day trips into the sun-dappled countryside by train. It's springtime. The countryside is green and hilly, not unlike Wisconsin. Each Basque village seems to have its own specialty in cheese or beer.

Exactly ten days into your month of bliss, you detect some itchy red spots on your shoulder. You wake up scratching them. It was only yesterday that you told yourself to watch out: you're thirty years old, and you know enough about unadulterated happiness to be wary of it. Here is one area where you and Ricky differ. He's from California, where sunny days last for months on end. Ricky moved to Wisconsin for graduate school. He hasn't lived long enough in your home state to have his character permanently altered by the weather. You're like most Wisconsinites in that sunny days unnerve you. On sunny days, you know there's always a storm ready to blow in from somewhere, whereas, in poor weather, you have nothing to long for but the sun.

So, when you find the spots that morning in bed, you're not exactly surprised. You're even a little relieved, but anxious too, considering your history of rashes and allergic reactions. Your former job with the county parks required you to be often in the field, and you bore the physical effects, what your mother called your "usual pox and palsy." But despite the frequency of these outbreaks you never grew accustomed to being constantly itchy and scabbed.

Until today, you thought you had left all that behind. Now, you can see the familiar spots in the big mirrors that line the closet doors next to the bed. They're in a straight line on your shoulder, perhaps a dozen raised red bumps. You turn over to see Ricky's wild head of hair on the pillow beside yours. He's still sleeping at 10 a.m., his long white torso uncovered. He doesn't have any bumps on him. None you can see, anyway. Even now, at this innocent stage, a small part of you suspects he is to blame, but you're able to rationalize this feeling away.

The rash is likely a reaction to poison ivy, or the Spanish equivalent. Three days ago you went hiking in the Pyrenean foothills around Ordizia. You picked wildflowers in a grassy meadow. You made love against a tree. You must have gotten into something. This rash will be uncomfortable, you realize, but it shouldn't linger too long.

You wake your shaggy husband and show him the spots. He inspects them, carefully poking you with his fingers. You watch in the mirror. He stretches the skin so the red spots turn white, shrugs, and says, You're fine. Probably sand fleas. Or a hungry spider.

This from the man who lived in a mud hut for a year during his Peace Corps days a decade ago and suffered all manner of indignities, including goiters, of all disgusting-sounding things, from a lack of iodine. You've noticed another difference between you two that seems at odds with the first: that is, Ricky doesn't seem to mind discomfort, or rather, he doesn't expect always to be comfortable. He must have developed this attitude from traveling so much abroad, and you hope that you can develop it too, a thick skin like Ricky's. Now, however, you're distressed about having bumps on your delicate skin. This is your honeymoon, after all. Not only do the spots itch, but they're unattractive.

The next day, when you count more spots, you decide to visit the *farmacia*. The first prescription, a topical anti-itch ointment, succeeds in stopping the itching for several minutes at a time, and you apply it generously. But three days later, after a second pharmacy visit and a second tube of greasy ointment squeezed empty, you find that your rash has spread. You have spots on your shoulder and around your shoulder blade, a new crop of bumps on your hands, as well as a few groupings on your stomach. The bumps seem to be cropping up willy-nilly. Anywhere you have bumps, the skin is raised and red and itches like mad. You can barely keep yourself from tearing into these angry patches with your fingernails. It's as if each of the red patches has a heartbeat of its own, pulsing under the surface of your skin.

You make a third trip to the *farmacia*, and this time you show the pharmacist your afflicted arm. He suggests a visit to the doctor. The doctor can give you a stronger prescription, he says, but this will make you *soñoliento*. Drowsy, your pocket dictionary says. Not even Ricky knew that one.

You want to avoid *soñoliento*. This is a new life you're starting, and you want to be alive to it. You're already sleeping more than usual, sometimes ten or eleven hours a night. And then you wake up tired. Ricky, too, is sleeping more. But he says it's probably normal, gives his litany of reasons honeymooners need more sleep: unrelenting sex, sun, the salt sea, decadence, wine. Did he mention sex?

So, you hold out two more days with the new maximum-strength medicated cream, staying in the apartment as much as you can and applying the cream every two hours as directed. But the rash worsens, throbbing mercilessly. It's become unbearable to be in the sun at all. This ruins your daily trip to the beach. Now you have to wear a long-sleeved shirt, especially conspicuous because so many of the Spanish women go topless at the beach. You're irritable and quarrelsome. You chastise Ricky for gawking at the women and their bare breasts. Ricky explains that he's a Third World traveler. This is his first trip to Europe, so of course he's not suave enough to enjoy bare breasts in public while appearing as blasé as a European. Give him time to become more sophisticated.

Your new husband has an asinine streak, you've noticed. You're in no mood for his brand of humor. It's time to see the doctor, you say, finally. This isn't a normal reaction to marriage. You extend your blotchy arm as proof.

Fine, Ricky says. He gathers up the beach towels. Let's get this taken care of now, before we waste any more of our honeymoon with the mopes.

You try to lighten the conflict. You say you have the measles, not the mopes. The ointment appears to be merely a gateway drug. You need some stronger dope. But despite your wisecracks, Ricky walks back to the apartment ten steps ahead of you.

The next day you spend the entire morning learning how a doctor visit works in Spain. Instead of sitting for hours in a waiting room as you would at home, you stand for hours in several long queues. At the end of each long queue, a bureaucrat waits to be apprised of your affliction. At home, you could whisper demurely to the receptionist that you have a rash on your shoulder. The Spanish translation, *Tengo una erupción*, is difficult to whisper. *Tengo una erupción!* seems more like a pop song and begs to be shouted. Four hours after arriving at the hospital, you finally see the doctor. Ricky offers to come in with you, but you decline. You'll not have two experts examining your pock-ridden body.

Your doctor is a woman, which is good. But she's a little too pretty, like a doctor you would see on TV. The first question she asks, after her brief examination, is something like ¿Dónde estás durmiendo? which you translate, Where are you sleeping? This a rude question. She sounds like your mother. Does she think you're a prostitute? Some American floozy living in Spain? You mention that you have an apartment on Calle Teatinos, near the cathedral, and that you rent from Doña Ester, who lives next door. This, you hope, will sound Catholic. The apartment is very clean, you say, and Doña Ester fastidious. You realize as you're saying this that San Sebastián isn't *that* small—the city sprawls well beyond the confines of the village-like Parte Vieja, where you feel self-contained, safe from the degradation of freeways and concrete tenements.

The doctor asks you another question which you're not sure you understand. You translate, What are you doing here?

This doctor seems more a customs agent than a doctor. You answer the question anyway, again trying to show you're an upright citizen. I'm with my husband, you say in your best Spanish. Mi esposo nuevo. You try to think of a translation for honeymoon: *Luna sucre*? *Luna dulce*? Instead of telling the doctor you're in Spain on a sugar moon, you point to the hallway, where the waiting room should be. In English you say, My new husband, of the U.S. Foreign Service, waits out there.

The doctor stares at you with a look your mother would describe as knowing. What her look insinuates is that Mr. Foreign Service, waiting there in the hall, is causing your skin to break out. But you're not ready for this drastic diagnosis, so you change the subject to poison weeds. You've been hiking in the woods. You're allergic to poison weeds. You must have gotten into something. You need some strong medicine for the weed rash.

The *doctora* prescribes a strong narcotic-based antihistamine and walks you out of her office. The medicine will clear up the *erupción*, she says, standing in the doorway, but it will make you very *soñoliento*.

If it doesn't completely take away the bumps, you may have to . . . to what? You didn't catch the last part. To go to sleep someplace else? You're confused, but you find that you've been ushered to the door. You have no choice but to thank the pretty doctor and go find Ricky. There he is, sitting on the floor in the hallway like a schoolboy sent out of class.

What did he say? Ricky says, still sitting down.

She.

Oh boy. What did she say?

Poison ivy, you say. Or something like that. You wave the prescription.

She said poison ivy?

Well, not exactly. I told her poison ivy. She gave me the prescription.

Christ, Ricky says. He gets up off the floor. You should have let me come in.

Why?

What did I say? I told you don't go in there and diagnose yourself. You let the doctor do that. Doctors love it when you diagnose yourself. They don't argue, they just send the little idiot home with the wrong medicine.

Little idiot? Look, I've had this sort of thing before. Besides, you seemed pretty confident in your diagnosis. Sand fleas? A bitsy spider? Have you seen my body?

But we're not doctors! Ricky's shouting now. We're in a foreign country!

To that, what response but silence? People are staring, people who don't speak your language, people who know you have an *erupción*.

Ricky must realize his asinine streak has shown through. He looks around, embarrassed at his public outburst. Like most men, Ricky often loses his temper, but unlike most men, Ricky is naturally humble, and he won't hold a grudge for long. This is one of the reasons you agreed to marry him. He's quiet now.

Ricky heads off to the Foreign Service office and you walk the other way, toward home, finding a *farmacia* on the way. Walking the six blocks to your apartment, you notice that the streets in the Parte Vieja seem noisier and more crowded than usual. This could be a local holiday or a bus strike. It's so difficult to keep track of special occasions in a foreign country. You're already very tired, and the loud voices of the people grate on your nerves. By the time you get home, you're ready for a nap. But you encounter Doña Ester in the hall. She's an officious, aproned woman who seems always to be just around the corner with a feather duster. She's just cleaned your apartment; it's included in the cost of the vacation rental. You exchange pleasantries. Yes, our apartment is very clean, thank you, but, say, isn't the Parte Vieja rather noisy today?

Es Semana Santa, Doña Ester explains, looking startled.

Oh, yes. Sí, sí. Semana Santa. Holy Week. You had forgotten. How stupid. You had read about Holy Week in your *Lonely Planet*. In Spain, they celebrate the whole Easter week instead of just the weekend. The people from the provinces flock to the cities to witness the medieval processions. You and Ricky, both recovering Christians, try to ignore religious holidays. But since the religious holiday is in a foreign country, it seems somehow more authentic and worthy of respect. You're embarrassed to have forgotten Holy Week in the presence of Doña Ester.

Tengo sueño, you say apologetically, but Doña Ester is still affronted. She lifts her feather duster to squash a spider.

Hay mucho alboroto durante la Semana Santa! Doña Ester exclaims, shaking the duster. As if her country is too rowdy for frail Americans. She shuffles off to her own apartment next door. You go to take a nap. The noise from the distant streets doesn't bother you in the least.

For most of Holy Week you are either sleeping or sleepy. Ricky is often gone from the apartment when you awaken, either at work or out with his coworkers. You wake up to take another pill and go back to sleep. The red spots have faded to pink, but they're still tender. Lying in bed, you count the spots. This counting makes you sleepier still. On your left hand alone you count fifty pinkish spots. On your groin, some eighty. There are hundreds on your left arm and shoulder. For some reason, your right side is all clear. The affected areas aren't nearly as angry as they were. The medicine must be working. Another day passes. Three days?

Ricky doesn't want you to be alone, so he invites a trio of his fellow Foreign Service initiates over for a potluck. Don't worry, he says, he's told them about your illness, and they've promised to treat you gently. His friends are all American, vegetarians by the looks of their potluck contributions, but they have designer Spanish names, as if this were Spanish 101 and you had to choose your name from a book. Too, they're all given to gab. You're soft-spoken, and all your life you've attracted people who talk too much. You've never been more thankful for this trait than now. You're so sleepy. You make one comment, about the doctor visit and the *doctora*'s strange question, Where are you sleeping? and the dinner conversation sustains itself. Wary of your delicate condition, your exotic dinner guests are very polite, sticking to their conversation cue but still managing to wedge in their own life stories. You doze and listen, itchy and sleepy, delirious from the narcotics and the burning pulse all across the surface of your skin.

Adrianna says she's sleeping alone in a double bed. She calls herself a recovering anarchist, her new job with the government akin to an ex-rummy running a liquor store. The anarchy was her ex-husband Kristof's idea, she says. Now, with Kristof and all that anarchy behind her, Adrianna could really use a single bed. A double bed with one person suggests incompleteness. Adrianna is complete in herself. At least she's trying to be. She doesn't need a double bed gaping at her every night and every morning to suggest she's incomplete sleeping without Kristof.

Gregorio, the lovelorn linguist, agrees. He, too, has been sleeping alone in a big bed. But he would just as soon keep it. He has half a bed saved for his Malaysian sweetheart, Simone, whom he met in graduate school in Athens, Georgia. She has another year of graduate school, and then, when she graduates, Simone owes her country two years of service. He wants Simone with him here, of course, not in godforsaken Malaysia, where the language—of some three hundred characters—could reduce even the most gifted linguist to gibbering. Would you believe, Gregorio says, two lovers stuck in separate countries, one in the Domestic Service, and one in the Foreign?

Gabriella, the eldest of the group, has been sleeping just fine in a single bed, thank you very much. She has sworn off men in favor of culture. Whenever she has a hankering for a man, she treats herself to a good meal or a gallery visit. Gabriella says she doesn't consider herself American. She's a dual citizen of France and California. *Califonia*, she says. She's come to Spain to escape those bourgeois Califonians and their lack of culture. She doesn't find the Spanish very cultured either, mind. They make her feel superior, which was how she felt in Califonia among the bourgeois millions. In France she always feels inferior. The French have so much culture and good taste, and the Califonians have so much money. It's easier to be in Spain.

Your guests have brought two bottles of *vermut,* and they pass these around the table, toasting their plum jobs and polishing off their vegetable medleys. The only difficulty, they agree, is not knowing where they'll end up. Could be any place. But wherever they go, they'll have the Foreign Service to greet them—Salud!—and cultured friends among their coworkers—Salud! It's like the Peace Corps that way, only more sophisticated—and with better pay—Salud!

The women commiserate with you; it is surely most difficult for the spouse of a Foreign Serviceperson. The spouse has to tag along from country to country, reinventing herself at every port. Never mind children.

Ricky gives you a squeeze, mindful of what you've both begun to call your eruption, and says how lucky he is to have married you before entering the Foreign Service, since so many Foreign Servicemen end up lifelong bachelors. You look at Gregorio, practically crying in his vermouth, then at your husband, his hair wild, his left eye drooping from the booze. Yes, you say, how lucky for you.

You're dog tired and itching like mad, but relieved. You've made it through dinner without interrogation, and Ricky's friends have been polite enough to ignore your horrendous eruption. But as the shoptalk continues, you grow weary of Ricky and his worldly friends. You can't help but think that the pretty doctor knew something you did not. She asked, What are you doing here? You begin to wonder. Your mother would never have found herself so far from home, and in such strange company. She warned you. But Ricky seemed so sure you were the one for him. You, who are never sure of anything, were astonished. He began his marry-me speeches shortly after your first night together, and you finally agreed. It was all so dizzying, to be the chosen one. Certainly effortless. You made the easy drive to the Sauk County courthouse, which your mother said was a fitting place for your wedding, given the looks of Ricky. Why, oh, why, did you settle on this one?

Now, here you are, a new bride in a new country, with a rash the likes of which you have never seen. Your new friends include an anarchist, a linguist, and a snob. You never answered your mother. If you had, you suppose, the reason would be this: Ricky settled on me, Mother.

It's 10 p.m. You can safely excuse yourself. You get up from the noisy table, but Gabriella, that old culture fanatic, catches your arm, releasing it quickly when she realizes she's grabbed hold of your eruption. Not so fast, she says. Here we are, running at the mouth, and we haven't heard from our hostess. We know where you're sleeping, dear, but what's the rest of your story?

You were nearly passed over in all these big fish stories of loneliness and loss, but now you're called upon to match what's come before. Where should you begin your maudlin tale? The throbbing on the surface of your skin deepens, sinking down into your flesh. It feels as if there are two of you, each with your own heartbeat, crammed into just one body. The pressure and heat are almost unbearable. You drink deeply of the spicy Spanish vermouth.

You can shut them up and send them home. Grotesqueries from the rural life always shut them up and send them home. Since it's been on your mind anyway, you tell them how, when you met Ricky, you were a county parks employee forced into service as a sharpshooter. Wisconsin's southern deer herd had been infected with chronic wasting disease, and your hometown of Mount Horeb was ground zero. The deer just wandered around in the woods, dizzy, bumping into trees. CWD had begun to show up in hunters who had eaten venison, and the Department of Natural Resources decided to eradicate the entire herd. Some two hundred thousand deer. The DNR hired local hunters to pot them. It was like in the old days of buffalo hunting. You got paid a bonus for each carcass. Twenty bones for a bag of bones.

Your dinner guests are staring as if your story has come from nowhere. You feel opposing urges to put them at ease and make them more uncomfortable still.

The reason I mention that, you continue, is because my mother liked to say that she had the CWD, and couldn't I please pot her like a dizzy deer. She said she was going out in a slow cooker, even a tough old bird like her would be tender, stewing nice and slow in the chemo.

She lived at home in a single hospital bed, you say. She could raise it up and down with a little button. Into this pretty story walked my big galoot—you give frizzy Ricky a pinch—and promised to get me out of Dodge.

You've silenced the table. You may as well have dropped your dentures into your gazpacho.

Good old Mount Horeb, Ricky says, coming to your rescue. The whole place is built on a pun. You should see it. They call Main Street the Trollway. Front yards all down Main Street display a gauntlet of hand-carved wooden trolls. There's Chicken Thief Troll and Carp Carrier Troll. My favorite is Transfer and Storage Troll. Dairy's gone in the tank, and trolls are the new export commodity. Sundays after church they have carving sessions like old-fashioned quilting bees. Locals call it "Going Trolling."

Ricky's coworkers are at ease again now that the hayseed story has swerved back toward comedy. You take the opportunity to get your pills from your purse. You want to make your getaway before Ricky starts in on your mother, whom Ricky called the Troll Queen Troll. You say your good-byes and good lucks and disappear into the bathroom. Your guests thankfully arise from the table as well.

After they leave, Ricky acts as though nothing were wrong, so it's easy for you to do the same. He's good about that. The pressure abates. In bed, as if he doesn't have a care, your husband falls immediately asleep. You've noticed you're always the last to fall asleep. It doesn't matter how tired you are when you lie down, as soon as you're in bed, in the dark room, you begin to worry. Tonight you're worrying the big questions. What am I doing here? Why am I married to this man?

You don't believe all the storybook nonsense about marriage. Your mother cured you of that. At best, she said, marriage is an end of freedom. At worst, it is just making the bed for death. Stay single, your mother said, and stay put.

But what's a girl to do? And what kind of advice is that for a mother to give? If you were an anarchist like Adrianna you could go a different way. But what anarchist was ever born in Mount Horeb, Wisconsin? Oh, the flower girls on State Street in the capital might go in for the communal life, but Mount Horeb is a different world entirely. You have a deep and abiding feeling that marriage is a normal part of a full life. It's part of the big story, and if you don't participate, well, there's something left unknown to you. Men, too, march up the aisle, eager to be part of that big story.

You're prepared well enough for marriage by the months you spent at your mother's deathbed. You suppose it was natural enough to exchange your mother for your husband. But it happened too soon, this changing of the guard. When your mother left you, it was the first time she had ever left you. You were supposed to be the one who went away. She was supposed to be standing in the driveway, waving you away, awaiting your return.

All those pictures you have in your mind of your mother waving good-bye while you set off are canceled by your last picture of her. The ambulance pulled out of the drive while you stood and watched: that was your mother's final emergency.

To put yourself to sleep, you try counting spots. In the darkness you feel with your fingertips the angry Braille of your skin. How many had you counted the first time a few days ago? You count the spots on your groin and lose track somewhere north of one hundred. You look at your husband with a mixture of worry and disdain. Where, pray tell, are Ricky's spots? Your eruption, you finally concede, is not poison ivy. The spots don't seem to be spreading as much as multiplying. There are simply more and more. The next morning you will go back to the hospital. With that simple decision made, you worry no longer, and fall asleep.

You have a different doctor this time who doesn't give knowing looks or ask tricky metaphysical questions. Typical man, he's all business, and within minutes of entering his office, you're bent over a gurney receiving a hydrocortisone shot in your backside.

Walking home, you realize Holy Week has been passing without your realizing it. The last of the processions weave through the Parte Vieja, the participants dressed like clansmen in their white robes and masked, conical hoods. You're stuck for a long while in the slow procession, behind two hooded pallbearers carrying one of the grisly floats of the crucifixion. The float is heaped with a blinding array of white gladiolus and calla lilies. Your hip hurts where you got the shot, and you would like to crawl onto one of the floats and be borne slowly along. Instead you find yourself in slow lockstep with the procession, tilting from one stiff leg to the other in time with the rigid pallbearers

By the time you get home and undress for bed, the spots have all blanched, and they don't itch anymore. You're so tired. Ricky too stays home. He mixes a pitcher of mojitos, closing the blinds against the Holy Week processions, and watches the steamy telenovelas in Spanish.

You sleep twelve hours that night. The spots abate. The next day, the narcotic apparently wearing off, you get some energy back. For the first time in more than a week, you're not bone-tired. All the fretting from before begins to seem like silliness.

That next night, you and Ricky go out to dinner. It's a warm, summery night, so you choose an intimate outdoor plaza, hidden in the old city. You haven't been out to dinner in some time. You toast to the end of the dreadful eruption, which is somehow not contagious. Ricky jokes that you must be the only one who's allergic to marriage, but now you're breaking down, resigning yourself to the inevitable.

Ricky grins. Truly, he says, I'm glad to have you back. I'm sorry that you've been laid low by the mopes, or whatever they are, but all that's over now.

You smile. Maybe Ricky's right. Maybe he's always been right. He orders another bottle of wine and you toast to your future. You have only a couple of weeks left here in Spain. Then back to the Trollway to pack your lives. In two months, you could be living in any of the world's twenty-three Spanish-speaking countries. Salud!

Whereas in the past thinking of this move has made you nervous, now it makes you giddy. If you had your choice of countries, well, that could be nerve-wracking. But you don't have to choose. The choice has been made for you, and you've simply agreed to go along. You must go along, and that's some comfort in itself. You will be assigned a country, and that country will be home. It will be a surprise, something like a destiny, but not quite as permanent. There is no pressure on you. You're not responsible, after all, if the placement turns out to be a disaster.

As you get ready to leave, a breeze arises. The salt sea air refreshes your blemished skin, blowing away the warm, stale air trapped in the city. Within a matter of seconds, the breeze gathers into wind and then rather suddenly into an alarming gale. Plastic tables wobble and tip. Silverware clatters onto the cobbles and placement settings take flight. You and Ricky, along with the other diners, hold on to your glasses and each other as you take shelter beneath the portico. Shrieks of delight and surprise accompany the sudden change in climate. Seconds more, and tables and chairs are skidding across the court-yard. Sounds of shattering glass fill the courtyard, and the tenor of the shrieks changes from rapture to terror. Everyone is hanging on to something solid. You've never had this sensation before, that the wind could pick you up and blow you away. You drop Ricky's hand and grip the stone threshold. A disaster is imminent. At any moment, you will be swept through the old stone portal of the plaza and out to sea.

But the wind dies, turns to rain mixed with a few hard nuggets of hail. Disaster is averted. Only things are broken. Some of the diners are crying. You leave the stoic waiters to reassemble their lives. Wet and cold, you cling to your husband the whole walk home. At the old port below your apartment you're surprised to see a group of young Spanish boys swimming shirtless in the deep water along the high harbor wall. What are they doing in the water on a night like this? The boys call out to you, reaching up out of the water and shouting. Are they calling for help? Ricky seems to know what they want. Watch this, he says, and flips a silver coin into the water. The boys dive for the coin, reaching it before it hits the bottom, and one comes up holding the shiny reward. Otra vez! the boys shout, and Ricky flips more treasure into the harbor.

For the first time in two weeks you don't itch anywhere. Even the throbbing has subsided. You feel as if you have lived a whole life in these few weeks. Your mother warned you would learn a secret. On her honeymoon she learned that your father wore a hairpiece. He was balding prematurely and had managed to hide it all through their courtship. During a honeymoon, however, all secrets are aired. Perhaps you have learned your secret. It has more to do with you than with Ricky. You're a small-town girl, after all, pretending to be a grown woman in a bigger world. Everything you know very well at all lies between the two ends of a single street. The eruption wasn't so bad: your mother would call it a slight hitch in your get-along. Now, a strong dose of hydrocortisone and the elements have cured you.

That night, invigorated by the parallel sensations of grace and danger, you make love. But, because of your eruption, there are precious few places safe to touch. You keep your eyes away from the mirrors and all they reveal. The lights are dim and your bodies covered by the sheets.

The next morning you wake up at noon and your husband is sleeping next to you. You haven't slept until noon since you were in high school. You don't feel lazy, however, more mischievous, as if you've gotten away with something. You stretch, yawning the sleep away, stretching your arms to the ceiling. You blink. There, on your arm—your other arm—is a line of fresh red spots. The skin is raised around the spots, and they have a heartbeat all their own.

Your own heart quickens. Ricky is a snoring lump beside you. He truly is a boy yet, with no regard for life's dangers. You want to wake him, but at the same time you want him to stay sleeping while you make your own decision. Almost anything can set off an allergic reaction, you know well. You can even catch a faceful of poison ivy from wood smoke, or from the fur of your pet. Your mother at the last had hives in her throat.

You think carefully about the whole mess, how it started. This is a mystery that you can solve by certain clues. At first, all mental trails lead back to Ordizia and the noxious Spanish weed that must have been lurking there among the wildflowers. Now, you see that all trails lead back to the man sleeping next to you. The wise doctor asked, Where are you sleeping? Her sage question was another way of asking,

How well do you know your husband? Implicit in the question was the answer. Harboring some disease, your new husband has been injecting you with his poison in unrelenting bursts.

Perhaps. You continue to ponder. What if your translation was wrong? What if she had asked, Where did you sleep? the way your mother asked the first time you stayed out all night with a boy, as if to suggest you were a dirty girl who had done a hideous thing. For the first time, you think of the question quite literally, removing poor Ricky from the equation entirely. You are sleeping in a foreign country, in a strange apartment, in this strange bed, and on these strange pillows. You roll over to examine your cream-colored pillow. Looking closely at the pillow, you see two small red spots. Blood stains, the size of pin pricks. In the sheets you find more of these stains. You ruffle the bedding and from the folds falls a small brown insect. It's been crushed. Not a spider. It looks more like a deer tick. You pinch the bug in your fingers and drop it on the nightstand.

You're on your knees now on the king-sized bed, peering into the sheets. Get up, you say to Ricky.

Ricky rolls over and yawns. What time is it? he says.

It's noon. Get up. I'm looking for something.

Ricky does as he's told. He yawns and stretches, then just stands there staring at you, your nose inches from the sheets, your fingers tweezers.

Who let this crazy woman into my bedroom? he says.

In the bed, you find several tiny particles and gather them in your palm. The particles are innocuous. They could be dandruff, or lint, dead skin, the broken wings of mosquitoes.

I think we've got bugs, you say to Ricky. Look, these might be babies. I have a big one on the nightstand. You go to the nightstand but the smashed bug is gone. Instead, you show Ricky the airy chaff in your palm.

I don't see any bugs, he says.

Back on your knees now, you search the floor around the bed. Look, here's another one. You hold up a tiny husk no bigger than a flea.

I don't believe this, Ricky says. I have to go to work. What are you doing?

We're living with insects, you say, holding forth the proof. I don't have a rash, Ricky. I have *bites*. I'm being eaten.

You're crazy, he says. If you're being eaten, what about me? Don't I taste good?

I don't know, you say. You're still inspecting the floor. I just know there are bugs in here. I think they're shedding.

I think you're obsessed, Ricky says, or cracked. So what if they're bugs. Those might be normal here. They're probably just dust mites or something. Look. Sweetheart. You've got to get over your small-town hang-ups. We're in a foreign country. You can't always bring your Midwestern baggage with you when you travel in a foreign country. You're going to have to get used to things being foreign.

You stand up now, and look directly at your husband. Ricky. There are bugs in the bed. I don't know what they do in California, or any other country, but in Wisconsin, we don't sleep with insects. Period. This is not normal.

To this, what response but silence? Ricky pulls on his pants and leaves. Alone in the empty apartment, you look through Ricky's backpack for his English dictionary. You look up the word bedbug. You're surprised to find the word there in plain bold print, and even more surprised by the definition. Bedbug: a small, wingless, blood-sucking insect. Small-town hang-ups, Ricky? you say aloud. I'm not crazy. Next you look up bedbug in Ricky's Larousse. Nothing. They must not have bedbugs in Spanish. They must be an English-speaking phenomenon.

As you put the dictionary away, you spy Ricky's fruit-colored journal, lying demurely in his backpack. You've looked through this before, of course, but not for some time. It's full of his scribblings and etchings, what he calls field notes. You finger the heavy cotton pages, flipping to the last entries, from this week. The pencil etchings catch your eye. Well, Ricky's drawing has certainly improved. The last is quite an interesting likeness. It's a sketchy nuptial image of you and him, but you're both crouched low on the curb, looking over Main Street, Mount Horeb. Your features are grotesque: he's given you a hunchback and himself a bulging neck-full of goiters or hives, but your faces are quite angelic. He's made your face softer somehow, prettier than you imagine it.

You hear keys in the door and stuff the journal away, quickly. There is Ricky, contrite, as usual, too soon. You can't take seriously a man who forgets his grievances so quickly. You're not as apt to forget a grudge, and now it's your turn to storm out. You pass Doña Ester dusting in the foyer and head out into the old city looking for a café with Wi-Fi. On every street you pass evidence of last night's storm: broken windows and strewn debris. At Café Donostea you're amazed that a simple search yields dozens of sites about the insects. It's as if you're discovering something for the first time that is commonplace to the rest of the world, that bedbugs are not just a bedtime story. They live in the creases of your mattress, under your headboard, any place safe and dark and near your body while you sleep. At night, awakened by your heat, they come to feast. They crawl onto your tender shoulders, forming a feeding line where they chisel their mandibles into your flesh. Blood-engorged adults may reach the size of a tooth. Like spiders and snakes, they grow by shedding their skins.

The sites you explore are quasi-scientific, the squalid descriptions often laced with humor. No one, it seems, has ever died from bedbug bites. The people who collected this information had, like you, unknowingly gotten into something. You learn that bedbugs are remarkably efficient animals. While feeding, they secrete toxic saliva that helps them break your skin and digest your blood. The poison induces sleep. The longer the bedbugs eat, the longer their meal stays at table. Theoretically, the host could fall into a state of continuous unconsciousness.

The other question, of course, is what about Ricky. Nothing in your search exonerates him, nothing suggests the bugs would choose one bedfellow and ignore the other. You explore some other sites of general interest about bedbugs. You find bedbug in a list right above cochineal bug, largely responsible for the rapid colonization of Mexico, a bug that clothed the entire British army in its blood.

Enough. Armed with the knowledge of where bedbugs live, you return to the apartment to check the mattress. You turn back the dust ruffle and aim a flashlight at what you've been sleeping with. There, in the mattress creases, hundreds of tiny insects crawl in a moving hoard of their own bodies. You suppress a shudder and lower the beam lest you send the little bloodsuckers into a frenzy. You close the bedroom door and wait in the living room for your husband to return. Sitting on the couch, you can't keep your fingers from exploring the seams on the underside of the couch cushion. But your fingertips read nothing but dense fabric. You feel an abiding sense of relief. All this will be over soon. You need only find someplace else to sleep.

When the doorbell rings, you realize you've drifted off. Sleeping again. How long were you out? You're expecting Ricky, probably holding a bouquet of flowers, but instead you find Doña Ester. It's cleaning day, evidently. At her side is a man she introduces as Don Rodrigo, her husband. Strange, you hadn't realized she was married, but of course she is. Don Rodrigo holds a big wrench. He looks like a plumber. You decide now is a good time to broach the delicate subject of infestation.

You have, you say to Doña Ester, many bugs in the bed. You attempt to translate. Muchos bichos, you say, de la cama.

Doña Ester looks at you blankly at first, then her eyes alight with recognition.

Oy. Pulgas, she says, laughing. Pulgas no son un problema.

No son pulgas, you say. They're not fleas.

You take Doña Ester into the bedroom, her husband in tow. You flip back the dust ruffle and point the flashlight into the mattress seam. The gasp uttered from Don and Doña is loud, synchronized. Don Rodrigo's big wrench hits the floor.

When Ricky comes home, holding a glaring bouquet of calla lilies, you're still packing. He has his friends in tow, the anarchist, the linguist, and the snob. They're lonely children of the Foreign Service, sleeping in empty beds. Polite to the last, or perhaps afraid of Ricky's monstrous wife, they wait in the doorway.

What's going on? Ricky says, gesturing at the luggage and the pile of clothes.

Sweetheart, we've been evicted, you say.

What do you mean evicted? We're on our honeymoon.

It's Doña Ester, you say. She didn't react well to the infestation. She seemed upset about the exotic disease we brought from Wisconsin.

Evicted? Ricky says again dumbly.

You take the flowers from your husband and bury your nose in their enormous white bugles. They're pretty but don't smell like much. Ricky will have trouble imagining a life on Main Street, Mount Horeb, a street where everything you could ever need is contained between its two ends. For your own part the return seems inevitable. Your roots are deep in the Mount Horeb soil, and your mother, the Troll Queen Troll herself, has bequeathed a place for you on the curb.

Writer's Elbow

Today, Graves will get a haircut. In the meantime, he will take out the garbage. The last thing Graves needs to hear is how he needs a larger cock and balls. But that's exactly what Shizzam Jizzam in his emails keeps telling Graves that he needs. It's his brain—that bifurcated lobe dangling between his ears—that could use enlarging. His wife, Camila, complains that he eats too much and exercises too little. She says he's a pig, but in that saucy Argentine way of hers that makes it seem as if she likes it. She gives him a bulleted list every morning before she goes to work. Today, it reads:

- Remember to take out the Garbage! Today is Garbage Day!
- Get a haircut! You look shaggy!
- Write something Brilliant to make your wife proud!
- Do some push-ups, hey Mr. Philosopher! They help you think!

Camila detests complacency. She gives orders with gusto. She does not, however, complain that anything is too small. He manages to give her pleasure, say, 50 percent of the time, which, according to an article he scanned in *Men's Room*, is statistically better than average.

Graves himself is able to achieve noticeable pleasure nearly 90 percent of the time he penetrates his wife. Yes, everything in the cock and balls department seems A-OK. Knock on wood.

His problem is that he needs to be smarter and more ambitious. Graves is on summer break from Evergreen Community College, where he teaches two sections of Intro to Creative Writing and three sections of College Writing per semester. He has the summer free. What's more, Camila is teaching double her normal load of tango lessons at Fitness Inc. because her colleague Audra is on maternity leave. The resulting arrangement leaves Graves with seven hours of virtually interruption-free writing time from 7 a.m. to 2 p.m. each day. He has squandered those hours for exactly seventeen days to date, checking his email, rearranging his files, losing at computer solitaire, thinking about cigarettes, chewing nicotine squares, thinking how he's a raving nicotine addict, thinking how he needs a dog—a large dog, maybe with a bit of wolf in him—breakfasting, lunching, napping, making a haircut appointment.

Never, until today, has he wasted his writing time thinking that the answer to his creative sterility is a larger cock and balls. As a teenager, sure, Graves believed that an extra inch or three would have made all the difference, would have made him an object of desire rather than one who desires, therefore altering the course of his life, or at the very least getting him some action, which would have been life-altering enough. Now, because he is a more mature thinker, Graves knows that larger genitalia, at this stage of the game, would be wasted on him. A book, now, or a brain. If he could buy a larger book and brain online, that would be a different kettle of fish altogether.

Graves sits at the breakfast nook in his rented, two-bedroom bungalow and fingers his skinny laptop. He will sit here for the morning. If he can do nothing else, he will at the very least keep his ass planted in this chair. He feels compelled to utilize his writing time, not because he particularly wants to but because he must make good sooner or later, on his reputation as a writer. Also, he must have some good reason to avoid taking tango lessons from Camila. She keeps nagging that he needs a little more blood to the brain, but beneath the nagging, Graves suspects, is Camila's doubt that her husband finds any particular value in what she does.

True, Graves finds the prospects of a life of the mind more stimulating than a life of the body. He's borrowed from some continental philosopher the idea of the instinct/intellect paradox; the way Graves understands it, intellect and instinct are turned in opposite directions, the former toward the mind, the latter toward the body. Generally speaking, the instinctual person is the happier one, and therefore, to Graves's view, the shallower. Lately, though, he has had precious little mind or body exercise. He feels no particular intellectual or instinctual urges. And for all her body enhancing, Camila remains intellectually nimble. She beats him in Scrabble nearly every time, though Scrabble, Graves reminds her—like the crossword, like spelling—measures rote more than intellect.

Three years ago, Graves married Camila to keep her from leaving him. That same year he completed a novella and a stimulating low-residency MFA degree in creative writing. It was a dizzyingly productive time. Graves wrote his novella about a Sunday watercolorist and sometimes-adjunct art professor who marries an aerobicist. Upon finishing the book, Graves procured an agent at Otis and Otis, New York, who called the book, titled *Housework*, "a perfectly gorgeous meditation." Nothing much happens in the book plot-wise, but according to his agent's cover letter—the good parts of which Graves has memorized—he, the author, "portrays the aesthetics of domestic intercourse with such relentless sincerity that the mundane actions of each spouse—his taking out the trash, say, her boiling of the okra—becomes the architecture that bears the weight of their entire relationship, and of the work itself."

Most of the book takes place in the breakfast nook, the very breakfast nook, in the very bungalow, where Graves now sits dallying with his email, staring at Camila's list of chores with no items checked off. Graves himself prefers to think of his book as "not unintelligent." It was his first book, after all, and it would be crippling to heap too much praise upon it. The agent is trying to sell his novella as a shorter novel, though it barely stretches past seventy pages in the biggest font—Courier Old School—Graves could find. It would be nice, the agent had said, if his book were larger. Every artist must question the size of his gift. Still, with the font-fattened manuscript in one hand and the agent contract in the other, Graves felt like a writer.

Lately, especially since the end of classes seventeen days ago, Graves feels like a fraud. He believes this feeling has something to do with his (he calls it his) instinct/intellect paradox. The intellect seeks things it can never find. The instinct could find the things the intellect seeks but would never look for them. This, Graves suspects, is why writers are so enamored with folks who work for a living, romanticizing and fetishizing every turn of their grubby lives. This, too, is why he loves Camila. Here Camila teaches tango and she's a tango fanatic. She does it because she likes to, because it feels good, not because it has any particular philosophical worth. She has learned the names of all the muscles in her body that will improve her tango agility, and she stimulates these muscles while she's doing other things. She does glute-tightening exercises when she's washing the dishes or vacuuming the house. When she watches TV and even when she first gets into bed, she does ab crunches, numbering aloud well into the hundreds. The effect on Graves is like counting sheep, and he falls into a liquory sleep beside her well-toned body.

Graves, on the other hand, prefers to do one thing at a time. He teaches writing, but aside from email and copious marginalia on student papers, he hasn't written a thing in three years. He doesn't even read very much anymore. During his three-year stint at Evergreen Community College, however, he has somehow fanned the flames of a rumor among his students and colleagues that he is indeed hard at work on a book, his second book, a novel. Sometimes Graves even catches the thread of a rumor that a few of his students and colleagues suspect that he, Graves, is a genius.

His students—and his colleagues, come to think of it—are so starved for a creative outlet that all Graves has to do is utter an aphorism like Writing is a philosophical mode—it's a way of thinking, with a certain sagacity he learned in graduate school, and his class practically weeps. They think he's Socrates. It helps that in Creative Writing all the work is about the students themselves. This is a subject his students find endlessly interesting. They want to study more of themselves, and they give Graves the credit for coming up with the pedagogical justification to let them. In College Writing, only the first assignment can be a personal essay. After that they get down to serious work. In Creative Writing, the students spend the whole semester writing personal essays, confessional poems, and self-referential fictions. They love it, and they love Graves for it. Since his tenure decision at Evergreen Community College is based mostly on whether or not the students love him, Graves has decided to make it his first priority.

Yet, in his own mind, Graves feels like a talented piano teacher who never touches his instrument. Every so often a doe-eyed sophomore with graceful prose and low-rise jeans will ask to read some of his work. I've heard you write like Kafka, she'll say. Then she'll smile a smile that manages to be innocent and hopeful and seductive all at once. Such smiling comparisons goad Graves, threaten to keep him awake through the bourbon-lit evenings and the ab-straining sheep counting that ensues. Sooner or later, Graves knows, he'll have to put out.

So, Graves has decided to use this summer to make good. Perhaps his students and his wife are correct. Perhaps he is brilliant, and perhaps the last three years have been a gestation period for Something Bigger. For seventeen days now, however, veritably chained to the breakfast nook, Graves has caught no glimpse of Something Bigger. Today, after looking at the screen for a couple of hours and checking his email—which he does with increasing frequency because he's expecting an important message from Otis and Otis—he's going for a haircut. He'll have to shower beforehand, of course, and take out the garbage. Surely the good news from Otis and Otis will propel him toward Something Bigger.

Each time he checks his account, however, Graves finds another notice from Shizzam Jizzam, Sin Amin, or Mei-Loine. Sometimes the taglines are cryptic: *Inflate your ego*, *Expand your capability*. Other times the messages are unambiguous and vulgar, vaguely ungrammatical: *Get a Larger Cock and Balls*.

How long has this been going on? For several months at least, but surely more frequently since classes ended. The first few times the messages appeared last fall semester Graves was confused and a little paranoid. Wasn't this something the internet people fixed years ago? He remembers getting messages like this back when he still had Hotmail, but not since then. He's checked with Camila, and with a colleague from work. They're not getting messages like this. Is Graves the only one?

Why me? he asked Camila. Why now?

Because you're a pervert, she said, and pinched him.

After trying unsuccessfully to unsubscribe himself from the mailing list, he simply deleted any messages with questionable subject matter. Lately, however, since he's had more time on his hands, Graves has become more curious. He sometimes opens the personalized messages, reading how larger genitalia will give him more sex appeal, more sex drive, and how this will make him, Graves, a pleasure factory. Sometimes, after reading the enticements, he even clicks on the links to begin his order. He can use his credit card to pay all at once, or he can make four easy installments of $19.95 or $29.95, depending on how enormous he wants to be.

Graves intuits now, late in the morning, his haircut encroaching, that he hasn't really been getting more dirty messages; rather, he has been rereading the same dirty messages more often. The problem is that he's checking his email too frequently. Once per day should be sufficient. Yet he finds himself on the goddamn email every ten to fifteen minutes, randy for an important notice. No wonder he can' do any writing. This bad habit is not unrelated to the vulgar subject matter of the emails themselves. The medium is the message, as it were; therefore, email itself is cock and balls. The important word Graves awaits will never come by email, he understands, yet he cannot help himself looking for the message where it will never be.

This is about more than the watched pot, surely. Yet the more Graves watches the pot, the more Shizzam Jizzam appears peddling his pornographic snake oil. Fine, so Shizzam Jizzam is the only one who cares enough about Graves to send him an email. Graves should reciprocate. Fine if the rest of the world turns its collective back to Graves. Graves will turn his back to the collective rest of the world. So, to show his appreciation this morning, after playing computer solitaire for three hours, checking his email a dozen times, chewing seven nicotine-replacement squares, and drinking four cups of coffee with cream while describing the florid wallpaper around the break-fast nook and Camila's mysterious window-ledge herb garden in a limpid paragraph and a half, Graves instinctively follows the links and purchases a pump device that will surely enlarge his penis and testicles by 20 percent—the $29.95 package, what the hell—or his money back, guaranteed, personally, by Shizzam Jizzam himself.

He shuts his laptop and goes to shower. His haircut is in half an hour. Camila is off somewhere in aerobic bliss, sculpting her der-rière. He imagines her looking at him in the shower, his widening girth threatening to cast a shadow on his love. Look at yourself, she says. You're disgusting.

Yes, but disgusting good, or disgusting bad? He can never tell with her. In the shower, he thinks that perhaps some material en-hancement would be just the thing.

Graves towels off. He is enamored of his new idea. Perhaps, if he were better endowed, he wouldn't need to write anymore at all and he could just live and be happy. After all, isn't that what writing has been for him, a way to get a woman and feel more like a man? If he had a literal enlargement, he wouldn't need the symbolic enlargement that writing has provided him. It was his writing, after all, that had most attracted Camila to him. Graves understood that Latin women had more respect for poetry than women from his own culture, so during their courtship he made sure always to be scribbling furiously and wadding up paper. English was her second language, so it wasn't too difficult to impress her. But now he's married her, this woman who dances all the time. He doesn't need writing to keep her. He only needs to accomplish his chores. Too, Latin women are supposed to be more amorous than white women. Maybe a 50 percent success rate is on the low side for a Latina. And what about Latin men? Did they have an extra something that Graves didn't have? Shizzam Jizzam's rescue package certainly couldn't hurt.

Brushing his teeth with his vibrating toothbrush, Graves remembers Hannah, the Swedish dental hygienist he dated before Camila. After they had been dating for a year, she went on a vacation with her girlfriends to sunny California and came back with fake breasts. They looked terrific and they were tremendous fun to handle during lovemaking. However, the silicone implants caused a lack of sensitivity in Hannah's nipples. Before her implants, Graves could easily stimulate her by rubbing, licking, or suckling her nipples. Now, she claimed that she couldn't feel a thing. That part of their foreplay was shot, but Graves kept paying attention to her nipples anyway because it seemed a requisite step. Too, he hoped the feeling might come back with use.

They're numb, Hannah had said, exasperated. You may as well suck on my elbow. Their relationship then began its inevitable decline, and the elbow became a metaphor for all that was wrong. Before too long, Graves didn't feel a thing either.

Never fear, says Shizzam Jizzam. It's right in the contract. You'll experience no abatement of sensitivity. Perhaps you'll even experience an increase in sensitivity to accompany your increase in size and virility.

More sensitivity, Graves thinks wistfully, banging the spit off his vibrating toothbrush. That couldn't hurt. He addresses the pile of clothes at his feet, the same clothes he had taken off before showering. He dresses, buttons his trousers, slips on his sandals, and turns to leave. There he is in the mirror, long hair obscuring his ears. A haircut will sure be nice.

Then Graves hears a noise. It's just perceptible at first, one of the many daily noises that skip across the surface of one's consciousness without causing a cascade of recognition. The little noise skips along harmlessly until suddenly it delivers to Graves a terrifying message—garbage truck—that wreck of short vowels and glottal stops that spells, for Graves, trouble. Then, out the window, he sees the deep-green signifier the noise had foreshadowed, idling. He remembers Camila's mock syllogism from this morning. Today is Thursday. Every Thursday is garbage day. Therefore, take out the fucking garbage, you dope. Why can't you ever remember that, hey Mr. Philosopher?

Graves hurries to grab the overfilled garbage bag from the can under the sink. In one fist he carries the garbage bag, and in the other fist he carries the recyclables. He bangs out the front door hollering, Hold on, just as the garbage man is pulling away. Graves has the vague feeling of déjà vu. He sees the yellow school bus pulling away, the silver train leaving the platform. Wait for me, Graves hollers. He's late, perpetually, left standing alone while the object he desires leaves without him. Yet he exists here on the vacant platform just the same. He has, he tells Camila, *negative capability*, the capacity to live just fine without ever being quite ready when the time comes.

Nonsense, she says. You're just lazy.

The garbage truck stops and Graves trundles toward it, garbage bags banging against his thighs. Up close, he notices that this is a different garbage truck than the usual. It's bigger. From around the driver's side comes the garbage man, a new, bigger garbage man.

Jesus. What's going on? Graves stands mute before the new and improved amalgamation of garbage truck and garbage man. He holds
the white garbage bags by their white necks. The outsized garbage
man seems to know him.

There's no need to separate the garbage anymore, Mr. Graves,
the man says. We have a new system. We have a conveyor belt where
people stand on each side and sort the wet garbage from the dry stuff,
milk jugs, egg cartons, beer bottles, and so on. They call it the Slime
Line. Don't worry. They wear rubber suits and gloves and gas masks
and . . . Mr. Graves? You seem confused. Don't you remember me,
Mr. Graves?

I have an inkling, Graves says. The garbage man is really just a
big boy, flannel-clad despite the heat, with thick glasses. He smiles
broadly.

You couldn't forget me, Mr. Graves. Intro to Creative Writing?
You gave me an A-. My best grade of the semester.

Oh, Graves says. Yes. Wilson. How are you doing? It's been
what, three years? Graves grips the white garbage bags in each hand,
feels the tug in his shoulder joints. They hang like dead swans.

Wilson was more of a poet, without much of a knack for narra-
tive. He doesn't remember Wilson's poems per se, but he remembers
a poetics essay the boy wrote about poetry being like a dance and
prose like a sullen walk. Poetry was an end in itself, and prose was
merely a means to an end. The essay had its obvious flaws, and Graves
thought he might have come across that analogy somewhere in graduate school, yet overall, Wilson was earnest if not completely convincing. A means to get somewhere else, sure. But where?

You had a big impact on me, Mr. Graves, Wilson says. Before
your class I had no idea what creative writing was. Now I got my
associate's. You made me see my own life as an asset to my educa-
tion. I never knew I was interesting before your class. I'm what you'd
call a round character, Mr. Graves. Remember how you used to say,

Give them warts? You couldn't invent a character as good as me, the world's first garbage-trucking poet.

Well, Graves says. Good for you, Wilson. It's good for a poet to be gainfully employed. Wallace Stevens sold insurance, remember.

You still writing, Mr. Graves? Published anything yet? Three years ago you had a book ready to be published, remember? I'd love to read your books.

Another day, Wilson, Graves says. I have a haircut. He walks forward and heaves the bags over the low tail end of the garbage truck, onto the other bags, some white, some black, some with crimson ties.

These are all sorted out, anyway, Graves says. Two less bags for your guys on the slime line to paw through.

Fewer. Are you testing me, Mr. Graves? You mean fewer, right?

Yes, that's right, Wilson. Two fewer bags.

I'll see you, Mr. Graves. Keep writing, like you told us. I'll be checking in on you every Thursday. From now on, I'm your regular garbage man.

You bet, Wilson. So long.

Wilson gets back into his garbage truck and motors away, honking as he turns the corner. Standing at the end of his driveway waving, Graves feels vaguely that Wilson is getting away with something, making off with some bounty. He feels the urge to run after the garbage truck and swing aboard the back platform where the garbage man's partner would go.

Instead, he stands empty-handed in the drive. He looks at his watch. Nearly two o'clock. Hoo boy. He'll never make his haircut. If he shows up late he'll put his barber behind for the whole afternoon. The line of men waiting for haircuts will look at him hatefully, and the barber might gouge him out of spite. Better to wait. Camila will be home soon. She'll be sweaty and happy from her dancing, and she'll want a shower. She'll chide him about his long hair but congratulate him for taking out the trash. She'll tease him about the strong, handsome men whom she taught to tango. And she'll have a bag of healthy groceries for Graves to put away. In the shower she'll sing something in Spanish. Then she'll call out for him. Make yourself useful and bring me my towel, hey Mr. Philosopher?

Next to the driveway is the homely tin mailbox. Some teenager has taken a bat to it. Its little red flag is bent. Graves feels a throbbing somewhere near his groin and gropes his pocket for a nicotine chew. There's one. Thank goodness. Yes, when she calls for him, he will bring her a towel.

Add This to the List of Things
That You Are

After she has utterly denuded it by removing all her furniture and every trace of her, move from the lovely cabin you shared together. The lovely cabin in the Santa Cruz Mountains with views out over the redwoods to the sea is now haunted, and you can't stay there. Understand that the rules you lived by are no longer true. The former first principle, time alone in the woods cures all distress, is now a falsehood. Understand that to survive this loss you'll need new rules.

Create Rule Number One: Any beautiful body can be replaced with any other beautiful body.

Create Rule Number Two: Beautiful or not, always keep a body close by.

In the meantime, learn to beg. Send begging letters. Call all of her relatives to beg them to beg her to come back. Please, you beg.

Get back in touch with your self-destructive side. Drink heavily. Start smoking again. Drive recklessly on dangerous roads.

Create Rule Number Three: Buy now, pay later.

Refer to Rule Number One: Call all the women you know who might possibly sleep with you. Of all the women you know who might possibly sleep with you, choose the married one. Stipulate in your oral contract that this relationship will solely concern sexual gratification.

Be surprised when the married one agrees to your terms.

Now, add home wrecker to the list of things that you are.

Add Rule Number Four: When you do the right thing, you will pay for it.

And Rule Number Five: When you do the wrong thing, you will pay for it.

Armed with these new rules, quit your job. Get back in touch with your pathetic side. Move across country from California to Wisconsin to be in the vicinity of your mother. Put everything you own in a 10×10 storage locker, the sight of which, lined with all the other 10×10 storage lockers, makes you sink down to the asphalt so that cars must avoid you.

Now, go to a foreign country. Don't pick the country arbitrarily. Choose a country where you don't speak the language, the country where you are most likely to be beaten for the perpetual scowl on your face. Choose Russia.

Make the mistake of choosing to travel to Russia via Finland. The one for whom you created these Rules is from Finland.

But of course you don't find her there. So, in Finland, have an affair with a Swiss woman and pay for it later.

In Russia have an affair with a Russian woman and pay for it later.

Keeping always in touch with your self-destructive side, create the situation where one of your bones is broken just to see if that helps. Decide the broken bone hurts, but it helps. Medicine has advanced. You now have your choice of colorful fiberglass casts. Choose black.

You are smart enough to understand that there is some pattern here, but not smart enough—and this, you think, might be the tragic part—to understand the pattern itself.

So. Urge the woman whose home you wrecked to visit you in Russia and pay for it later. By now she has fallen in love with you and asks you difficult questions that violate your original contract. When you fuck her, she asks, do you imagine the other one?

Don't ever speak the truth. Don't ever say, Only then do you not. For now, give thanks for this time of abundance.

On the way back through Finland, prolong the Swiss affair by urging the Swiss woman to meet you there. You will pay for that later also.

Return to your own country. Learn that the Russian has been cheating. Her lover sends you a ranting email in broken English telling you he is the one that you fucked too.

Deny all offers of love. Understand for the first time this term that women use: emotionally unavailable. Tell all the women that you didn't mean what you said.

In your own country adhere to your failed rules for another year just to see. Be surprised when another year turns into three. Continue to deny all offers of love. Realize just how long this is going to last.

Finally, empty your 10×10 storage unit. But decide to keep the unit. Locked. Empty. Indefinitely. Let the fines for unpaid debt accrue.

Admit you have become one of those who keeps a locked room he can never enter.

Add this to the list of things that you are.

Barrel Riders

I

Timothy's new landlord, Fred, has put a wren house out, and the annoying creatures have moved in with a vengeance. It's as if they followed him from Blue River. His mother always had a wren house out too. The wrens chatter every few seconds, incessantly, no variation. It doesn't even sound like birdsong, more insectile, like the unholy coupling of a locust and a cockroach. It's 8 a.m. and they've been at it since before dawn. It's impossible to sleep. Why invite such pestilence to your doorstep?

So, this is Milwaukee. This is June. Lilacs shroud the dooryard, crabapples sprout in the cracks of the alleyway, and Timothy's not the only charity case at Rooms for Men. So, Timothy's escape from Blue River has landed him here. He had imagined a further escape. California somewhere. But for a bargain hunter, Milwaukee is turning out to be a fair deal.

What brings you to Milwaukee? Fred had asked, the day he signed the lease.

It's as far as I could get from where I'm from, Timothy had said.

170

And that was close to the truth. There was more to the equation: his new teaching job, starting in August. But it came down to trading in simple binaries. Urban for rural. Strange for familiar. He likes to tell the story this way: At the farm, Timothy had been bucked off. Rather than get back on, he moved out.

Timothy's landlord, he realizes in his first week of residence, is what's called a payee. Several of the local derelicts in the other boardinghouses on Marshall Street receive Social Security Income—SSI. But they can't get their government checks delivered directly to them or they'll squander their money, so a payee doles out their monthly check in weekly increments. Enter Fred. Timothy didn't know this when he signed the lease, but otherwise he can't complain about the place, or the cheap rent.

Also, there was no deposit, no first and last, and Timothy's lease is month to month. He knows what else he can get in the city for this price. He's made the rounds. On the west side, five hundred dollars gets you a basement room with bars on the window overlooking the expressway. In River West five hundred dollars buys you the same basement room, but this room in a house full of live-action role-players who leave their swords and chain mail scattered about the living-room battlefield.

Last place I looked at was a room in this old guy's house in River West, Timothy tells Fred. As he recounts the story, Fred's showing him the features of his upstairs studio. It's old, that's for sure, but it's got character. Fireplace encased in marble used to burn coal and an old brass chandelier still goes on gas. The high ceiling and the ornate fixtures give the studio a grandiose air, but there's still just the one room. Timothy can see everything from where he's standing. Nice big windows look out to Marshall Street. Little sink in the corner to brush his teeth, or if he has to get up to pee. Bathroom is down the hall, shared with the three other tenants. Cute white enamel appliances look like they belong in a dollhouse.

Timothy continues his story. Old guy's a cripple, a veteran, so he's offering a deal if you can help out with house chores. Phone interview is going fine. Asks me how big I am. I tell him not so big, but I've done farm work around Blue River. Says farm work is a definite plus. Asks me how old, I tell him twenty-five. I figure he wants to know if I can handle the work. Says he needs a hand getting in and out of the tub, and I say that's cool.

Fred's stepping on a piece of the subfloor as Timothy talks, a section that's got a little wave to it. He says he'll finish the floor tiles in a day or two, then Timothy can move in if the place suits him. He's wearing a red-plaid flannel and blue jeans. Bifocals. Black work shoes. Like he just walked off the factory floor. Except he's too old, of course. Retired clock puncher, Timothy would bet on it.

So, I'm thinking this is going to be great, five hundred dollars a month, and I just have to haul in groceries and lift a guy in and out of the tub. Of course, then comes the catch. Old guy asks what I do for a living and I say, Schoolteacher. Then he asks me if I like men. I say, Excuse me? He repeats the question. Do I like men? What a question, right? I figure out he's asking me if I'm gay and I say, No. No way. He says, That's too bad. I was sort of looking for someone who liked getting head.

Even then, retelling the story, Timothy feels a surge of anger similar to what he felt when it happened. He notices then for the first time how retelling a story allows you to re-create the emotion of the experience. Caught so unaware, and somehow violated. Yes. His trust and friendly instincts violated.

Timothy stops to measure Fred's reaction. But this old man seems more interested in his remodel job than Timothy's theatrics. He's gotten some spackling on the marble fireplace he's scraping off with his thumbnail.

Can you believe it? Timothy says.

That's too bad, says Fred. I'm sorry to hear that happened to you.

Tell you what, Timothy says. He's lucky we were on the phone. I don't know what I would have done to him in person. Sort of shocked me, I guess, because I wasn't expecting nothing, anything, like that.

No, says Fred. I would be shocked too.

Black leather chaps with silver studs. A black mask like the Lone Ranger would wear. Videos, some with Western motifs: *How the West Was Hung.* This is what Timothy finds in the closet in the third-floor attic. Snooping around, looking through some of Fred's antiques, and then finding this little cache of carnal goodies. At first Timothy didn't believe that Fred could be gay. Then he couldn't believe he could be this *kind* of gay. By which he meant what exactly? *So* gay? Exactly what you would think of when you thought of gay.

Chip is another of the renters. He's in his forties, according to Fred, though he looks Timothy's age and has the face of a cherub and the body of a Greek sculpture. He's also on SSI, Timothy has learned. Fred derisively calls him *that boy toy.* He has no job and spends most of his time working out at the Y. In the evenings, Timothy often sees him picked up by older men in luxury sedans, one night a Lexus, the next night a Mercedes. The men don't get out of their cars. They pull up in front of Fred's house and honk their horns, waiting for Chip to come to them. This seems like ghetto behavior to Timothy, announcing to the whole neighborhood you've arrived in your bad wheels.

Fred seems more like Timothy than like these other men. Fred even trusts Timothy, not his longtime tenants, to water the flowers when he's out of town.

Timothy felt a certain buoyancy at moving to Milwaukee. From Fred's house, you could walk to a theater, an opera house, art galleries, and ethnic restaurants of your choosing, or even an NBA game. Not that Timothy did any of these things. Who could afford them? But the fact that you could meant something to him. Timothy once

walked under the ornate wrought iron portico of the old brick Pabst
Theater after the shows let out. It was easy to convince himself that
he too had just come out into the fresh air after the intoxicating
dream of the theater. For the first time in his life, Timothy felt he was
someplace he might belong.

It was at a little gallery with a foreign name—the Pesti Est—on
Water Street beyond the Pabst that Timothy met Reka. Timothy
was on an evening stroll and passed by the street-front gallery announcing the *Milwaukee and Vicinity* art show. The floor-to-ceiling
windows beckoned, and Timothy watched all the well-dressed sophis-
ticates inside drinking wine and eating grapes and dainty cheeses.

The door opened for him.

Don't stand out in the cold. Come in. A high-pitched voice
dressed in a foreign accent. It belonged to the blonde holding the door.
She was a statuesque woman about sixty, Timothy guessed, dressed
in a tight cashmere sweater that accented her large breasts, and a
vibrant red sash that rested upon them. She held a glass of sparkling
white wine, which she handed to Timothy. When she passed him the
drink, Timothy noticed her withered hands, the hands of a much
older woman. She wore designer glasses and bright-red lipstick that
was a little smudged. She seemed like she might be half-crocked. She
took him by the arm. Here was an artist if Timothy had ever seen
one.

Of course, he had never seen one. It turned out this woman
owned the place.

My name is Piroska and I come from Hungaria, she told him.
Pesti Est is my gallery. When she said the name of the gallery, it
sounded like she was shushing him. *Peshty-esht.* It's a nice gallery,
Timothy said.

Don't be shy. Come, there are some people I want you to meet.
Timothy could smell the liquor on her breath as she navigated the
room, pointing out the bright paintings on the walls and the artists
they belonged to. She led him past the oils to a wall of black-and-white

photographs and finally to a brown sculpture that looked like soft-serve ice cream or a heaping pile of dung. There Piroska found the person—it turns out there was only one—that she wanted Timothy to meet.

Young man, this is my daughter, Reka. Reka, this young man would like to meet you.

Reka looked up from the sculpture she had been studying. On closer inspection, Timothy saw that it was a coiled serpent.

Hello there, she said. She seemed surprised, though not unpleasantly.

Just like that, Timothy thought, plucked off the streets of Milwaukee and fixed up with the best-looking woman in the joint. At an art opening, no less. This was Timothy's first. No mistaking that Reka was her mother's daughter, now that Piroska had pointed it out. She was also blonde, and similarly statuesque, but slimmer, and she wore looser-fitting, earth-toned clothing and leather sandals with her toes showing. Organic was the word that came to mind. Then the word his mother would have used. Earthy.

You two stay as long as you like, Piroska said. Then she said, Pussy dear, kissed her daughter, and walked off into the blotchy tableau of painters and paintings.

Did she just say that?

Puszi, Reka said. It means kiss in Hungarian.

I guess I like Hungarian, Timothy said.

Reka laughed. My mother is such a pest. Pleasure to meet you. She extended a hand. Not so young. Not so young as Timothy. But a beautiful hand. Timothy accepted her hand and for some reason, perhaps because it was so picturesque, perhaps because this is how he imagined one behaved at an art gallery, he kissed her hand.

My, Reka said, this one fancies himself a gentleman.

As he kissed her hand, which smelled of smoke and fruit, he noticed the scars on her wrist, thin filaments running both ways in a little crosshatch. Reka was a woman with many scars, he would learn.

Later that night, in front of his place, in the cab of his small truck, Timothy foraged for a goodnight kiss. Leaning in close to the wispy fronds of her blonde hair, he got a stronger dose of Reka's strange musky perfume that had lingered about her at the gallery.

You live in a boardinghouse, Reka said. How cool.

Yeah, Timothy said. I guess it's cool. It might be the last cheap studio left in the city.

You're lucky, she said. That's my new nickname for you. Lucky.

Well let's see it, Reka said, excited. Both of her hands went to his neck when she kissed him. Let's have a look at your little room, Lucky Boy. Don't make me beg.

II

To get what you wanted, Timothy was quickly learning, you never really had to leave the snug harbor of Milwaukee's east side. The freeway encircled the city on the west side, while Lake Michigan formed the eastern limit. There seemed to be a force field around the neighborhood that shielded Timothy from everything that happened at home. There were no visitors from Blue River. His place was too small for that. And he was far enough away that no one expected him to visit on a whim. He was safely hidden here, and all the news from home had to come by phone. If Timothy didn't want the news, he didn't answer his phone.

Timothy had landed, he found out from Fred and later from Reka, in a neighborhood that had been Italian. Then came the white flight and the black tide to fill in the vacuum. Two decades later, new condominiums began to rise from the ashes of the historic bungalows, and white-collar workers and investors began to leak back in. Marshall Street, perpendicular to an abandoned freeway spur, was still intact with its old Victorians, but most of these were boardinghouses, like Rooms for Men. So, the neighborhood had transformed into a mongrel collection of yuppies, gays, holdover blacks, and old Italians—and low-wage earners and SSI recipients who lined the porches of the Victorians not yet renovated.

Reka and Timothy sit now at the Y-Not II, just a couple blocks from Timothy's new home, drinking seven and sevens and smoking Reka's Camels. The advertising has done its work on him over a lifetime. There is nothing in the world sexier, Timothy thinks, than a woman who smokes. Reka has hands built for a cigarette ad. My God. Slender, white fingers tipped with red nails. Hands fragile, but also agile. Promising. A ring the size of a broach with a syrup-colored stone—amber, Timothy has learned—dazzles her index finger.

The Y-Not II seemed like a good neighborhood bar when they walked in, but Timothy wonders now if it's a gay bar. There's plenty of neon, and the clientele seems hip in a way that Timothy can't quite be sure about. They wear tight jeans with the bottoms rolled up. Chuck Taylor tennis shoes. Others wear black on black with heavy steel-toed boots. Reka calls them skull crushers. Many have silver chains attached to their wallets. Black horned-rim glasses. Serious-looking piercings in their eyebrows, noses and lips. Even the name of the place seems to invite subversion. Y-Not II. Why not what?

So, is this a gay bar? Timothy asks.

You're so clueless, Reka says. You have no gaydar whatsoever. This place is industrial, not gay. Reka seems to know everything about what's hip. She takes another cigarette from her handbag. Everything about Reka is sexy. Even the handbag. Leather, petite, classy, but slightly used. When she picks it up to put it on her shoulder, Timothy wants to be the handbag.

OK, but they look strange. Fred doesn't even look strange. He looks like he could be from my hometown.

Oh, come on, Reka says. I knew Fred was gay the minute we pulled up to your place.

How did you know? Timothy says.

Painted lady, she says. Geezer fixing it up. He might as well have shouted *I'm gay* from the widow's walk. He couldn't be gayer in ruby slippers.

Painted Lady? Timothy says.

That's the house you're living in, Lucky. Victorian with the bright woodwork. You don't get around, do you?

OK, says Timothy. I get the picture. But he was wearing blue jeans and a flannel.

Well, you said he was from Iowa. And where did you say you found the leather goodies?

Right, says Timothy. In the closet.

Reka grew up in one of the wealthy suburbs of Milwaukee. Elm Grove. Her father is a surgeon who flies his own plane for a hobby. Her mother is Hungarian. A refugee. Patron of the arts. Timothy hasn't been to her place yet, though she's living there with her folks until she finds her own place.

My mother thinks loneliness is a disease she must fight against daily, Reka says. Doesn't matter if it's her divorced daughter moving back from the coast or some single bumpkin walking around a gallery. She just has to cure them.

It's true, Piroska had spotted Timothy on the street as a lonely new immigrant, a perfect playmate for her daughter, who was also new to the city. Rather, Timothy was new and Reka newly returned. She had lived in San Francisco for the last decade but had come home for what she called the Return Tour.

You'll have yours someday, she says. You'll see what it feels like to come home with your tail between your legs.

That won't happen.

Oh, I say it will, says Reka. But first you'll have to get a little more distance from the homestead. I mean, who runs away to Milwaukee, Wisconsin?

Timothy responds by sipping his drink.

That was a question, Lucky. Who does?

How do I know? Now he stares away at the entrance, his only escape.

You have a big secret, Lucky? You think being mysterious makes me want you more.

I guess so, Timothy says.

My Lucky Boy. Runs away from home and doesn't even make it over the crease in the map.

Good thing the men at Rooms for Men don't seem to mind Timothy bringing a woman home with him. After drinks at the Y-Not II, they return to Timothy's, where they both cram onto the trundle bed that came with the place. Timothy teases her that she's slumming with him, but she just laughs, in a way that makes Timothy feel belittled. The dismissive laugh tells Timothy she could teach him a few things about slumming. Already the feet of the trundle bed have worn grooves in Fred's new tilework. Timothy will have to bring that up to his landlord, but how embarrassing. See here Fred, when I fuck my girlfriend on your bed, I leave marks on your new floor.

They're entwined in the trundle bed nude. Fred's metal fans clatter away on the floor. Timothy traces an areola with his finger. Scars surround both of Reka's areolae. Each time with Reka he learns something new. He didn't need to ask about the scars lacing her wrists, but these scars on her breasts are an enigma. This time he finally gets up the courage to ask, and he learns these breasts have been reduced.

Her ex-husband, she says, couldn't get off with a woman with large breasts. He was very particular. First of all, Reka had to be on top, and from that vantage point her large breasts were evidently a distraction.

I never heard of anything like that, Timothy says.

Everyone has an ideal, Reka says, and I wasn't his. All his life he'd been jerking off to nymphs with pert tits, and along comes a leggy blonde with D cups.

I think your breasts are beautiful, Timothy says. He tries to imagine the devotion one must have to undergo such a surgery on behalf of another. But what happened next? She had the surgery like he wanted. Why then the divorce?

Well, big surprise, she says. It wasn't my breasts. There were all sorts of other problems. Problems on top of problems. Funny part is the world is full of men who love big tits. And I end up with the lone male who can't abide them.

I'm sorry, Timothy says, retracting his hands from her breasts. It seems indecent now, to be touching them.

That leaves me where I am, she says. Back home in Momma's house. Back on the market. Getting too old to play the game. My number one asset reduced by my own stupidity. Reka gets up to pour herself a drink of water from the little sink. When she comes back to bed, she puts the cool glass on his sweaty chest and offers this one bit of unsolicited information. Nobody will ever love me again like he did.

It shocks Timothy to hear this. How did he love her if he forced her to cut herself? Then, without thinking, Timothy says, I love you.

Thanks, Reka says. But you don't love me. So don't say you do. That's cruel.

I'm sorry, Timothy says.

So, what did you do? Timothy says. After the surgery and everything. How long did you stay married?

Another three years. She hesitates, finishes her water, and then puts the empty glass back on his chest. We stopped having sex altogether.

What did you do? Timothy asks, driven by genuine concern but also morbid curiosity.

Jerked off, stupid. And went to bars.

Went to bars? Timothy couldn't stop himself.

You like to play dumb, don't you, she says. You keep your secrets but want me to tell all. You think only men can sport-fuck. Look, I

wasn't penetrated by my husband for three years. I went to bars to
sport-fuck.

For a while Timothy is silent, letting this new information sink in.
He doesn't want to be judgmental. He doesn't want to be cruel. What
does he feel for her? Not love. Pity, yes. Lust. Anger now. Then he says,
You don't have to go to bars. You can go to your mother's gallery.

I prefer bars, Reka says.

Ouch, Timothy says. Goddamn.

She picks up the glass and swirls an imaginary ice cube in its
emptiness.

III

Reka was a kind of honky-tonk tour guide. She seemed to know all
the eastside bars, and he noticed that if she didn't know a man in
each one, she usually met one quickly. This led Timothy to wonder
why her mother thought to intervene. Reka could obviously fend for
herself. What if she just left him one night, just decided to go home
with someone else? Tonight maybe? Clearly, she could have her pick.

Tonight Reka chooses a bar called the Foundation, just over the
river on a dark tree-lined street, nestled among a row of dark bungalows. You would never know the bar was here unless someone guided
you to it. Crowd inside seems to be similar to the Y-Not II. If the
Foundation were a new album, its reviewer would describe it as Edgy.
Punk. Grunge. Eclectic. Like most of Reka's choosings. And, Timothy
can't help noticing, everything that he is not.

They have a drink at the bar, the gruff bartender nodding at Reka
like he knows her before moving on to the next barstool. The bar top
is long and straight, salvaged from an old bowling lane, with a line of
three-legged stools parked all the way down, some empty, some not.
This place is darker and smokier than the Y-Not II, and without the
suggestive neon. Most of one wall is given over to a faded mural in
earth tones. The mural depicts short, heavily muscled men, hobbits

or dwarves, spinning on whisky barrels in a roiling river the way loggers spin logs. The dwarves embody varying stages of jeopardy, some in temporary command of their vessels, others about to be rolled. A waterfall down the river the dwarves can't see tells you they'll all lose it eventually. Underneath the old mural, a painted scroll reads, *Barrel Riders*. The barrels are at eye level, so you have to look up at the dwarves, which makes them seem giant. The dwarves look down at you peevishly. Clearly, the mural is from a different time. The script on the scroll is calligraphy. Maybe *Barrel Riders* was the original name of the place. Whoever renamed it the Foundation has tried for a more urban motif while still contending with the history. The hanging lamps are square and angular, and a few low-slung couches gather nonchalantly in the far corners of the room. Some tables scattered about hold couples and lone drinkers.

The gruff bartender, a gray-haired man with a deep, gravelly voice, pours them another drink. Reka introduces him as Garth.

Just as Timothy is considering how it came to pass that Reka knows this Garth, another man sitting at one of the bar tables beckons Timothy and Reka, waving as if he wants to be joined. He's wearing a tan leather coat, which makes him about the brightest thing in the place.

There you go, Timothy says.

You go see what he wants, Reka says.

Timothy walks over from the bar, and the man says, Sit down, I'll buy you a beer. One for your wife, too.

Girlfriend, Timothy says. Friend. The man looks drunk, but Timothy judges him harmless enough. He also looks familiar, but Timothy can't quite place him.

Girlfriend, wife, the man says, gesturing as if to say, Same difference.

Timothy waves Reka over from her seat at the bar. Man wants to buy us a drink.

Why not? Reka says. She sits down next to the man and he puts his arm around her, just for a moment, like he has a secret to confide in her.

What did you say? Timothy says. He wonders how men know Reka is the kind of woman you can put your arm around like that.

He says his name is Jerry, Reka says. Jerry, this is Timothy. But you can call him Lucky.

Timothy is lucky, Jerry says. We should all have a nickname. My wife, my ex-wife, used to call me Old Fat Baby. You two can call me Jerry.

How's it going, Jerry? Timothy asks. A stupid question. Clearly, things are not going well for Jerry. He's drunk, disheveled, unwashed. He looks like he could be a Brady Street bum except for the coat, which looks expensive, one-of-a-kind. It's suede, Timothy sees now, and lighter than tan, more the color of a palomino horse. He stands out at the Foundation because of the coat, and for his age. Jerry looks to be in his fifties, and this is a twenty-something crowd.

How's it going? Jerry says, echoing Timothy's question. Well, let's see. The wife's gone, the house is lost, and the dog is dead.

Geez, Timothy says. Sounds like I should be buying you a drink.

No, this one's on me. So is the next one. And that should about do it.

He reaches into the pocket of his palomino coat and pulls out a fistful of coins and drops them onto the table. Then he reaches back into his pocket and fishes around some more. He empties the last of the coins onto the same pile, some coins spilling onto the floor. Jerry doesn't bend to pick up the coins but instead calls for the waitress.

Timothy notices a group of five or six young hipsters on the corner couches at the back of the bar seem to have an interest in this table. Maybe not hipsters. What would Reka call them? Industrials? Industrialists? Timothy doesn't know how long they've been watching his table, but they don't seem shy about staring. Reka notices too.

That rivethead's giving you stink eye, she says.

Rivethead. Timothy thinks of Rosie the Riveter. Growing up in Wisconsin, he's always associated her with Milwaukee.

The waitress arrives. Except for her apron, she's dressed like she could be one of the industrialists—were they all rivetheads?—at the back of the room. Timothy notices her patent-leather high heels are thick as blocks, like combat boots. Skull crushers.

Another double vodka for me, Jerry says. Rail's good. And whatever these two lovebirds are having.

The waitress sighs. She's been serving Jerry for a while, it seems.

We're vodka sweet, Timothy says. From the rail. Then to Jerry. All those coins, it looks like you were on Marshall Street this morning.

Come again? Jerry says.

I saw a man drop a jar of change out of his car window on Marshall Street earlier and a herd of bums dived after the coins. Looks like you got a few.

Shit, I saw that too, Jerry says. Where do you think this loot came from?

No kidding?

Shit yeah. I was watching from the window.

Odds or evens? Timothy asks.

1537. Big brown Vic full of bums.

Well that makes us neighbors, Timothy says. I'm 1535. Rooms for Men. Timothy feels better now. This isn't some stranger, it's his neighbor. So, did you join the fray? Timothy says.

Naw, Jerry says. Sold my electric toothbrush to my housemate for a bagful. Jerry shoves the coins into a tight pile. You that way? he asks, cocking his pinky.

What do you think? Timothy says. He's grown to like this ambiguity. Timothy tells the story, which Reka hadn't heard, about the orange Caprice and how he thought for a moment the man had dropped a bomb, but how it was just a jar of coins. Timothy admits he felt an urge to run out to the street and join the mob sifting through the shards and coins. It was free money, after all.

It's been a strange day, Jerry says. Waitress ever gets her skinny ass back here we'll drink to strange days on Marshall Street. Timothy notices how the chairs at their table are arranged so that Reka's chair is closer to Jerry's. Someone just walking by might imagine that Reka and Jerry were a couple and Timothy was, what, their young friend? A little brother?

The waitress comes back with the drinks, and Jerry takes a long time counting twelve dollars from the pile of coins on the table. Jerry's suede coat is out of place in a way that Timothy can't quite name. It looks like maybe it could be a cowboy coat. But it could also be some kind of vintage number, so maybe it was trendy? These vintage stores practically outnumbered the bars on Brady Street.

Jerry smiles at the waitress in a hungry way that Timothy recognizes from somewhere. Gust, his brother-in-law back in Blue River. That's who Jerry reminded him of. Hungry not for the woman but for what she's doling out.

The waitress furrows her brow. She looks disgusted, like Jerry just spilled something on her.

Hey, it spends, shit, Jerry says as she walks away.

What a cunt, Reka says.

Timothy flinches, but Jerry does not. She's just young, Jerry says, taking a big drink before he says, Cheers.

Cheers, says Timothy.

What were we drinking to? Reka says.

What would you say if I told you I was hunting for bottom? Jerry says.

If we weren't in a dead-end dive bar in Milwaukee, I'd say you were hunting for pussy, Reka says.

Timothy flinches again. Jerry laughs. Not that bottom, he says. That's kid's stuff. To the other bottom. He holds his drink up to toast.

Amen to the bottom then, Reka says. Tits up.

Jerry gulps half the double, then explains how his wife had left him earlier that year for a younger man, what Jerry called a boy toy. They had to sell the house. The dog was a problem too. He was a rescue number, large, boisterous, and troublesome. Sparky. Wife's new man wanted no part of the dog, and Jerry, well, Jerry was in a boardinghouse now on a week-to-week and couldn't keep a dog. They decided to euthanize it. Euthanize him. Sparky.

I can't believe you had to kill your dog, Reka says. That's so sad.

As if to outdo himself, Jerry says, too loudly, Then I lost my job. I was a broker. Isn't that funny. Now I'm broker than I was.

Timothy notices the rivetheads still watching from the corner couches. A couple of them wear dark stocking caps, and their facial piercings glint in the dull bar light.

Now you're staring, Reka whispers, and Timothy turns to face the table.

This is the last of my money, Jerry says. He's talking directly to Reka now. The very last. When I wake up tomorrow, I'll have a headache and no money and no job and my roommate will still be a huge Samoan dude with tits bigger than my wife's. And that will be the bottom of the jar for Old Fat Baby.

After neither of them responds, Jerry says, Right?

I've got some bad news for you, Mister Baby, Reka says.

Timothy feels oddly like he's interrupting these two. That will be the bottom, he says stupidly, but Jerry ignores him, as does Reka.

You two getting hitched? Jerry asks brightly. Timothy and Reka look at one another. He says, You might as well get it all over with. Get married, have a kid, get a divorce.

Ha, Reka says. You are one jaded individual.

But Timothy is offended. This is too much. All of it. Let's go, he says, standing up. As he does, he sees eyes on him from the corner of the bar.

Hey, whoa there, Texaco, I'm just fucking with you. Don't be so touchy. Happy couple. Let me buy you another toddy. Things will probably work out great for you guys. I can tell they will. You're quite a bit older than this one, aren't you? he says to Reka.

Wow, Jerry, Reka says. I can see why your wife left you. She offers this comment like her last one, with a flirtatious glint in her eye. At least it seems so to Timothy.

OK, I deserved that, Jerry says. But let me buy you another drink.

Jerry finishes his double.

He buys another round with the coins, and the same waitress waits impatiently for Jerry to pay up. Once he's paid, a small pile remains, and Jerry brushes these last few coins from the table with one cupped hand into the other, carefully, the way one clears bread crumbs from a table. Then he reaches for the waitress, catches her waist, and drops the coins into the pocket of her apron.

Don't touch me, she says, jerking back. You'll be out of here. Then she cuts Reka with a look as if to say, Control your animal.

Sorry lady, Jerry says. No offense. Just trying to tip good.

The waitress remains affronted. Just control yourself, she says.

Hey, sorry . . .

Then Reka interrupts. No, he's not sorry. Listen, bitch. No one forced you to be a barmaid. Why don't you go do what barmaids do.

Cowed, the woman walks back to the bar, her skull crushers crushing the carpet. Now it seems like everyone in the Foundation is watching them. Even the barrel riders stare down evilly from their precarious positions.

Wow, Timothy says. You put her in her place. She wouldn't have taken that kind of treatment from a man.

There was something about Reka. Some mysterious authority. When she gave an order, you knew you had better obey. Timothy remembered certain of his high school teachers claiming that authority, while others did not. But it was impossible to say for sure what separated the two groups. It had nothing to do with gender, he was sure of that. It had to do with a certain latent cruelty you knew you didn't want to see unleashed. Sitting at the table, it was easy to see. Of the three of them, Reka was the one you had better not fuck with.

Reka and Jerry drink their drinks efficiently, one matching the other. Timothy still has half of his drink left when Reka gets up to use the bathroom. Listen, we really do have to get going, she says to Jerry. It was nice to meet you, truly. She reaches across the table to shake his hand. Then she looks at Timothy. Meet me on the way out, OK, Lucky?

OK, Timothy says.

When Reka walks away, Timothy turns to Jerry. He wants to say something comforting but doesn't know what to say. We're pulling for you, he says finally. I think you're a good guy. I think tomorrow things will start to look up for you.

Thanks, Jerry says. This is my last night to party. I guess no more dough means no more drinks for Old Fat Baby.

That's a good place to start, Timothy says.

He gets up to leave and Jerry says, You've got your hands full with that one.

I know I do, Timothy says. He walks to the bar to nurse his vodka sweet and wait for Reka.

No sooner has he gone than Timothy sees two from the group of rivetheads approach Jerry. It's as if the group has dispatched the two as scouts. So, they weren't interested in Timothy after all. They were waiting for him to get out of the way. The others stay on the corner couches but keep vigilant.

At Jerry's table, all three seem to be laughing, just having fun. Or maybe they're taunting Jerry and he's laughing at his own expense. It's hard to tell, and maybe it doesn't matter. The rivetheads don't really seem old enough to be in the bar, but they're dressed for it, the black hoodies and death-metal T-shirts and all that hardware in their faces. Either they're too young or Timothy's too old.

Timothy watches one of the young men in the corner whisper to his girlfriend—he seems to be the head riveter and she's the only girl, Rosie—and she too approaches Jerry's table.

He can't hear what they're saying, but he can guess. The picture is becoming clear. Rosie touches him on the sleeve of his suede coat, and Jerry laughs and nods. He struggles to remove it, nearly falling down. Then he holds the coat up in one hand. It shines golden in the dusky bar light.

Reka walks out of the bathroom and meets Timothy at the bar. OK, Lucky, she says. Take me home or lose me forever.

Just let me finish my drink, he says. Then he nods toward Jerry. Our friend's being fleeced.

They watch as the young girl Rosie puts the coat on. The other two seem to distract Jerry, showing him their tattoos or something, as she walks back to her boyfriend.

Jerry doesn't appear to need much distracting. He's already forgotten about the coat.

They watch Rosie take the coat off and fold it elegantly over her arm.

Well, there goes his precious coat, Timothy says. That will be the bottom. I don't really want to be around for the end of this, do you?

You have to do something, Reka says. He looks at her as if she might be joking, but she's serious. You can't let them, she says, not pleading so much as demanding.

What do you care? Timothy says. He's punishing her now, for her earlier flirtation and all the unwanted news about her sporting ways.

What do you mean, what do I care? It's the right thing. I thought you were the Good Samaritan boy. Go do some good.

There isn't time to argue. Rosie's heading toward them with the coat, angling toward the door. Her boyfriend approaches Jerry to taunt him with the others while she escapes with the prize.

Timothy wonders what they want with the coat. It's not their style.

Do something, Reka urges again.

Reka was right. It wasn't fair. Jerry wasn't just a drunk. He was a good guy in a bad spot. And he had been generous to them. She wants him to do something. Something may be the wrong thing, or it may be the right thing. It doesn't matter. It only matters that if Timothy does anything it's going to end badly. Doesn't Reka know this? With all her worldliness doesn't she know this basic thing?

Timothy steps in front of the girl. You shouldn't take the man's coat, he says.

What are you talking about? Rosie says. She wears black eyeliner, and her full lips are colored purple.

That's Jerry, Timothy says. He's good people. He's having a rough stretch. You really should give him his coat back.

Mind your own business you fucking hick, Rosie says, and she tries to walk past.

How did she know? They had been talking about him too. Timothy grabs her wrist. Give the coat to me, he says. I'll give it back to Jerry and nobody will know any different. Her boyfriend, Head Riveter, looks up and sees Timothy confronting his Rosie. He leaves Jerry and comes to her rescue.

What's going on bro, Riveter says. He's a head shorter than Timothy but broad in the shoulders and across the chest. Timothy is more afraid of him when he sees how he's built, but he tries not to show it.

Your gal Rosie here was just going to give my friend his coat back, Timothy says.

Rosie's pouting now, and she starts to slide the coat off her arm. Timothy reaches to take it, but Riveter stops him.

Yo bitch, the man says. Hop off.

Timothy says to Reka in disbelief, Riveter just called me bitch. Look, he says to the two thieves. You're out of line. Just give the coat back and I'll buy you a beer. I'll buy you both a beer.

Riveter gets up in Timothy's face. Dude gave us the coat, dog, he says. Dude don't even want it. Then he says to Rosie, Let's go, man.

Timothy looks at Reka, who seems content to be the observer. It's clear what she wants. He's a schoolteacher. He's the adult in the room. He should say something stern and practical and put an end to this nonsense immediately.

Timothy tries one more time. He catches Rosie's wrist. Listen, he says, trying not to tremble. Jerry is a friend of ours. His wife just left him and he doesn't have a dime. You shouldn't kick a man when he's down.

But then Riveter is in Timothy's face again. From the corner of the room, Timothy sees the other industrialists watching, waiting to pounce. The only one who doesn't know what's going on is Jerry. He has his arms out like he's trying to balance on one spot.

Let's just get out of here, Ray, the girl says.

That's the right call, Timothy says.

Step back outta my road, Riveter says. Then he reaches for Timothy's face and tugs at the soul patch growing under his lip. Check it, man. Dog's got a little prison pussy, he says.

Timothy's mind reels. In front of him there's an antagonist calling him names, and the man has just grabbed his face. Timothy looks to Reka for help, but she stands dispassionately to the side. Why won't she do something? These two would listen to her. Timothy looks around the room, but everyone seems to have chosen this moment to mind their own business. Only the hobbits watch, spinning on their barrels. The downstream hobbit has lost his balance. In the next moment, he'll be in deep water.

Doesn't Riveter know what happens when you touch a man's face? Why does he take Timothy for a pushover? He somehow came to the conclusion that Timothy was harmless, but it was the wrong conclusion. In Blue River this would be settled already.

In the right hand Timothy holds the rest of his drink. His left hand is empty. On the bar, on the edge of the bowling lane, he finds an empty beer can. Pabst. They're drinking this stuff again. Everything is still. His left hand holding the beer can arrives squarely on Riveter's nose. The can crumples and the man crumples with it. Blood spurts from his nose. He's on his knees, holding his bloody face. The beer can is on the floor crushed flat like the waitress had taken her big heel to it.

Rosie shrieks and unfolds the coat. She throws it at Timothy and runs toward the door.

Timothy wheels to face the onslaught of the other rivetheads, but they're all streaming by him for some reason, out the door, running.

The bartender, Garth, has made it around the bar now, just as Riveter stands up from the floor, his face a bloody mess. Timothy expects Riveter to stand and fight, but he too lurches for the door.

And just like that it's over.

Timothy stands, holding the coat. He walks over to hand it to Jerry.

Jerry seems dazed. How did you get my coat? he says. He had missed the whole scene.

Those guys tried to steal it, Timothy says. I got it back for you.

No shit? he says. That old thing. He nods at the coat. I said they could have it.

Garth has decided someone should pay for the mess he has to clean up later. He puts his hand on Timothy's shoulder. You're out of here pal, he says in his hoarse voice. There's no fighting in this place. I don't care who started it.

He started it, the waitress says, pointing at Timothy.

A couple of other bystanders nod. Timothy is the guilty party. It doesn't matter. They're leaving anyway. He grabs Reka's hand, but she pulls away and walks out ahead of him.

On the sidewalk outside, Riveter has regained his bravado, but he's like a dog on an invisible leash, barking but held back.

Bitch coldcocked me, he says. I'd tear his shit up, but my paroley'd have my balls.

The threat seems to be over, but out of the darkness Rosie walks up and spits in his face. She's accurate, and the hot heavy glob of mucus clings to his eye. He wipes it away, but it lingers there like a wet kiss. Now Timothy expects Reka to come to his rescue, but she's way out in front of him, already getting in the truck.

Timothy drives the darkened streets toward home. Reka's been silent for a long time. Finally, she says, How could you do that? How could you just hit someone like that?

Timothy doesn't answer. He's still spinning. When they get out of the car at Rooms for Men, Timothy's surprised to find he's wearing Jerry's coat. The suede has absorbed a lot of heat. It's too hot, and it's too fucking big on him.

IV

It's August and the wrens are still at it. Timothy's mother told him that the male makes the nest and then sits on his little perch singing his song while the females come to inspect his handiwork. If she likes his remodeling, she'll move in; otherwise, she'll move on. The male seems unfazed. He sings the same incessant tune, all morning long, day after day. The females come and go. Then in the afternoon the male makes some adjustments to the nest, hoping—in the small fretful way a bird must hope—these adjustments will lure a new tenant. One day, finally, the female goes in the hole and she doesn't come out and there's a blessed silence. The male bird finally gets to do something besides sing and remodel.

Timothy laces up for a run. Before he gets to Downer Avenue and the walkway down to Lake Park, a dark sedan pulls up beside him. A BMW. The sedan looks familiar. The tinted passenger window lowers to reveal a driver wearing dark sunglasses asking for directions to the art museum. Timothy takes a minute to orient himself, Downer being a one-way. Then he gives the simple directions. Stay on Downer until North Ave. Then head down the hill until you get to the water and come back south along Lake Shore about a mile. You can't miss it.

Hey, thanks a lot, the man says. You make it sound easy.

No problem, Timothy says, and continues running. It feels good to have someone ask you for directions and then to produce the correct directions. It's a simple, wholesome transaction. It means you have been taken for a local, an insider, and you've lived up to your billing.

Rather than pull away, the man in the BMW continues to drive slowly alongside Timothy. Excuse me, he says again, and Timothy comes near. I hate to bother you on your workout. He leans over the passenger seat and lowers his sunglasses. With his close-cropped salt-and-pepper hair and pressed white shirt and black trousers, he gives the impression of a restaurant waiter. You know, the man says, your build, you could be a model.

Surprised, Timothy feels his muscles tense, then relax. That line doesn't even work on women, he says, backing away.

The man doesn't give up easily. I work for a talent scout. I know it when I see it.

Now Timothy feels annoyed and even somewhat bullied. This is what women must feel like, he thinks, when they're harassed by men.

Let me give you my card, the man says.

What's the matter, Timothy says, is Chip busy tonight?

Caught out, the man pulls away, the wide tires of the BMW chirping as he pulls into traffic. Timothy continues his run. Just a month earlier such an altercation would have flustered him. Now it humors him. He feels a small boost actually, to receive the compliment, no matter its source, and he picks up his pace. He runs over the Lake Avenue Bridge and out onto the wide lawn of Lake Park. Everyone is out in the park today, enjoying the fine weather, riding bikes, flying kites, or picnicking. When he passes other runners, Timothy waves, like they belong to the same fraternity.

He runs down by the harbor and hears the seagulls arguing and the tinkling of the sailboat riggings in the wind. A few lone fishermen cast bright spoons out into the harbor for browns or chinooks, but not much action today. At Bradley Beach, a scum of dead alewives has washed up on the sand, hampering the swimmers and raising a stench.

Veering away from the water, Timothy hits his stride. On some runs you feel the effort of every step and you can't get your mind off the end of the run. But today isn't like that. Today is the rare day when Timothy feels like he could just keep running. He feels a kind of bottled energy inside that he can uncap as needed to run faster and longer.

Timothy thinks of the Old Gent running on the horse trails or around the country roads when he was a boy. Running wasn't popular in the country and you never saw runners out on the roads. Kids on the school bus said, I saw your dad running down the road. Did his truck run out of gas?

Timothy used to think the Old Gent was so stupid, running up one country road and down the next. Even in winter, with big mittens on his hands and snot frozen in his whiskers, he ran. Then the Old Gent came indoors with his face and hands frozen, and Timothy's mother said, Stay away from me with those hands! The Old Gent turned to the easier target, his cold hands finding Timothy's neck, or sliding up Timothy's shirt, sending him squealing from the room.

Now, inexplicably, Timothy has become one of those who runs to no purpose but the running. He's on the homestretch now, feeling good. *You've got to be rugged*, the Old Gent would say, coming in from a run covered with hoarfrost.

Timothy sees the gleaming white wing of the new art museum puncture the blue sky, and there, parked along Lake Shore Drive, a black BMW sits idling while a leggy runner leans in the passenger window. Another potential model has just been identified.

Timothy runs back up the hill and now he's cruising down Brady, carried by adrenaline, past the hip pub, the Nomad, and the trendy coffee shop painted lime green, Rochambo. Then past the old places, Brady Street Hardware and Listwan's Tavern and Glorioso's Italian Deli. In front of Peter Sciortino's Bakery, with its colorful ceramic mosaic portraying an overflowing breadbasket, Timothy thinks about what he'll have to eat when he gets home. There are eggs in the refrigerator and a good loaf of wheat bread, and he can have egg-in-the-nest and fry the little golden nest to a crisp, golden deliciousness.

The glass bakery door swings open suddenly onto the sidewalk and just about hits him, and who's standing in the doorway but Reka, her armload of fresh bakery nearly sacrificed to the encounter. Both of them shocked still at this near collision. It has been a week since the incident at the Foundation. Timothy, out of breath, means to apologize, means to say, Let me carry that for you. But instead he sidesteps her and continues his dash toward home. Call me, he says over his shoulder, even as his feet carry him away.

Coasting in the last half mile, he thinks about Reka and how things will end. It's easy to be in love when you're saying good-bye or hello, Timothy decides. Now is the time for good-bye and he's practically gushing with feelings for her. He tries to understand this feeling. No person is insignificant, after all, and when you welcome someone into your life, or usher her out of it, you do feel love. At least Timothy does. If not love, what is it? As he thinks about his dilemma with Reka, his mind is clouded by thoughts about sex with Reka. Stop it, he warns himself. But he doesn't stop. He picks up the pace for the last two blocks so exhaustion will trump his lurid thoughts.

Back at Rooms for Men, he sidesteps Fred painting the front porch and heads straight up to his apartment. He guzzles a glass of water and then fondles the coveted after-run cigarette. Reclining in the easy chair by the window, he lights the cigarette and blows the first lungful of smoke out the window. This is dependably the best cigarette of the day. For some reason, it feels like the smoke can't possibly do any harm after a good run. It's like the final step of a purification.

On his knee, he holds the small brass slipper that he had slipped into his belongings when he left home two months ago. An ashtray. It was his mother's, when she was a smoker. The ashtray holds only one cigarette, and it needs to be emptied each time. Not very practical. Yet it might be Timothy's most unique possession.

Cigarette finished, snubbed into the brass slipper, Timothy feels a strange new appetite, some combination of hunger and desire and a vague cramping sickness. The cigarette didn't satisfy him like it usually does. He wants another. But he knows that will make it worse. Maybe it's the effect of the nicotine on his quickened metabolism. But it's a new feeling. The full slipper rests on his knee, which is bouncing involuntarily. All these memories of home. Where were they coming from? Timothy understands then exactly what he would like to eat. Dirt. Good rich black earth from the Old Gent's garden. He imagines putting his nose right into the freshly turned earth, then opening his mouth, eating a loamy, gritty mouthful, and breathing it into his nostrils at the same time.

His phone rings and it's Reka.

You wouldn't believe what I was just thinking, Timothy says.

I bet I would.

Not that. Well, that too. But I was thinking about dirt. Eating dirt from my dad's garden. Just pushing my face right into it. Isn't that fucking weird?

After a pause, Reka says, I think it's cute.

Cute? God, I can almost taste it.

Baby's homesick, she says. And before he has a chance to argue, it strikes him as the correct verdict.

Why don't you come over tonight? Timothy says. Then, without censoring himself, he says, I want you right now. I couldn't stop thinking about it on my run.

Reka doesn't respond for a moment. Then she says, That's a good idea. I come over to your place and we talk about breaking up for an hour, and then you fuck me until you come, and then we fall asleep. You first.

I didn't know it was so bad, Timothy says.

You don't know a lot of things, Reka says.

Like what don't I know? He's feeling playful and full of unspent energy from the good run and the week apart. It doesn't matter what she says, as long as she comes over and satisfies this urge.

I shouldn't tell you on the phone.

Oh, come on, when have we ever been so formal? He gets up and puts the full slipper on the counter by the sink and sits back down. He'll empty it later.

Well. OK. You don't know, for instance, that I'm moving to Chicago.

Oh? Timothy says. You're moving to Chicago?

I'm moving to Chicago.

He recovers himself. I knew that, he says.

You knew that?

Yeah, I knew it, Timothy says, even though he didn't know it. He feels a certain giddiness, though he knows he should express sadness. But there's a little trickle of relief, some of the tension draining away. This might be easier than he thought. Tell me something I don't know, he says.

Not on the phone.

You want to send me a smoke signal?

All right smartass, she says. I'm pregnant.

Don't joke around about that.

I'm pregnant.

I said that's not funny.

I said I'm pregnant.

Timothy ends the call. To keep her from saying it again, he tells himself. He paces the room. It couldn't be possible. Of course it could be possible. How could it not be possible? He sits down at the table in the center of the room. Then he stands up and bangs his head on the gaslight. Fucking light. He hits it with his fist and one of the glass shades falls to the table and shatters.

He hears himself saying, That was bright. That will teach it. Then he calls Reka back. Can you come over, he says.

The bed is still unmade, and the rumpled covers invite him in. For a long time, he doesn't move. The sweat dries on his body, and he wraps up like a mummy in the blankets. So, this is how life happens, he thinks. Timothy, his parents had admitted, was an accident. But Timothy's parents were married. He's known Reka for what, six weeks? He doesn't have any money. But this isn't the first surprise in the history of the world. And who has any money? Yes, this is how life happens. You're confronted with an obstacle or an opportunity, and you react to it. The way you react to it says more about who you are than the opportunity or the obstacle. Right?

Timothy drifts off to sleep in the cozy sarcophagus of blankets. When Reka arrives, he's still foggy from sleep, and he grapples with her at the door. He puts his hand over her mouth when she tries to speak. She presses her hand over his own, as if to shut herself up, and they stand like that for a while. Then she moves her hand up his arm, and that's all it takes.

A long, loud, guttural, determined lovemaking begins, first in front of the little apartment-sized sink, then over the kitchen table, carefully with the shattered glass, and then finally over the sink again. Timothy's always fantasized about doing it that way. No talking, no kissing, just tearing off clothes and getting to it. But not all clothes. Undressing only what needs undressing, pushing the rest to the side and entering unannounced before she's had a chance to open her mouth to voice objection or invitation. But Reka does open her mouth then, with that surprise, and commences responding like she never has, bucking and writhing against him and almost knocking him off his feet. Taking everything and giving more back. Timothy feels a new sweat seeping through the crust of dry sweat, then a cauldron of lust and anger and confusion and revulsion and still that arcane hunger for good black garden earth in his mouth and nostrils. Home-sickness, Reka called it. Whatever it is, it rises to a boil in him before he unleashes it finally into the naked body draped over his sink, finishing like that, his hand over her mouth again to keep her from yelling this time, and her taking the offering in her teeth and biting down hard.

And then the cauldron simmering. Reka rests her cheek flat on the dirty counter. This is a kitchen sink and a bathroom sink and also a toilet. Her blonde hair mingles with all the sink stuff. The broken wedge of bar soap, the rusted core of an apple, breakfast dishes scabbed with breadcrumbs and the mess of butter and jam. A noose of used floss girdles the hot water handle. The toothpaste rests uncapped, its lip a bulbous yellow crust. And there's the red toothbrush itself resting in a cruddy puddle of shaved whiskers and soap scum. It's a fairly new toothbrush, but already its bristles splay out as if it's been used for months. Either Timothy has been using it too long, or they just don't make toothbrushes like they used to.

Reka looks back, extracting her hair from the sink. That was amazing, she says, pushing back and standing up, wiping a wetness from her face. Where has that been all these weeks? I didn't know you had that in you.

I'm sorry, Timothy says, feeling tenderness now. But also sadness and self-pity. He sits down on the unmade trundle bed and hangs his head.

Sorry? she says. You deserve a medal or something. But Timothy's not cheered. He sits dejectedly on the bed. Oh, don't act so guilty. I needed that too. More than you know. She sits down beside him, both of them naked.

What are we going to do? he says. I mean, I feel like we barely know each other.

Shhh, she says. She goes to the sink and returns with the brass slipper, its opening fit snugly with the single cigarette butt. She hands it to Timothy and he tips the slipper into the can by the bed. Then he lights a new cigarette and passes it to Reka.

You don't understand, Timothy says. What are we supposed to

do? I like you. I told you I loved you, and you told me I don't love you. That's just confusing. And I don't know if you love me. I suppose I could love you if we just give it time.

Reka shushes him again. You talk too much. She lies back on the bed naked and Timothy wraps some of the blanket around her. They share the cigarette.

What happened anyway? I thought you were on the pill. I mean, I figured you must have been.

Well, I was. The pill wasn't working out for me and I switched to an IUD. There was some time in between.

Here was the mistake. A mistake that wasn't his own. *Some time in between.* You should have told me, he says. That wasn't fair, keeping that from me. He feels his confidence rising. For one thing, he says, how do you know it's even mine?

Do you have to sound like a fucking ass? God, why did I ever get into it with a kid? I broke Rule Number One: No dating little kids.

What the fuck is that supposed to mean?

It means you're too used to being pleased and not used to giving pleasure. You're selfish, Lucky Boy. You think this is what I need in my life? I was supposed to be starting over. Now I have to start over from starting over. Reka begins to cry.

I'm sorry. Shit. I never should have said that, Timothy says. But still he wonders. He supposes there are tests you can do, if it comes to that.

Reka is too strong to cry for long. Listen. You don't have to worry. I'm going to have an abortion.

Those words he didn't know he wanted to hear until he heard them. Those saving words. No taking them back. Now that those words were spoken, he can afford a new generosity.

Of course I'd support you either way, he says.

I know you would, Reka says. Look, I need to be going. I'm not staying here anymore.

I just feel like we never even got started.

There's just one more thing I need from you. Reka stands and begins to dress, recovering her clothes from the floor in front of the sink. Can I count on you for one more thing?

Turns out the abortion clinic is right there on the east side, right next to Shank Hall, where Reka said they play some good blues. They can walk to it, and they do. A line of protesters guards the entrance. They're standing across the street from the gauntlet waiting for the light to turn.

Timothy holds Reka's hand tightly. She seems so brave and mature but also somehow younger. She's wearing makeup today, which is unusual for her. Something about the heavy mascara and the loose-fitting clothes reminds him of the older girls in high school and how sophisticated they seemed to Timothy when he was an underclassman. He passed them in the halls with their exotic clothes and smells and curvaceous bodies and hoop earrings, and he felt like he didn't belong in the same building with them. He couldn't wait until the day he could exist on the same plane as those heavenly creatures, leaning against their lockers and speaking secretly with them while the unlucky ones trundled past in the hallway lugging their stupid books. One of the senior girls had an abortion when he was a freshman. Trina Miller. Trina was a rare beauty, slightly bow-legged, which seemed about the sexiest thing in the world. Timothy had doubted that she would let someone even touch her. She was gone from school for a few days. Word got around. Afterward, when she came back, she walked the same halls. Now she seemed to float even further above them. Nothing could touch her. Just being in her proximity was enough to sustain Timothy's imagination for the entire school day. Timothy remembers that when he got to be the same age as Trina Miller and the other worldly girls, he never felt worldly himself. The plane on which the ones with the secret knowledge lived seemed always just two or three levels ahead, and Timothy was a perpetual underclassman.

The little man in the stoplight turns from red to green, and Timothy and Reka cross over. He feels ashamed that his thoughts are off elsewhere instead of on this current emergency. He wonders briefly what Reka could be thinking. Then the wall of protesters with their ugly signs demand attention. The protesters shout murderer and sinner and coward and one of them uses the word profligate and another one says Mom and Dad. Reka has to drag him through. She's wearing new boots he's never seen before with heavy heels, like those skull crushers. The door is in sight when a man in a heavy flannel shirt grabs him by the arm. Timothy turns. The man doesn't look malicious, but the pressure on his arm is such that Timothy knows there's no resisting it.

Hey, the man says. Listen here. His voice is pleading and friendly. There's still time, he says. Just take another day to think it over. You know, that's your little fishing buddy in there.

Let's go, Reka says, and pulls Timothy in the door.

Later, in the waiting room, Timothy wonders how the big man knew exactly what to say. Like the riveter girl in the bar, this man seemed to be able to see right into him, into his weakness.

V

Kidney stones, Timothy tells the tenants at Rooms for Men. Reka would stay with him for a couple of days to recover.

How's the patient? Fred asks when he passes Timothy in the hallway. Fred roams the hallways at Rooms for Men like a gray ghost, always some project underway, unclogging a leak or puttying some tile.

She's doing fine, Timothy says. Recovering. Not moving around too much yet.

Let me know if you need anything, he says.

On the second day, Reka's feeling good enough to get up and around. I could use some fresh air, she says. You know, there's someplace I've always wanted to see.

Name it, Timothy says. I'll show it to you. Fresh air sounds great, anything to escape the humid shroud in the little apartment.

I've always wanted to see that widow's walk.

I'll get the key from Fred.

Now that she's had the abortion, Timothy wonders if maybe he does love Reka after all. She made that sacrifice for him. Like the sacrifice she had made for the other lover, her ex-husband. Not everyone would pay such a cost, and it seems to Timothy like a thing of value.

Timothy leads her gingerly into the attic. A bare bulb burns from the ceiling cord, revealing Fred's little chest of Western wear, and his stockpile of antiques. Several chandeliers and gold chalices are piled in disarray on one side of the room. The other is stacked in framed panes of stained glass. There are dozens of these panes. In between rests a jumble of old copper and tin street lamps, stacks of tin ceiling tiles and boxes of brass fixtures, door knobs and plates. Even without realizing the value of these items, Timothy knows it's a treasure trove. Fred has been collecting for decades, since back when old junk was just old junk, not yet varnished with the stately term, antique. When they tore the buildings down for the Park East Freeway, for instance, Fred just wandered through and took what he liked.

Fred's attic was once part of the boardinghouse. It was amazing to think that whole families lived up here, before Fred bought the place, before it was Rooms for Men. Fred told Timothy the story of the German immigrant woman who raised five children in this attic. She lived her whole adult life in this house, moving to Timothy's apartment only after all her children had left and her husband had died. Timothy sees a little sink, like the sink in his apartment, covered in dust.

Timothy guides Reka carefully past the sharp edges of the antiques toward the trap door in the ceiling leading to the widow's walk. Besides being valuable, everything in the room seems dangerous for a woman in Reka's condition. All these corroded old objects, angular and sharp like elbows ready to jab. He keeps her close to him as they step around the minefield of antiques to the trapdoor. Timothy is aware of his own tender feelings as he pulls the string and a stack of wooden stairs is revealed, leading up into the darkness.

Ladies first, Timothy says. He follows Reka up the dark ladder toward the padlocked roof cap, which he unlocks with the key and lifts away.

Well, this is my first widow's walk, Timothy says after they've emerged into the light.

Mine too. She's so reticent. Reka is clearly not yet herself.

The flat patch of roof is bordered by an ornate wrought iron fence. The brick chimney rising another six feet above them could use some tuck-pointing, and Timothy makes a mental note to tell Fred. It's a sunny day, but they're bathed in the shade of the big maple tree and the chimney. There's not much of a view, except to the ground. A widow on this walk couldn't have seen very far. Timothy climbs over the decorative fence and looks down the steep pitch of roof. From here he can see the roof of the little wooden wren house outside his window. One of the wrens, who can tell which, climbs into the hole with something in its beak.

Looking down from the roof, Timothy wonders if the fall would kill him. The height, maybe forty feet, along with the hard gravel, seems sufficient to do the job. As long as you went head first, you wouldn't have to suffer much. He feels the telltale weakening behind his knees and in his groin.

Why don't you stand away from the edge, Reka says. You're making me queasy.

OK, Timothy says, but he doesn't step over the railing just yet.

Aren't you scared of falling to your death? she says in an exaggerated tone.

It would be a quick death, Timothy says in the same mood. I'm not afraid of a quick death. Just a slow one.

Aren't you maudlin, Reka says. Life is a slow death.

Wow, Timothy says. I mean, that's the most depressing thing I've heard in my whole life.

Timothy peers over the side edge of the widow's walk and catches sight of Fred, setting up his ladder. Fred struggles with the ladder, and it occurs to Timothy for the first time that he's getting too old for this work. It's dangerous for a man his age to be climbing ladders. Then a commotion from next door pulls his gaze the other way. He steps back to safety, next to Reka.

They watch a man leaning over a moving box. He's just dropped it on the porch, and the crashing of the box is what they heard. They watch as the man picks up the box up. That's Jerry, Reka says. Good old Jerry.

Jerry has a station wagon out on the street. He fits the box in the back end and heads back into the house. An overweight man sits on the porch with his shirt off, smoking a cigarette. They're arguing. The big man is giving Jerry some moving advice, and Jerry is telling him where to put his advice.

Listen to this, Timothy says to Reka. Jerry, he calls. Oh Jerry. We're watching you. He pulls Reka behind the chimney.

They watch from behind the chimney as the men strain their eyes into the leafy tops of the maple.

Who's there? a voice calls.

Reka calls out too, her voice a high chirrup. Old Fat Baby, she calls.

The fuck is that? Jerry says to the trees. He sways a bit, and Timothy can tell then that the man is drunk. The old bottom hunter still looking for his way.

As if in answer, one of the wrens pipes up. It must be the paranoid male, singing danger, danger, danger.

Timothy and Reka laugh at that. They crouch behind the chimney holding one another. Huddled together with Reka in this good hiding spot, Timothy feels a giddiness he knows Reka must share. It's a lightness that comes from knowing you're safe here. That no one will find you until you give yourself away.

Acknowledgments

Dear reader: If you've read anything of these pages, I owe you a debt of gratitude. Raphael Kadushin at UW Press, for your faith in this project, I thank you. And to the talented staff at UW Press for helping to pull this book off (and even helping to name it!): Thanks! Cheers to all my writer pals; you never (well, almost never) let me down — Christi Clancy, Chad Faries, Christopher Grimes, Jayson Iwen, Kristen Iversen, Phil LaMarche, Cris Mazza, Scott Sublett, Kyoko Yoshida. Scott, you love the forest, and this project needed someone to see past the trees. Dan Libman and Molly McNett, you were essential readers, and I owe you. Thank you to the astonishing number of journal editors who somehow said yes; the slow trickle of story publications has sustained me. Thanks to my good colleagues and friends at Beloit College. Beloit students too; I'm daily more thankful for good students than almost anything. Except my family — who puts up with this strangely inaccurate parrot's flapping — thank goodness for you, and thank goodness you don't watch what you say. (I know you remember it all differently.) And of course, Breja, best wife, awesome person, thank you for believing in me always. And Iris, you little spandoozler, you are a blessing.

These stories appeared in somewhat different forms in the following publications: "High Hope for Fatalists Everywhere" in *The Pinch*; "The Bush Robin Sings" in *Rosebud*; "Three Ps" in *Phoebe*; "First One Out" in *Elixir*; "Lazy *B*" in *North Dakota Quarterly*; "Strings" in *Witness*; "Birds of Paradise" in *Clackamas Literary Review*; "Trollway" in *Fifth Wednesday*; and "Add This to the List of Things That You Are" in *New Orleans Review*.

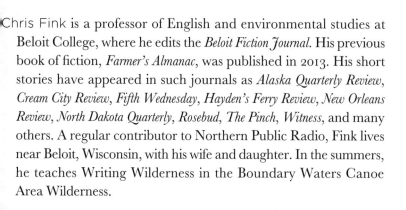

Chris Fink is a professor of English and environmental studies at Beloit College, where he edits the *Beloit Fiction Journal*. His previous book of fiction, *Farmer's Almanac*, was published in 2013. His short stories have appeared in such journals as *Alaska Quarterly Review*, *Cream City Review*, *Fifth Wednesday*, *Hayden's Ferry Review*, *New Orleans Review*, *North Dakota Quarterly*, *Rosebud*, *The Pinch*, *Witness*, and many others. A regular contributor to Northern Public Radio, Fink lives near Beloit, Wisconsin, with his wife and daughter. In the summers, he teaches Writing Wilderness in the Boundary Waters Canoe Area Wilderness.